FERAL AS A CAT

Sons of Wonderland Book 3

KENDRA MORENO

FERAL as a CAT

Sons of Wonderland Book 3

Kendra Moreno

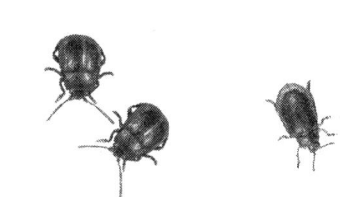

BLURB

Weapons don't weep...

Calypso is only trying to make it through life, raising her little brother and taking care of her ailing mom. She doesn't have time for fairytales or pipe dreams, so when two men show up at her door talking about Wonderland, she sends them on their way.

But life has a way of taking trips down rabbit holes...

Cal gets dragged to Wonderland and told she's the savior of their world. She's destined to end the reign of the Red Queen, to destroy the Jabberwocky, all while dealing with the teasing grin of the Cheshire Cat.

In this epic conclusion to the trilogy, will Calypso be able to give everything to a world not her own, or will she let it die and Cheshire right along with it?

Let's go to war...

COPYRIGHT

Please do not participate in piracy.

Copyright © 2019 by Kendra Moreno

All rights reserved.
No part of this book may be reproduced in any form or by any electronic or mechanical means, including information storage and retrieval systems, without written permission from the author, except for the use of brief quotations in a book review.

This is a work of fiction. Names, characters, businesses, places, events, locales, and incidents are either the products of the author's imagination or used in a fictitious manner. Any resemblance to actual persons, living or dead, or actual events is purely coincidental.

Edited by Michelle Hoffman

Cover art by Ruxandra Tudorica with Methyss Art

Formatted by Nicole JeRee at The Swamp Goddess

ISBN: 9781091550216

CONTENTS

Trigger Warning	xi
Prologue	1
Chapter 1	7
Chapter 2	13
Chapter 3	16
Chapter 4	18
Chapter 5	25
Chapter 6	27
Chapter 7	32
Chapter 8	36
Chapter 9	38
Chapter 10	43
Chapter 11	46
Chapter 12	50
Chapter 13	56
Chapter 14	59
Chapter 15	64
Chapter 16	67
Chapter 17	69
Chapter 18	71
Chapter 19	74
Chapter 20	76
Chapter 21	83
Chapter 22	87
Chapter 23	94
Chapter 24	97
Chapter 25	100
Chapter 26	109
Chapter 27	116
Chapter 28	119
Chapter 29	126
Chapter 30	136

Chapter 31	144
Chapter 32	150
Chapter 33	155
Chapter 34	158
Chapter 35	164
Chapter 36	166
Chapter 37	169
Chapter 38	174
Chapter 39	191
Chapter 40	194
Chapter 41	198
Chapter 42	200
Chapter 43	202
Chapter 44	205
Chapter 45	209
Chapter 46	212
Chapter 47	215
Chapter 48	218
Chapter 49	221
Chapter 50	226
Chapter 51	232
Chapter 52	235
Chapter 53	240
Chapter 54	246
Chapter 55	251
Epilogue	254
Riddle for glimpse of Spin off:	257
Acknowledgments	259
About the Author	261
Also by Kendra Moreno	263
Clockwork Butterfly	265

To Aunt Martina
I hope this final book would have made you proud. I miss you. I love you.
RIP Martina Knight 1968-2019

To Uncle Mark
I wish you could have been here to tease me about my books. I wish you could have chosen to stay. You are loved.
RIP Mark Salsberry 1966-2019

TRIGGER WARNING

Feral as a Cat includes descriptions of gore, extreme violence, and sex. I always want you to read my book, but please, take care of yourself first. If you ever have any questions, never hesitate to reach out to me.

Prologue

Cheshire moves through the thick trees, his feet silent, his whole body tense and alert. He can feel the tingles that shoot up and down his arms, the awareness that he can never quite figure out where it comes from making his hair stand on end.

"Do you feel that?" he whispers, so quietly no one should be able to hear him.

"Yes," Danica breathes beside him. "Something big is happening."

Cheshire straightens and listens, his ears twitching with the sounds of the forest. Creatures caw around them. Something scuttles through the underbrush. In the distance, a howl pierces the air, so full of sadness that Cheshire feels his heart skip a beat.

"We're being called," Danica says, rolling her shoulders. Her own ears are twitching with the sounds, aware of every moving part around them.

They are being more than called. The sense of dread that spreads down Cheshire's spine almost makes him shiver. If he was a different creature, he might have run in a different direction. Instead, he straightens his shoulders and prepares to Fade. His tail moves back and forth behind him, already sensing the growing stress, their first sign that whatever they find on the other side won't be pleasant.

"I don't think this is a normal calling," Cheshire whispers, not daring to raise his voice.

"Do you think it has to do with Alice's return?" Danica asks.

Cheshire doesn't answer. He doesn't need to. They both know it has everything to do with Alice's return. She's come back a vengeful woman, full of hatred. Cheshire had watched her rip the heart from the Hatter's chest for making the mistake of thinking her the same little girl she'd been the first time. That little girl was gone, and no one knows what happened between then and now.

Cheshire draws his sword, his little sister doing the same beside him, as they begin to Fade. When Wonderland calls, they don't have a choice. If the Hands of Justice and the Hope Bringer are needed, they're pulled from whatever they are doing by the powers of the land. There's no ignoring it.

When they reappear, Cheshire looks around quickly to take stock of the scene and nearly stumbles back when he realizes what's going on.

"How sweet of you to join me," Alice coos, her dark eyes zeroing on Cheshire and Danica. Danica raises her chin, ever the fighter, and draws her sword from her back. Danica's role as the Hope Bringer is an odd one. While Cheshire is the Punisher, Danica tips the scales with kindness. Her role is always to encourage a change of heart.

"Alice, what have you become?" Danica asks, her voice strong, but there's a twinge in there, a thread of sadness that Cheshire barely picks up on.

"I've become exactly who I'm meant to be," Alice replies, a smile curling her lips. She's covered in blood, and there's no question of where it came from. Around them, bodies litter the ground, some obviously castle guards, others unrecognizable.

"Where are the King and Queen?" Cheshire asks, his sword resting on his shoulder as if he doesn't have a care in the world.

"Where's Alexander?" Danica adds, her voice a hiss that Cheshire crinkles his brow at. Danica's role is not to get angry. Her role is to reason, to persuade. His is to get angry.

Alice's smile grows wider, her pointed teeth peeking over her bottom lip.

"The Prince is alive," she says. "Although, I'm afraid he's rather lost himself. The King and Queen, well, they lost their heads."

"Where's Alex?" Danica asks again, and Cheshire looks at her out of the side of his eyes. He's not sure what's she's doing, but he prepares himself to protect her regardless. They're two sides of a coin, meant to keep Wonderland in order.

Alice turns from her spot on the dais, her large blood-red dress hardly shifting at all. There's a gleam in her pitch-black eyes, an inhumanity that hadn't been there as a little girl. Something had happened in-between. But what?

"Knave!" Alice coos.

Behind her, the sound of footsteps are immediately heard. Both Danica and Cheshire tense as a man steps out from behind Alice. He wears the armor of the Prince, and one crystal-clear blue eye looks out at them without emotion. Beside him, Danica gasps and takes a step forward, but Cheshire reaches over and stops her.

There's something wrong. Half of Alex's face is ripped away, and in the mottled flesh, bright-red roses bloom. Similar blossoms grow where his heart should be, in the gaping hole left behind. Alice runs a finger down the side of Alex's face, a touch the Prince doesn't react to. The red roses stand out starkly against his pale skin, as red as blood, as red as Alice's dress.

"What have you done to him?" Danica snarls, raising her sword.

Alice giggles, the sound just as innocent as it had been as a child. It makes her more of a threat, Cheshire realizing that something is terribly wrong. Alex doesn't even spare an eye for the siblings, as if he doesn't recognize them at all.

"I don't think it's Alex anymore," Cheshire tells her, but Danica isn't listening, her face morphing into absolute fury.

"What have you done to him?" she screams again.

"I've given him purpose," Alice answers, studying her nails. "And I'm tiring of this already. Knave, get rid of them."

Prince Alexander advances forward without a second thought, his sword raised for battle. He attacks Cheshire first, his sword curving down so fast, Cheshire barely has time to block it. Danica watches in horror as someone they called friend attacks her brother. He's going for the kill. There's no resistance in his eyes.

"You take him," Cheshire snarls, shoving Alex away. He doesn't even react besides a small stumble before righting himself. "I'll take Alice." Cheshire's blood sings with punishment, Wonderland urging him to act. He storms right up to the woman, who to her credit, doesn't even flinch as he raises his sword.

"Wake up, Alex," Danica tells the prince, dodging his sword but not raising her own. "Wake up!"

Just as Cheshire prepares to bring his sword down across Alice's neck, the tingles on his arms stop, and his limbs lock in place. Sweat breaks out on his skin as he fights to bring his arms down, only for them to remain infuriatingly still. Alice tilts her head to the side.

"Did you think I would not prepare for the Punisher and the Hope Bringer, Cat?" she asks, studying Cheshire's eyes as they flick between human and feline. "Did you think it would be so easy to kill me after everything?"

"I don't know what you're talking about," Cheshire snarls. "But you'll die for the crimes you've committed against Wonderland."

"We shall see," she replies, taking a step back. She looks over Cheshire's shoulder towards Danica and Alex.

"Wake up! Alex, wake up!" Danica stumbles back a step when Cheshire turns to look at the pure agony in her voice. She doesn't raise her sword. She doesn't fight back.

"What are you doing?" Cheshire snarls, taking a step forward.

"Knave," Alice calls, and the prince turns a blue eye towards her. "End her."

"No," Cheshire growls, jumping from the dais and running towards Danica.

There's a flicker of something in the Prince's eyes, perhaps something of the man before, but whatever it is isn't strong enough. He turns, almost in slow motion, towards Danica and raises his sword.

"Protect yourself!" Cheshire snarls as he rushes to her side. "Move! Danica, move!"

Danica looks into the eye of the Prince, tears welling in her own and slipping over her lashes.

"Alex, wake up. You have to wake up. Please." She whispers something, something that Cheshire can't hear even with his sharp senses, even as he hurries closer.

"Danica!" Cheshire screams, realizing he's moving too slow, as the sword is thrust towards his little sister. "Move!"

Alice's laughter follows him, taunting, tinkling, childish.

Cheshire hears the sword slice through flesh, hears the gasp on Danica's lips as the blade pierces her sternum, sees the shock on her face as he presses down until the hilt is flush with her skin.

"No!" Cheshire screams, sliding to a stop beside Danica just as her sword drops to the ground, and she collapses into his arms. "What's wrong with you?" he shouts at Alexander, his anger filling his body. The Prince stumbles back, and Cheshire looks at him in time to see a tear slide from the corner of his good eye, before the emotion is wiped clean from his face.

Danica stares at the Prince, a trickle of blood slipping from the corner of her lips. The green ringing her eyes dims, her breath wheezing from her chest, rattling as if it's trying to escape.

"Wake up, Alex," she breathes, her voice barely loud enough to hear. "Alex, wake up." Her eyes stare off into the distance, unseeing, and Cheshire shakes her, a sob caught in his throat.

"Danica," he tries to growl but it only comes out as a hoarse grunt. When the first tear falls from his eyes, anger fuels him even more. He jerks his head up to Alice and meets her amused stare.

"I'll kill you, if It's the last thing I do, I'll rip your head clean from your body."

Her laugh fills the air, her shoulders shaking with the movement.

"Good luck, Grimalkin." She turns her eyes to the Knave where he still stands staring down at Danica. "Come along, Knave."

Cheshire's sees his feet hesitate for a split second, his hands clenched into fists.

"I said, come along, Knave," Alice snarls, tapping her leg like one would call a dog.

Whatever fight the prince had in him leaves his body, and he turns like a puppet to follow his master.

Cheshire looks back down at Danica where she lies in his arms. The breaths come slower as they leave her lips, her eyes glazing over.

"Cheshire . . .," she breathes, and her chest freezes, no more breaths left. Everything stills around them, Wonderland mourning the loss of the Hope Bringer.

Cheshire gives into to the agony and shakes her hard.

"Wake up, Danica," he growls. "Danica, wake up." The Hope Bringer doesn't move again, her light slowly fading from her body as they lay in the middle of the carnage Alice left behind. Cheshire sobs, hugging her body close, begging Wonderland to spare his little sister.

But Wonderland is an odd world, and she doesn't come when she's called.

Danica, wake up....

Chapter 1

The entryway for the Helping Hands Nursing Home always makes me feel cold. It's the first thing you see when you walk inside, these white walls and sterile room supposed to make you feel relaxed and homey. Instead, it makes me feel out of place in my dirty blue jeans and leather jacket. I'm incredibly conscious of the fact I could be leaving little scuff marks on tile floor with my motorcycle boots, but I try my hardest not to turn and look. Last time, the prim and proper receptionist had given me the stink eye when I'd tried to clean up a fleck of mud I'd brought in. Apparently, even if I was making a mess, it's frowned upon to actually clean it up and look like they aren't doing their job.

I hate this place.

"We're here to see Diana Yoshida." I tap my fingers on the counter to get the receptionist's attention as she taps away on her computer. I immediately stop when she glances at me with disinterest and points at the clipboard.

"Sign in."

"I hate this place," Atlas whispers to me as he signs us in.

We know the drill. We've been here too many times to count, coming to visit at least three times a week. Today, we come bearing takeout from the Tex-Mex place close to home. It had always been her favorite.

"Me, too, Attie." The receptionist pretends like she doesn't hear our conversation, ever the professional. *Except not*, I think, as she blows a large pink bubble with her gum.

"Head on back." She doesn't even glance at us this time as she points down the hall in the general direction we've walked a hundred times.

We've been coming to the Helping Hands Nursing Home for the better part of two years now, and it's a constant thing hanging over our heads. Contrary to its name, the nursing home hasn't been so helpful except for comfort. Before this one, it was the Country Oaks Nursing Home. It had been nicer but triple the price. We hadn't been able to afford it.

We stop at a doorway partially open, and I peek inside to make sure everything is okay. A doctor leans over a clipboard as he scribbles some sort of chicken scratch across it. No matter how hard I try, I still have yet to be able to read his handwriting. At our arrival, Dr. Frank looks up and smiles. His greying, side-swept hair is perfectly placed as usual. The age lines around his eyes crinkle the tiniest amount at our arrival. Dr. Frank is still young and spry, always able to make a joke, but today, no joke meets our ears. Today, he's serious.

"Ah, right on time," he says, gesturing for us to come in.

I push the door the rest of the way open, and Attie immediately goes and sits across from the woman taking up the couch. We'd tried to make the room as comfortable as possible, but it's difficult when the walls are as white as freshly fallen snow.

My mother had always liked bright colors. Now, she doesn't even question the glaring white.

"Is today a good day?" I ask Dr. Frank, and his tiny smile grows sad. He shakes his head.

"Good morning, Mrs. Yoshida," Attie says softly, smiling at our mother. "How has your day been?"

Mom smiles at Attie, bringing her attention away from the sitcom playing on the television.

"It's been uneventful, unfortunately. I had lunch and then I've been watching my favorite TV show. Oh, what was it called again?"

"The Best Days," Dr. Frank answers helpfully.

"Of course. That's it. I've been watching that show. It's terribly dramatic."

I watch my mom and my little brother interact for a bit, smiling when Attie laughs at something she says. Even with Dementia, she still has her sense of humor. Nothing could take that away. Unfortunately, the disease took away her children.

Dr. Frank stands and motions for me to follow him outside the door. I turn and lead the way, my heart squeezing at whatever it is he wants to tell me. We never discuss her diagnosis in the room. My mom can be violent if she gets worked up. We'd found that any mention of the disease could cause her distress, so I leave Attie to talk to her.

"Are you going to tell me why she has an IV in her arm?" I ask the doctor as he exits the room. We don't go far, just enough that we can talk quietly. I can still hear the conversation between my mom and Attie going on. My eyes meet my little brother's for a moment, and he barely nods his head, letting me know he can handle it. Attie is so strong.

"I'm afraid it's not good news," Dr. Frank says, his eyes meeting mine in an attempt to get the information across. I'm sure he comes into contact with patients and families that refuse to listen, but he doesn't have to worry about that with me. I listen to every word.

I bite my cheek to prepare for whatever it is he's about to tell me, knowing it can't be good. No doctor ever says it's not good news if it's not terrible news.

"Your mother has begun deteriorating at a rapid rate."

"What does that mean?" I ask, shoving my clenched fists into my pockets.

"It means she's stopped fighting the disease, and her age isn't helping. It's like her body is shutting down because her brain is. It's not uncommon for a person to decide it's their time, and their body seems to know it."

"Can't we give her more medicine?"

"Your mother is already on ten different medications daily. Her liver can't handle any more."

"So, what does that all mean?" I ask again, meeting his eyes.

Dr. Franks sighs and runs a hand through his hair. I can't imagine this part is easy.

"Your mother only had one good day last month. She's had none this month. The rest of the time, she spends asking the nurses and caretakers if they can find her husband and tell him to bring her babies to her. She's been on emergency oxygen for the last three months. Her liver functions are failing. I'm afraid to say, your mother doesn't have that much time left."

I bite down hard on the inside of my cheek again to keep tears from springing to my eyes. I have to be strong for Attie. I turn to look at him again as he discusses the weather with mom. For the first time, I take in her appearance, really seeing. Her skin looks paper thin, pale, her veins bright blue underneath. There are bags around her eyes, and her hair is more unkempt than usual. When she reaches for the remote, her hand shakes as if it's too much to bear. I swallow hard.

Attie continues his conversation even though mom has dropped off, her attention no longer held with the weather. Attie always talks to her, whether she's aware or catatonic. Some days, she'll say nothing at all, just stare blankly at the wall.

"Mrs. Diana, have you been working on your needlepoint?" Attie asks, glancing at the unfinished piece on the table.

Mom smiles and leans forward to pat Attie's hand.

"You're such a respectful young gentleman," she says. Hope fills my body that perhaps, today can be a good day. "I hope my son is as respectful as you when he grows up. He's only a baby. Come to think of it, where's my Atlas? Do you know where my husband has gone off to?"

I can see the tears glisten in Attie's eyes, and it's a struggle not to have them spill over my own lashes.

"No, ma'am. I'm sorry. I don't know where he is." Lie. We both know that Dad died ten years ago. But Mom is stuck in a loop, thinking it's fourteen years prior, when Attie was only a year old, and I was fourteen. To her, we should be much younger, so she no longer recognizes us.

"Blasted man. Always wandering off. He probably has his nose in a book somewhere. He never could resist a good book."

Truth. Dad was a professor who studied mythology. I remember his bedtime stories being full of the Greek gods and Roman battles. I'd heard the Odyssey more times than I could count by the time I reached teenage years. He's the reason I bear the name Calypso, and my brother, Atlas. He was cool like that.

We used to tell mom the facts, let her know what's true and what's not. That's what they always say. Bring in things that can remind her, things from home, items she would know. So, we followed their directions. We brought in everything we could think of, artwork from school, Dad's journals, her favorite blanket. And it worked for a little while. We would tell her stories, and she would laugh as if she hadn't been there to witness them herself.

But eventually, the facts began to upset her. We'd tell her a story, and she'd begin to thrash and call us liars. She'd throw things at us, scream at us to get out, to bring her babies to her, to find her husband. She'd be so uncontrollable that nothing we said would break through. When she got violent with a nurse, the doctors advised us to go along with whatever she said to ease her pain. So, we did, and the violent outbursts stopped. It had eased our mother's pain, but it had increased ours, instead.

"I want to take my mom home," I tell Dr. Frank suddenly, my decision made.

"That isn't wise. Your mother needs constant medical attention. If she continues to decline, her organs will start failing, more than just her liver."

I watch Attie wrap a shawl around my mom's shoulders, her smile up at him so gentle, appreciative, but without a single hint of recognition.

"She deserves to be home. If this is her end." My eyes don't leave the sight of Attie making sure she's warm, of my fifteen-year-old brother taking on too much responsibility, too much pain. The least I can do is make sure we can spend as much time with her as possible, even if she doesn't recognize us. "She would want to be home," I whisper, biting the inside of my cheek so hard, I taste blood.

Dr. Frank studies me for a moment, looking for some sign. He won't find one. I won't let any of my emotion cross my face. I need strength right now, not tears. Finally, he nods his head.

"It'll take some time to get the paperwork together. She'll be registered under the hospice program. We'll make sure she's comfortable. There's also the matter of medical supplies, and things that will need to be done to prepare for her coming home."

"That's fine. Whatever we need, we'll get it." I meet his eyes, my shoulders back in a semblance of calm.

"Can you afford to?" Dr. Frank looks worried. He's been the attending doctor since we first came to Helping Hands. He remembers everything, including the two bounced checks we'd had this year. I'd had the money, but the jobs I had took a little longer than planned.

That hasn't happened in months, though. It's fine. We can handle it. We will.

"We'll make it work," I tell him, my hands clenched tight enough to ache in my pocket. "We have to."

Chapter 2

When we push through the doors and exit the building, I take the deepest breath possible. It always smells like disinfectant inside, and bleach on the deep clean days. Today had been a bleach day, and my nose hairs burn with the scent of it.

We walk through the busy parking lot until we get to my vintage Harley, parked in the back; away from the idiot drivers who might back over it. It had happened before, back when I'd had a cheaper version. Now, I don't take any chances.

The beauty had cost me a small fortune and is the one thing I've been able to treat myself with. I had saved pennies to buy it, the sleek black machine beautiful, fully restored to its glory. It's my pride and joy, after my little brother.

I unhook the helmets from underneath the seat and pass one to Attie before buckling my own. The mood is tense, somber. Attie is always the one to break the tension.

"So, when am I gonna get my own bike? The guys at school have been teasing me about riding on the back of my sister's."

I chuckle, knowing full well that the guys tease him about it. I'm not worried about bullying. My brother has a great group of friends, all ones that I've met before. In fact, one of them had recently gotten up the courage to ask for my number. I'd laughed and asked if he needed a babysitter. The kid had blushed so hard, I thought he would explode.

I'd been the only face they'd all seen for years, my mother's illness common knowledge around town.

We'd known she'd had dementia for a few years before the nursing homes, but it hadn't been extreme. She'd forget which street to take, forget things at the grocery store that she needed. One time, she got everything to make hamburgers except the meat. Those were the small signs. Once, she got lost and ended up three towns over, trying to get inside someone else's house she swore was hers.

Then one morning, she'd woken up and started screaming that there were strangers in her house. Attie and I had just watched her, terrified, as she called the cops because we were trespassing. When she pulled the gun from under the bed where dad had kept it and pointed it at Attie, that had been the last straw. We'd had no choice, and she'd been admitted to Country Oaks that day.

Attie had only been ten, and I had just turned twenty-four.

That day, I became the guardian of my little brother. It had been tough to keep him out of the system. The courts didn't seem to think that a twenty-four year old could handle her little brother, even though there were teenagers having babies and handling it all the time. When I pointed out that I was family, and that I was able to support him, they'd finally relented. Not without costing me a good amount of court fees, though. They couldn't do something good without taking from people who need it most.

I'd worked my ass off to open my own mechanic shop, something that my dad and I had dreamed of since I'd been a little girl working under the hood of his '69 Chevelle. The shop's successful, and well-known in the city, but every now and then, work could get slow, resulting in a bank account far too small to pay for the expensive nursing home. Some days, we'd survive on Ramen noodles. But I always set aside a little money every month, a nest egg I'd been building for Attie's college. He probably wouldn't need it, not with how good he was at baseball, but it would be there just in case. I want to make sure my little brother doesn't have to struggle, even if I have to take on all the struggle myself.

"Another year, and you'll be able to drive," I remind Attie, smiling at him wearing the helmet. He always complains it ruins his hair, but he dutifully snaps it on, knowing how important it is to me. "Besides, I know you're just eager to get that girl you like on the back of it." Attie blushes and itches at his shoulder. "Have you asked her out yet?"

"No, she doesn't even know I exist." Attie looks down at the ground, so oblivious.

I doubt that girl has anything but feelings for my little brother. Every morning when I drop him off for school, she only has eyes for him. She probably thinks the same thing, that Attie doesn't know she exists. Oh, teenage love. So much simpler, and yet so much more dramatic.

I smile, trying to hide the sadness from creeping in. I understand why he might be too scared to ask the girl out.

"You just need a few seconds of courage. That's all." I open my mouth to tell him what the doctor said, but think better of it. Now isn't the time to burden him with the details. There's always later. "Mom is coming back home to live with us," I say instead.

When Attie's eyes meet mine, I realize I don't need to go into details, after all, not right now. He knows. He knows that mom isn't coming home because she's getting better. He understands that the news isn't good. My fifteen-year-old brother just nods his head and climbs onto the back of the motorcycle. I follow suit and start her up.

The rumble of the engine soothes my soul, at least for a little while.

Tomorrow. I can always deal with everything tomorrow.

Chapter 3

CHESHIRE

Something slaps me in the face, making me growl softly. When I sit up and hold up the offending material, I realize it's my leather pants, and not the threat I assumed it was. I blink my eyes to clear the sleep from them before looking towards the door.

"Get dressed," White says, slight disdain in his voice. "Now."

I yawn, stretching my arms above my head until my bones pop.

"What's got ahold of your cotton tail this morning?" I taunt, the corner of my lips ticking up.

White's eyes drop to the naked female beside me, out cold from a night of exploration. Her blonde hair spills over the pillows, a mess of curls and stickiness. She smells like peaches and hairspray, a scent my nose absolutely hates. But she'd fucked like a mad woman, so it had been worth it to spend the night inhaling the fumes.

White sighs and scrubs a hand down his face. "We're here to find your mate, Cheshire, not so you can whore yourself out to the general population."

I grin at that and roll my eyes. A soft sigh escapes the woman beside me, and I fight the urge to frown. Annoyance fills my body as I realize I've been here too long.

"I'm trying to help. How else would I know if she's my mate or not?" It's stupid to taunt White this way. I've already seen the prophecy come true twice now. But still, I can't help but brush it off, and pretend that there's nothing in it for me. I won't let my life be decided by a few rhymes.

White shakes his head, no anger on his face. That unsettles me more than anything else he could have said. White had been angry with me the first couple of times he'd found me in bed with a woman. A few times, I'd invited him to join in, only for him to scowl and storm away. I knew he would never actually jump in, not without Jupiter anyways. White was well and truly smitten with his mate, as he should be. Jupiter was perfect for him, a light that chased away his darkness. For me, my darkness is a permanent part of me. It can't be chased away by a dainty little redhead.

"You'll know without having to get into her pants," White says. It's the same line I've heard him say since we came to this world, and I ignore it just the same. I doubt there's a woman out there that's so perfect for me, it'll change everything. There's no way. My luck doesn't run that deep. And I have no urge to give away any more feelings only for them to be taken away. "Get up," White orders again. "I have this tingling. We're close. This sleepy little town has promise."

I frown and look down at the woman snoring beside me, blissfully unaware that there are two predators in her room that could easily kill her if they wanted. These people could be so dense sometimes, or perhaps just as self-destructive as I am.

"It's not her," White says, disgust on his face. "Get dressed. We're going out."

White storms from the room with another look of disdain, no doubt waiting for me to follow. I'm getting really sick of his orders, as if he's the general here and not me.

I sigh and climb from the bed, tugging on my leather pants. The woman rolls over and groans in her sleep, the scent of hairspray smacking me in the face again. I wrinkle my nose, my tail flicking from side to side in annoyance.

Her hand reaches out towards the other side of the bed, but when she opens her eyes to look for me, I'm already gone.

Chapter 4

The sounds of classic rock echo around the mechanic shop, the noise both comforting and soft, competing with the high-powered fans trying to keep the shop cool. My mechanic shop is a decent size, four bay doors for pulling in the vehicles, but today, there's only one project.

I'm leaning under the hood, tightening a bolt, cursing the older black Impala while also crossing my fingers that this is it. We've been chasing problems on this thing all day. The owner said it had been flooded recently after a southern freak rainstorm, and after drying it out, it began to understandably have problems. The things with the cars 1980s and newer is all the electrical. An engine can survive flood waters once it's drained and dried out, but the wires and electrical bits can't. And all the newer vehicles can't run without the electronics.

"Try it again," I shout to Rob, my partner.

Rob has been in my life as long as I can remember. He'd been a good friend of my dad's and after dad had passed, he'd stuck around. He's always been a sort of uncle to Attie and me. He'd been the one to help me get my mechanic shop off the ground. He's the reason I don't go running and screaming every time a new problem arises. He's our rock.

Rob cranks the key in the ignition, and there's a hard click from the engine compartment.

"Shit. Now the starter has gone out," I growl, dropping the wrench from my hand.

I have the insane urge to kick the old-school Impala, but I'm sure the customer wouldn't like a foot-sized dent in their car. Every single time we fix one thing, something else goes wrong. It's like searching for a needle in a haystack, and I'm getting real sick of it.

"Do we have one lying around for this model?" I ask, scraping my hair back away from my face.

"Nope," Rob answers, sliding from the driver's seat and closing the door. "But I can order it in. Should be here by the end of the day if we're lucky. If not, then tomorrow morning."

"Figures." I sigh. I'd hoped to get the car out of my shop today but no dice.

I glance at the clock and realize it's already three in the afternoon. Normally, I would have taken a break around two to go pick up Attie from school. He likes to hang out at the shop sometimes and do his homework. But his best friend had recently gotten his license, so he's been catching a ride with him. They were going to the movies after school. I wonder if he finally asked the girl he likes to go with him.

With nothing better to do, and the shop closing in a few hours, I wipe my hands clean and toss my tools back in the tool box.

"You can go home if you want, Rob. I'll clean up."

"Are you sure?" he asks, eying the tools scattered around the floor. We usually have one other employee, a younger kid who knows his way around an engine, but he'd called in sick today. He's a good kid, but sometimes he really puts us in a bind. Luckily, we hadn't been that busy today.

"I'm fine. I'm just gonna work on Bertha until closing and then head home."

"I can help with that."

I wave him away.

"Go home to that sweet little grandchild of yours. Give Timmy a kiss for me."

Rob's son had recently moved back in with him, bringing along his one-year-old son. The mom had skipped out on them, and Rob had offered for them to come live at his house until his son could get his feet back under him. I've known his son, Rob Jr., for as long as I've known Rob. He's a good man and it shows every time I watch him with his baby. Little Timmy is adorable, and I always look forward to baby cuddles when we all eat dinner together.

Rob is so excited to have his son and grandson home with him. He adores the baby, and that child will never want for anything. Hell, even I'm known to show up with a toy or two when the funds allow. He is just too cute not to spoil.

"If you're sure," Rob says, trailing off. He's already wiping his hands clean and heading for the door. I smile at the sight, perfectly happy to give him some time off. Now, if I can just convince him to go on vacation. "Don't forget to lock the door behind me," he calls over his shoulder.

"We're still open. I can't lock it until five." But he doesn't hear me. He's already out the door.

I listen for the sound of his truck starting, the husky rumble penetrating the metal walls and forcing my eyes closed to absorb it. I love the sound of deep, loud pipes. There's something about the purr that always makes me feel better.

I turn towards Bertha, my 1940 WW2 Harley I'd slowly been restoring to its former glory. I'd bought the bike from an old man who'd had it rusting away in his backyard. It came with tons of history, including the story of being ridden by the man's father during the war. I have plans to get the man's name and rank painted on the gas tank once I get to that point. It has been hell getting the parts for it though. It's gonna be worth it, but I still bitch about it on the regular. The gas tank for it had cost me a whopping twelve hundred dollars. The parts are collectibles now. It slowly coming along because of that fact, but I can't wait for the first chance to start her up.

Cranking up the radio, letting the sounds of classic rock flow through me, I start to bob my head as I take a seat at the workbench. Bertha's engine is in pieces, spread out, so I can see each one. I'd had to improvise some of the parts, the mechanics no longer safe and available, so the engine will be a little more updated than the motorcycle. I wish I could keep the whole thing stock, but that just isn't the case. It's a shame, really.

I'm so deep in my work, slowly putting pieces together, that when a thump sounds to my right, rattling the work bench, I jump. When I search for the source of the disturbance, I scowl and immediately turn down the radio.

"What the hell are you doing in my shop, Jerry?" I ask, already feeling a headache coming on.

Jerry owns the mechanic shop down the block and is my closest competition. Dressed in a grungy work shirt and dirty jeans, his beer belly hangs over and gives him an imposing appearance. His receding hairline gives him the creep vibe. But his personality does that all on it's own.

Jerry likes to think his shop is superior to mine, but that's honestly just because he's a man. Sexist pig isn't a big enough word to describe the man standing beside me. Truth is, I run an honest mechanic shop, while Jerry likes to rob his customers blind. I've had to repair some of his "repairs" when customers have come to me after the disaster of his shop. One woman had come in after dropping three grand at Jerry's shop because they'd told her she needed all new pistons, only to bring it to me. She'd only needed a tune up. I didn't charge her; I never did if they were Jerry's "repairs". I always feel so bad that they've had to go through that; Jerry is such a snake.

I drop the ratchet I'd been using on the table top and close my fingers around the two-inch wrench beside me. I've never used the massive wrench on cars. No, this baby is for protection, large as a small baseball bat.

"I saw Rob leave. Figured I'd come check on you to make sure you're okay over here all alone." A grotesque leer pulls his lips, and I have to fight the urge to grimace in disgust. Jerry is known to harass women. The fact that I'm in the same career field as him and successful doesn't sit right. To him, a woman belongs in the kitchen and in bed. Nothing more. Fucking bastard. If there's anyone I hate in the world, it's this man.

"Unless you're here to pay me back some of the money you owe me for fixing your screw ups, you can see yourself to the door."

I have a file in my office full of the receipts for work I've done to fix his problems, just so I can throw that out there. I figure if I say it enough, he might pay me just to get me to shut up.

I stand from my stool and meet Jerry's eyes head on. I'm taller than him by about three inches, another fact he doesn't like. But he also assumes that because I'm a woman, I must be weaker. He should know better. My biceps alert everyone to the fact that I lift heavy shit. That'll be his downfall, though.

Jerry takes a step towards me. "I don't owe you nothing, bitch."

"Then get the fuck out of my shop before you leave here on your knees." I don't even snarl at him. My threat is calm and calculated, but it's exactly the type of thing you don't say to a sexist pig if you want them to leave. To be honest, I might be subconsciously goading him. It wouldn't be the first time.

He immediately fluffs up like a rooster, his masculinity so fragile that he can't stand my words.

"Listen here, you—"

"Is there a problem here?"

We both turn towards the new voice coming from the doorway, Jerry because he's been caught threatening a woman and doesn't want a witness, and me because it could be a new customer. When my eyes land on the man standing by the door, framed by harsh sunlight, my eyebrows go straight up to my hairline.

The new man is wearing rabbit ears on his head for some odd reason, but that doesn't detract from his attractiveness. He's clean cut, wearing an old style waistcoat and a fancy watch on his wrist. The bunny ears throw me off, but it's not that crazy, I suppose. People wear all kinds of stuff when the comic-con comes to town. I still blink just in case I'm imagining him.

"Who the hell are you?" Jerry asks.

The newcomer glances around the shop, seemingly looking for something. When he sees the Impala that has been causing us trouble sitting in the bay, he points to it.

"I came to check on my car. Unfortunately, I came inside just as you were threatening the lady."

This man is definitely not here for that car. The owner of the impala is a sweet little old lady who wears a scarf around her head with cats on it. She has no children—she'd told me her life story when she first came in—so this couldn't even be her son or a family member. He's using the car as an excuse, but really, I don't need his help.

"Why don't you mind your own business?" Jerry sneers, before reaching out his grubby, grease-coated fingers for my arm. When those digits wrap around my forearm, the newcomer lunges forward as if to help, but it's unnecessary.

I slide the wrench free from the bench and swing it towards Jerry's gut. It makes contact, and he doubles over. His fingers stay wrapped around my forearm, so I don't give him time to gather his wits. I bring my knee up and aim for his balls so hard, that he drops to the floor, his fingers finally sliding off my skin. I have the sudden urge to scrub that part of my arm until it's raw.

The newcomer comes to a stop in front of me, and looks down at the pig rolling around on the floor. His breathing is harsh, and it sounds kind of like he's trying to call me a bitch, but he just doesn't have the air.

The newcomer smiles and meets my eyes.

"Your eyes are very unusual," I say, tilting my head, a frown on my face.

They're like molten silver and almost glow even in the harsh lighting of the shop.

"I've been told that. Want me to take out the trash?" he asks, gesturing to Jerry still on the ground.

I shrug. "If you don't mind, sure."

The newcomer reaches down and grips a fistful of Jerry's shirt before dragging him towards the door. He doesn't even grunt with the weight, even though Jerry has a full-sized beer gut and has to weigh close to three hundred pounds. He literally kicks Jerry out of the door. I hear a satisfying groan of pain from him before Silver Eyes turns back to me.

I get the chance to study him a little closer as he walks back towards me. His waistcoat is definitely not a modern cut. It reminds me of the Victorian era a bit, and it's emerald green. But instead of proper slacks, the waistcoat is paired with dark-brown leather pants and combat boots. A goth, maybe? I don't think hipsters wear this kind of stuff.

"I have to ask," I point to his head, "what's with the rabbit ears?"

He grins at my question, but he doesn't answer it, changing the subject, instead. Well, okay, then.

"I have a friend I think you should meet," he says.

I frown, and set the wrench back on the workbench.

"Is this like trying to set me up for a date?" There's something off about the way he asked it, as if he's not quite expecting a date, but also wants it to be. I can't pick up on his tone, though.

"Call it introducing two people who would get along well." I swear I hear him mumble "or not" under his breath, but I don't comment on it.

"Look, I appreciate you taking Jerry out of my shop, but I'm not looking for a man, now or in the near future. I don't have time for one."

He glances at the intricate watch on his wrist, and I peer at it curiously before he can hide it away behind his back.

"I know all about not having time, unfortunately. I'm afraid I have to go." He glances at my Harley, spread out in pieces. "If I bring in a motorcycle tomorrow, could you work on it for me?"

I perk up, automatically switching into professional mode.

"Absolutely. Besides the Impala, I'm wide open. What do you need worked on?"

He grins again, chuckling at some imaginary joke. "It doesn't quite purr like it used to."

"It might need a tune up then. That's no trouble at all. Just bring it by tomorrow, and we'll get you all straightened up."

He nods and turns to leave without another word.

"I didn't catch your name," I tell his back, and he turns to look over his shoulder at me.

"You can call me White. See you around, Calypso."

It takes me a full minute after he's gone before I realize he knew my full name, even though my shirt only says "Cal."

Chapter 5

I pull a TV dinner from the freezer and toss it in the microwave, watching as it slowly spins in circles. Attie had called to let me know he's staying at his friends. Not unusual. The friends' mom, Becky, had already called to let me know they'd arrived. She's a sweet woman and never minds when Attie stays over.

The community had kind of all banded together when I first got guardianship of Attie. I'd been hopeless at first, burning everything I tried cooking besides macaroni and cheese. I'd never had to actually cook meals before. Mom would always cook when she came home, and while out and about, I'd survived on takeout and Ramen noodles. But Becky had stepped in to help and immediately taught me how to cook some of my favorite meals. Now I can make everything from meatloaf to enchiladas, all things I'd never needed to make before. Cooking for yourself isn't something I do, because there is always something left over. For a while, I had to cook for three, and now I cook for two. But tonight, I'm back to cooking for one, so a TV dinner, it is.

When the machine beeps, I pull the small tray out and plop it down on the table. *Nothing like microwave, frost-bitten turkey,* I think as I take a bite. I eat slowly, going through a mental checklist of things I need to do to prepare before mom comes home. She's scheduled to come in a few days. The nursing home had already called with a list of supplies I'll need to have available, and it includes everything from a first aid kit to an oxygen tank.

A nurse would stop by everyday while I'm at work and Attie is at school to take care of her. The service costs a pretty penny, but at least Mom will be home and happy. We're even going to tell her that Attie and I are just more caregivers, ones who stay overnight with her. She seems to accept that more than us actually being her own grown children. As much as it will hurt to do it, at least Mom will be comfortable until the end.

"Dad," I whisper, looking up towards the ceiling. "I'm trying to do the right thing. I'm trying to make sure everything is okay. I hope I'm doing it right."

I wish my dad was here to talk to. He'd always known the right things to say. He'd been killed by a drunk driver when I had been nineteen. Attie had only been five. It had been a shock to mom; they'd been the loves of each other's lives, perfect for each other and yet complete opposites.

Mom used to be a dancer in her younger days, ballet. When she couldn't dance anymore, she'd been the instructor. And dad, well, he was that mythology professor everyone thought was so cool and nerdy. They'd always been in love, always smiling. Losing dad had started her decline, spiraling from the little things into forgetting names and getting lost. It had all been manageable . . .

. . . until the gun incident.

"Who are you? Why are you in my house?

"Mom, it's me. Atlas."

"My Atlas is only a baby. Get out! Get out!" she'd screamed.

Then we'd heard the sound of the gun being cocked.

And so we'd lost our father and our mother, and it became just the two of us.

Chapter 6

"I seen Jerry limping into his shop today. Wouldn't happen to know anything about that?" Rob asks when he walks into the shop the next morning.

I fight the grin that wants to spread across my face, and I'm confident I meet his eyes without humor.

"Nope."

"Hmmm . . .," he scrubs his chin. "'Cause I also heard him talking about how three guys jumped him yesterday."

I can't hold the snort that comes out, and Rob raises his brow at me.

"Alright, alright," I say, grinning. "Not three men. Just little ole me and my wrench."

"I knew it!" he growled. "What did that asshole do after I left?"

I shrug and walk over to the Impala. The starter came in this morning, so we're set to replace it and hopefully, get this thing out of my shop.

"He got a bit handsy is all. I took care of it. And then a customer helped me take out the trash."

Rob shakes his head and runs his hand through his receding hairline. If he keeps that up, he'll be bald sooner rather than later.

"I'm glad you can take care of yourself, baby girl, but please be careful. Jerry isn't the kind to let something like that go."

"I know," I nod. "I'll be careful."

"Next time, he could bring backup."

"Well, then, it's a good thing I have you, old man." I clap Rob on the back, and he smiles down at me.

The rumble of a motorcycle grows in the distance, coming closer, and I tilt my head to listen as it gets loud enough to drown out the radio. It sounds good, and to any normal person, there wouldn't be a problem at all, but every so often, there's a skip in the rumble. It's slight now, but could be a bigger problem later. Either the engine is missing, or it's misfiring. Neither are good things.

The rumble stops outside the bay doors and shuts off, the sounds of classic rock suddenly filling the shop again. That motorcycle might be missing, but it sure is loud. I bet it's a beauty.

We watch the door, waiting for whoever it is to step inside. When White steps through the opening, I smile.

"Who's that?" Rob asks when he sees my smile.

"The customer who helped take out the trash yesterday. He's bringing his motorcycle in for a tune up."

Rob narrows his eyes on the man, and I wait for him to mention the rabbit ears White still wears on his head. They even quiver and twitch, like they're robotic or something. I bet they cost a pretty penny. When Rob doesn't even bring them up, I frown.

"What do you think of the ears?" I whisper to him. One of the ears twitches like White might have heard me, but there's no way.

"What?" Rob looks at me in confusion. "I don't know. They're covered by his hair."

My frown deepens, and I glance at the ears that I can very much see, but I don't bring them up again. White comes right up to us with a smile on his face. It's a gentle smile, but even I can tell there's more underneath there. He has secrets, just like everyone else. That's the beauty of my business and meeting people face to face. I can always get a good read on them, and somehow, White still ticks my danger instincts, even if he's the definition of kindness right now.

"Good morning, Calypso," White greets me, and I nod my head in welcome.

"Morning. This is Rob, my partner."

White's eyes flick to Rob and looks him up and down.

"Partner?" I hear a thread of confusion, so I feel like I should clarify.

"Business partner. Rob is pretty much my uncle." I elbow Rob in the side playfully, and he flicks me on the ear in retaliation. White watches the exchange with curiosity, taking it all in.

"Ah, I see. I brought my motorcycle for you to look at."

"Yes! You were right to bring it to me. There's definitely a misfire in your engine. I heard it when you pulled up."

"Really?" Surprise flickers in his eyes. It's not a usual reaction. "You could diagnose the problem from so far away? And just by sound?"

"It's her gift," Rob says proudly, slinging his arm over my shoulder. "She's the best in the city. It's like she speaks to the machines."

I laugh and shake my head. He's exaggerating, as usual. I'm not that great. But if you give me an engine to diagnose, I can do it. It's the reason we're doing so great with the shop. We guarantee the problem to be fixed before the customer leaves. And if we can't fix it, then we don't charge, simple as that. That's my dad's legacy, something I put in place to honor him. He would have never charged someone if he couldn't help them, no matter how much time he spent on the project.

Rob wipes his hand and scratches his head, before glancing at the clock.

"Mind if I take a quick break?"

"We haven't even started yet." I laugh. "What do ya need a break for already?"

"Timmy had a rough night." He rubs the back of his neck. "With all his crying this morning, I forgot to grab breakfast. I was just gonna hit up the burrito place across the street. I can grab you one, too."

"Go ahead." I wink at him. "The usual."

"The big one," Rob nods in understanding. "Be right back."

I watch Rob practically skip through the door on his way across the street. That burrito place loves when Rob comes in. He might always order me the same thing, but he tells them to surprise him each morning for his. One time, he got a Jalapeno, cheese, bacon, egg, and donut burrito. It literally had pieces of chopped up glazed donut inside it. Another time, they added pineapple. They've started getting pretty creative.

"So, you have the keys to your bike?" I ask White.

"Of course."

When he hands me a set of keys, and I look down at them, I snort. I hold the keychain up in front of me. Dangling from the metal hook is a lucky rabbit's foot.

"Really?"

"I couldn't help myself," he teases, laughing right along with me. "Also, I want to introduce you to my friend."

I sigh, already forgetting the joke we'd been laughing about. "I already told you, I'm not interested."

"Well, he came with me," White says, and I roll my eyes.

"You're not gonna let this go, are you?"

White smiles, but it doesn't quite reach his eyes this time. The hairs on the back of my neck stand up, but I don't know why. This moment feels important, loaded some how.

"Just meet him. That's all I ask."

I'm tempted to say no, to stick to my guns, but White helped me out, and he seems so earnest, I find myself nodding my head.

"Fine. Where is he?"

White points behind me, and I turn, my eyes immediately finding a man sprawled across the top of Bertha. Like White, he has ears on his head, though his are feline. They're grey with bright-blue stripes. I watch as they twitch and move, before a tail, which flicks over his hip, catches my attention. What are these guys into? Are they furries?

I take in the leather jacket hanging open, a chiseled chest on display beneath it. He's built, and hotter than any man I've ever met. Certainly, hotter than any man I've ever seen. He wears leather pants and combat boots, and he's exactly the kind of guy I'd normally feel myself drawn to even though I know it's a bad idea. This man reeks of bad choices. I've never met someone who so completely screams 'Bad boy.'

A Cheshire grin spreads across his face when he sees me ogling him, and those ears twist again, bringing my eyes up to his. They glow an electric, vibrant blue, a color so bright, I'm almost drawn to them like a bug.

"Hello there, Pretty Thing," he purrs, and his voice is like gasoline to my ovaries. They sit up and stand at attention. Hell, they probably would roll over if he told them to. But I don't focus on any of that. I don't reply to the obvious pick-up line, not with any reaction he might be hoping for.

Instead, I say very nicely, "Get the fuck off my bike."

Okay. So, maybe not that nicely.

Chapter 7

I can feel White's grin even though I'm not looking at him. There's a sort of giddy excitement coming from his aura in waves, and for some reason, it makes me bristle even more. What are these two getting at? Is this a joke?

My eyes stay fixed on the man with cat ears, his ass still parked on Bertha.

"Did I stutter?" I ask when he doesn't move.

This time, White actually snickers out loud, and I glance at him. There's absolute glee on his face, and I wrinkle my brow.

"What kind of joke is this?" I look between the two men, taking in their ears again, confusion taking over.

"What do you mean?" White asks, tilting his head even though the laughter is still in his eyes.

"Y'all two come in my shop, dressed in furry costumes, and expect me to not think this is a joke?" I grab my wrench from the workbench and hold it at my side. I no longer feel as safe as I had before.

"Calm down," Cat Ears says, his tail flicking again. He still hasn't moved from Bertha.

I take a step towards him and raise the wrench.

"What part of 'get off my bike,' didn't you understand?" I snarl.

"All of it. It's just a machine." He rolls his eyes, and I have the sudden urge to bash him upside the head with my wrench. *Deep breaths, Cal. You don't want to go to prison today.*

"You have three seconds to get off of my bike before I make you get off." Cat Ears raises his brow but doesn't move. "One."

"I'd listen if I were you, Cheshire." White smiles. "I watched her take down a man twice her size yesterday."

"Two." My voice is hard. I'm not even listening to what White says. My eyes are trained on the man in front of me. I take another step forward.

"What can she possibly do to me?" I know his name is Cheshire now. How fitting since he wears cat ears.

"Your funeral," White shrugs and takes a step back at the same time as I step forward.

"Three." I don't give him any more warning. I swing the wrench towards Cheshire's chest, intending to knock him off my bike. I don't expect him to be fast enough to block it, but that's exactly what he does. His hand shoots up and wraps around my wrench before it can make contact.

"Ah, ah, ah," he chides, his eyes flashing for a moment. I swear they look like they're slitted like a cat's for a moment before they're human again. "That isn't very nice."

I release the wrench when I'm unable to yank it from his grasp and throw my fist at his nose. I don't need the weapon to make my point. My knuckles connect with his face, and Cheshire jerks backwards with a snarl.

"What the fuck?"

I'm satisfied when blood drips from his nostrils, and his eyes narrow on me. He completely ignores the possibly broken nose as if it's a common occurrence. Who knows? For him it might be.

White absolutely loses it behind me, laughing so hard he doubles over to clutch his stomach.

"If you don't want a black eye to match that broken nose, I suggest you move." My voice is calm, even though my hand aches from the hit, and my anger is festering beneath my skin. White howls louder.

Cheshire grins, and it throws me off guard enough that I take a step back when he finally stands.

"You're a feisty little thing, aren't you?" he purrs. I narrow my eyes and turn to White.

"I don't like your friend, White. Leave your keys, and I'll take care of the misfire, but take him with you when you leave." I move back over to the Impala and lean under the hood. I can feel Cheshire's eyes on me, and it pisses me off that my body reacts to it and begs for me to wiggle my ass a little more. Instead, I say, "Keep your eyes off my ass, and you'll get to keep them."

Cheshire snorts even as White laughs again.

"Actually," he says between chuckles, "we have something to ask you."

I sigh and straighten. "If it's for a date, I'm going to be extremely pissed off."

"I don't date," Cheshire adds helpfully, but his eyes trail down my body in a way that suggests he does other things.

"Of course, you don't, Pussy Cat."

Cheshire growls and takes a step towards me, but White holds up his hand. Surprisingly, Cheshire stops and looks at him even though there's still fury in his eyes.

"What do you know of Wonderland?"

I frown.

"You mean like the story book?"

"Well," White shrugs, "yes and no. Do you believe it's real?"

"It's a book." I roll my eyes. "And I'm not a child anymore who believes in fairytales."

"No, you're certainly not a child," Cheshire mumbles, and I fight really hard not to look at him.

Cheshire is exactly the type of guy I would normally go for. The cat ears and tail are a bit weird, but everything else is perfect. Even now, I'm tempted to look at his naked chest. The only thing he's missing is tattoos, but those could be hidden. He's the spitting image of a Bad Boy, and I can't help but want to lick him.

But I have too much going on in my life to take him up on the invitation in his eyes. Cheshire doesn't seem the kind to stick around after a night of great sex, which is perfect, but White makes me feel like something bigger is happening here, and I can tell I don't want any part of it. Not with my mother getting sicker, and Attie going through his teenage years.

"What would you say if I told you it was all real?" White asks, his face so serious, it makes me pause.

I glance between the two men, confused, before laughter bubbles from my lips.

"Oh, I get it now," I manage between laughs. "That's what the ears are for, right? The White Rabbit and the Cheshire Cat. Y'all have too much time on your hands."

"It's the truth, Calypso."

Neither of the men are laughing, just watching me with solemn eyes.

"So, then you're just crazy." White shakes his head, and I glare at him before turning my eyes on Cheshire, who thinks he's actually the Cheshire cat. What the fuck? "I don't have time for this shit. I have work to do, so if you'll kindly leave my shop, that would be great." I toss the motorcycle keys back to White. "I don't think I'm the best mechanic for you. Try another shop."

"Calypso, wait."

For some reason, my eyes flick to Cheshire's instead of White even though he isn't the one who spoke. Cheshire's face holds more than one emotion. There's annoyance, sure, but there's also anger, lust, and a brief flicker of hope that's gone before I can study it closer.

"We need your help," White says, urgency in his words.

I shake my head. "Sorry, I don't have time for fairytales."

I turn and walk away.

Chapter 8

JUPITER

"They've been gone a long time," I comment, worrying my bottom lip. The Hatter's table is completely full and overflowing. There was a brief spell where there weren't any tea parties at all and then suddenly, the number of deaths tripled. It was Alice's way of making up for the brief lull.

We've had to find extensions for the table, and add more spots for seats. We're using anything we can find now as tables. Barrels, crates, I don't even know what some of the stuff is. It makes the tea room even more of a mismatched nightmare than usual.

There's a low hum in the room as all the guests talk to each other. There's so many that there's almost no room to move, and I can barely hear myself talk.

Across from me, Doe sips her tea delicately, watching all the creatures, a heavy sadness in her eyes.

"It could have only been a day in your world," Doe reminds me.

"Well, it's been two months here, and I'm slowly going insane with worry." I frown. "What if something went wrong?"

Clara reaches across and picks up my hand.

"They'll be fine. We know Cheshire's mate will be a tricky one. I'm sure the cat is fighting White every step of the way."

Hatter nods his head before he speaks.

"This will most likely be the most difficult part of the prophecy."

I sigh and glance at the Tweedles, sitting in their usual spot in the midst of the tea party members.

"More and more people are attending the tea parties," I comment, meeting Clara's eyes.

Clara can't hide the worry in her eyes. "We can only wait and hope."

"What do we hope for?" I ask. There are so many things to focus on. I hope Alice fails. I hope White comes back unharmed. I hope we can keep everything together.

"We hope that Cheshire's mate saves us all," Clara says solemnly.

I frown. That's so much pressure to put on one woman. Whoever she is, I hope she has a spine of steel, and that she can stay strong for us all. At least she won't be alone. At least, she'll have us to stand at her side.

There's a high-pitched ringing that fills the room, then, and makes everyone fall silent to listen. Doe jerks in her chair, and a tiny smile curls her lips.

"Be easy," she whispers when the room grows quiet. "The flamingo comes."

Chapter 9

"Now remember, the oxygen tank has to stay with her at all times. The day nurse will show you everything when she comes, but there's a lot of medication and steps. I have a sheet printed out for you with a checklist to complete every night."

The doctor hands me a stack of papers, and I stare at it without really seeing. So many medications. So many steps. Can we even do this?

"Is everything okay?" Dr. Frank asks, worry on his face. "It's not too late to change your mind."

"No." I meet his eyes, swallowing down the panic. "No. We can do this. The nurse will help. It'll be fine."

He studies me for a moment and gently takes the papers from me before scribbling across the top.

"If at any time, you have questions, or something doesn't seem right, feel free to call or text me. I'm sorry I can't help you any more."

I shake my head.

"Dr. Frank, You have been the one bright spot about having mom here. You cared so much more than you had to. Thank you for this. You might regret it when I text you at three in the morning."

He chuckles.

"Don't worry about it. I don't sleep too much at night anymore, anyways."

He turns and walks away before I can ask him what he means. I have a feeling it has to do with the high number of patients that don't make it out of here. Dr. Frank has apparently been the doctor at Helping Hands for years, and he's watched many patients come and go. His happy demeanor doesn't make up for the fact that many patients come to this place to die. It's a sad profession, and he does it anyways.

The poor guy deserves a vacation.

I turn to go into the room where mom and Attie are talking. Attie is prepared, wearing scrubs. He told mom that he's a volunteer, and she fawned all over him for that. I'd seen the blush on Attie's face at that, liking that she seemed proud of him for something. We haven't seen that emotion directed at us in a very long time, not from mom.

I hadn't thought to wear scrubs. I'm dressed in my usual jeans and leather jacket despite the humid weather. It's become a habit to wear the gear when I ride my Harley, and it's just easier to be ready to ride at any moment.

I take a seat beside Attie and smile at my mom. She's weathered, more than she's ever been. Her skin has a yellow tint and hangs on her skinny frame. She looks far too old at fifty-nine. Sick, she looks sick. I attempt to hide the sadness in my eyes, but I've never been that great at hiding things from my mother, even when she doesn't remember me.

"Why the sad look, Calypso?" she rasps, the sound of the oxygen tank almost carrying away the sound.

My eyes jerk up to hers, and I'm glad to see the recognition there that I need today. I want my mom, and for once, someone heard my prayers.

"Nothing, mom," I reply, blinking furiously at the tears in my eyes.

She holds her arms open, and I immediately kneel before her and wrap her in a hug. She feels so fragile, like I can easily break her if I move the wrong way. I'm so conscious of where I put my fingers that it makes my heart hurt.

"You never could lie to me," she chides, beckoning Attie forward. "My babies."

Attie doesn't even try to hold back tears as he wraps his arms around both of us, burying his face in the opposite side of mom's neck.

"We've missed you," I whisper, the urge to hug her harder overwhelming, so I sit back instead, and wipe the errant tears from my cheeks.

"I know, sweet girl. I know. I'm afraid this old disease is kicking my tosh. Even now, I can feel it creeping at the edge of my mind. You've grown so big, both of you." Her voice almost slows when she talks, like she's fighting a losing battle in her head. I'm terrified of where my mom goes when she's not right, what prison she fights against.

"What are we gonna do, ma?" Attie asks, his face still buried in the crook of her neck. "We want to help."

"You are helping, baby. But my time is coming. You must know that."

This time, I can't stop the tears from trickling over my lashes freely. I take my mother's hand in mine and hold it as firmly as I dare.

"We're taking you home today," I whisper. "We're getting everything ready now."

She nods her head.

"I think I would like to be at home, when the time comes. You've done so perfect, my sweet girl. I'm sorry I couldn't be there for y'all."

I shake my head.

"I don't know what else to do, Mom."

She smiles at me, but it's not quite as wide, and her eyes become just a little more unfocused.

"Keep going, Calypso. You're destined for something far greater than you can even imagine."

Her words trail off, her eyes going distant, as she stares just above our shoulders. Attie pulls away, and takes his seat again on the other side of the couch. My mother looks me right in the eyes, seeing but unseeing.

"Do you know where my husband is? Blasted man is always running off."

♠

Cheshire

I stand outside the window of Cal's house, invisible to any human eyes, and watch with sad eyes as Cal, and who I assume is her brother, lead an older woman around the house. The woman touches things, runs her hands lovingly over photographs, and yet doesn't seem to recognize her own children. I can understand a sickness of the mind eating away at her, having witnessed it many times in Wonderland.

Seeing Cal lead the obviously ailing woman around, I realize with a sudden clarity, that Cal will never come to Wonderland, not when her family needs her so much. If I ever had the chance to choose, I wouldn't leave Danica behind, nor my mother.

"She'll never come willingly," I whisper softly, but loudly enough that I know White's sensitive ears can pick it up beside me.

When I glance over at him, White's face is solemn as he watches Cal's mother pick up something she doesn't recognize and set it aside. A trophy, either Cal's or her brother's, I'm not sure, but it hurts them both either way. I can see Cal flinch even from where we stand outside the house.

"You would leave her here, knowing she's destined for you?" he asks.

I can hear the gears in his watch ticking, the noise getting louder and louder the longer we're here. I frown.

"I won't take a sister away from a brother, or a daughter away from a mother. I'm an asshole, but I'm not cruel, Rabbit."

White looks over at me then, his eyes searching for something I have no name for.

"Did you feel it?"

"Feel what?" I bite the inside of my cheek.

"The click."

I look away from White's knowing eyes to back inside the window. Cal lets her brother lead her mother down the hallway to what I suspect is her room. Cal takes a moment to step into the kitchen, and I watch as she breaks down, her shoulders shaking with the emotions she keeps hidden from her family. This strain is wearing on her.

"I don't know what you're talking about."

Cal hastily wipes her face, pulling tissues out to scrub it free. She's beautiful, her hair hanging down to frame her face, her slanted eyes framed with lashes. They're puffy right now, but normally, she appears completely put together. A sad smile pulls at her lips as she gains her composure, and the memory of another such smile flits through my mind. I immediately push that thought away, and focus on the vision of Calypso.

White shakes his head, and I catch the movements out of my peripheral.

"If you leave her here, Wonderland will die." He pauses. "And you'll see her face for the rest of your short life."

His words hit me so hard, I'm barely able to contain the emotions. Angry for being forced into this situation, angry that this is the only way, angry at myself for even coming here, I lift my hand and place a single claw against the glass. I don't expect Cal to look up as I do so. I don't expect her eyes to meet mine, as if she can see me, before she looks away again.

I feel the stones harden around my heart, the cruelty of the world I've grown up in bringing cruelty to my lips.

But in my mind, anger whispers about the destruction of my home, and I dismiss it for the innocence of a daughter trying to subtly remind her mother of her name.

"Then so be it," I whisper, and I turn and walk away.

Chapter 10

Saturdays are my day to relax usually, but with everything going on at home, it's hard to ease the tension in my shoulders. Attie had wanted to spend the day with mom, and I couldn't deny him that, not when he's had so much of his childhood robbed. I'd been lucky enough to be an adult when the disease hit. Attie hadn't, and he'd missed out on so much that I couldn't give him. So, the nurse and Attie had taken mom to her favorite park, a day of sitting by the pond to feed the ducks and eating her favorite meals.

I'd come into the shop to work on Bertha some more. I need the escape.

Last night, mom had woken up screaming, suddenly remembering that dad had died. She'd dreamed about it, and while she wasn't quite sure if it was real or not, she'd finally fallen back asleep after asking where her husband was. It had been a brutal night, made even more so by her cupping my cheek before sleep claimed her and whispering "my baby" as if she remembered.

I'd been almost grateful when Attie suggested the day spent with mom. He could always read me so well, and he knows my heart is hurting, no matter how hard I try to hide it.

I'm tightening down a bolt on Bertha's frame when I feel the same eyes on me that I had last night, the ones I had convinced myself were never there. The hairs stand on my neck, and I slowly turn to meet the electric-blue eyes of Cheshire standing just inside the door. I hadn't even heard him come in, but I'm certainly aware of him now. I sigh.

"I don't need this today, buddy. You can just see yourself out."

He tilts his head, studying me, that fancy tail twitching back and forth like a real cat's. I'm so curious to ask how he's made it work.

"What's so special about you?" he asks curiously.

I scowl. "Excuse me?"

He takes a step forward, and I tense.

"Why you? Out of billions of people, why you?"

"I don't know what you're talking about, and if you don't leave, I'll call the cops."

He laughs and takes another step forward. "What could they do to me?"

I raise my brow. "Throw your ass in jail and give you three square meals a day." That only makes him laugh harder, and I frown, before turning back to the motorcycle frame. "Whatever. Just make sure not to drop the soap," I grumble. I hear him step closer this time, still across the shop, but gaining ground.

"You're good with your hands," he comments, and I snort, meeting his eyes again.

"Is that supposed to be a sexual innuendo?"

He shrugs. "It was meant to be a compliment, but if your mind automatically went to fucking, well, who am I to complain?" He grins, and I have to fight the twitch at the corner of my lips.

Oh, yes. Under different circumstances, I would be drawn to the man in front of me. The cat ears on top of his head twitch again, swiveling as if picking up sounds. And that tail, it's so realistic, it almost has me fooled.

"Where do you get such believable ears and a tail? I've never seen anything like them."

He smirks. "Wanna touch it?" he asks, and his tail comes around his hip and hovers in the air like he has complete control over it. Wow. I can't help the small chuckle that escapes my lips when I meet his eyes again.

"I'm good, Pussy Cat. Was there something you needed?"

Cheshire growls at my nickname for him, but when I ask the question, sadness passes over his face so fast, I almost miss it, before it's replaced by that smug look again.

"I just wanted to see you again, one more time, before I leave."

And just like that, my heart squeezes. What the hell is wrong with me? I've met the guy for a few minutes, and suddenly, I care about him. I don't listen to the whisperings inside my head that say everyone is leaving. That's too much to bear right now. I don't need to be worried about a man I just met, let alone one who wears cat ears all the time.

"Where are you going?" I ask, dropping my ratchet and standing up.

Something whispers for me to stop him, to keep him here with me. It's an insane thought, one that I crush down hard, but I can't completely dispel the feeling.

Cheshire slowly begins to stalk towards me, and I back up, his intensity almost forcing me back, until the base of my spine hits my workbench. He doesn't stop, coming so close that I immediately tense. His arms cage me in, bracing himself on the counter on both sides of me.

His nostrils flare the same time as mine do, a thick smell of wild honeysuckle and woodsmoke filling my nostrils. Cheshire presses so close that my eyes close of their own accord, absorbing the feeling of this man pressing against me, and liking it far too much. He leans in and rubs his cheek against my neck, just like a cat, and I tilt my head to the side rather than push him away. I groan at the feeling, tempted to thread my hand through his hair and hold him closer.

What the hell is wrong with me? I'm letting a stranger rub all over me, and I'm not even pushing him away.

"What's so special about you?" Cheshire groans into my neck, asking the same question as before.

"I don't know," I breathe, my eyes still closed. I don't know how else to answer the question. I'm no one special, just a woman trying to raise her little brother. Nothing extremely special about me.

My words make him pause, and he yanks away. My skin grows cold where he'd been against me. When I open my eyes in confusion, Cheshire's gone.

The only sign that he'd been there at all is the scent of woodsmoke and wild honeysuckle hanging in the air.

Chapter 11

Hatter

I shift on my feet in the tea room, as anxious as everyone else. Clara stands beside me, and Doe and Jupiter stand beside her as we all direct our eyes to the double doors. Doe had said the Flamingo is coming, and he's an ally we desperately need in this war.

Even though Clara stands next to me, I can feel my madness creeping along the edges of my mind, feeding off of my nervousness. I manage to tame it down for now, barely, but if the Flamingo comes in and starts trouble, I know I won't be able to hold it back.

Eventually, it will come down to a fight, and we need everyone possible on our side. The Flamingo is the first step in preparing for war.

"What's he like?" Clara whispers, tilting her head towards me.

How can I explain the Flamingo? I'm not certain I can.

"Just wait and see," I reply, threading my fingers with hers. The touch of her skin on mine calms the madness again, and I sigh. My mind clears enough that I can remember Flam's story.

The Flamingo was never good, not in an honest to goodness way. He's never played for one team or the other, preferring to remain neutral in any fight. And then he met and fell in love with the Dodo bird.

I smile, remembering the night that they had formerly met. Flam had been in the process of beating the shit out of another creature. I can't remember who it was now, but I do know the creature had challenged Flam. It had been an idiotic decision really. Everyone knows not to challenge the Flamingo, even if his powers are a little diminished now thanks to the old King and Queen.

Flam used to have a penchant for trouble—he still does—but his powers got too out of hand for even him to control. So, he'd gone to the King and Queen, and he asked them to lock some of his powers away, inside himself. He's still powerful beyond knowledge, but he chooses to be less every day. That's what redeemed him in the eyes of Wonderland.

Flam's heritage makes him a prime example of 'you are what you make of yourself.' He could have become something far worse than anyone had imagined. His mother was a flamingo, just like his namesake, but his father, oh, his father was a Jabberwocky. I have no idea of their love story, or how a beast incapable of love fell in love with a flamingo. Flam's mother was far from weak, taming the Jabberwocky, and she chose to die with him when Wonderland deemed him too much of a risk after he'd razed the whole forest.

Flam was left behind, a child, appearing as nothing more than a flamingo. It had been easy to persuade everyone he was an innocent, until he wasn't. His powers awakened when he reached adulthood, and he rained down destruction wherever he went. But he never harmed innocents, not directly. And then he'd met Doe, and all of that had changed.

Flam is still bad, still powerful, but now he has a reason to love, something a Jabberwocky should never be capable of. And yet, the Flamingo lives.

The double doors to the tea room slam open and crash against the wall with a bang. I sigh dramatically. Bloody bird can't ever be gentle. Even now, a nice little crack creeps up the wall from where the door had hit.

The crash had made Jupiter jump, but Clara didn't even twitch. Her senses have been getting better since she came to Wonderland. No doubt, she heard Flam's footsteps the moment he stepped into my home.

I laugh when I see the surprise on Clara and Jupiter's faces when Flam steps into the room, his stance wide, his eyes searching.

"Where's my girl?" he asks, his voice thick enough that it even gives me chills.

His eyes scan our group until they fall on Doe, a wide smile on her lips. He storms forward and sweeps Doe into his arms, swinging her around. She laughs, pure joy in the sound, and wraps him tight in her arms.

"I've missed you, Pink. It's been forever."

"It's only been a few days," he reminds her, staring into her eyes, complete adoration reflected there.

Doe and Flam had been meeting in the woods rather than my house. He claims he's not fond of structures, that they make him feel caged, and yet he walks into my home today. I'm interested to see what he has planned.

"You're the Flamingo?" Jupiter asks, tilting her head. "I expected someone vastly different."

Flam sets Doe down and glances over at Jupiter, a grin on his face.

"Were you expecting someone bedazzled and flamboyant?" he teases, and I chuckle. Flam has dealt with the stereotype his whole life. I secretly think that's why he looks like he does.

The Flamingo is far from flamboyant. He's covered in tattoos, some depicting scenes from Wonderland, others just random tidbits all added in. A small mushroom is inked under his eye, just an outline, but it's enough to draw your attention. The tattoos even climb his neck and swarm around his jawline, but besides the mushroom, they don't actually touch his face. They only give the illusion that they could. Besides the tattoos, he's covered in piercings, his lips, in his brow, along his ears. If it's capable of being pierced, it probably is. I can't see from my position, but I know Flam's eyes are a bright-fuchsia color, and to top off the whole look, he's dressed in hot-pink leather pants. It does nothing to detract from his masculinity though. Even I can take that in.

"I was, actually," Jupiter laughs. "Although the pants fit with what I imagined at least."

Flam's smile turns soft as his gaze fully lands on Jupiter.

"I've heard lots of things about you, Fire Child. I heard you're the one that saved my girl."

I watch as Jupiter shifts on her feet, a slight blush rising to her cheeks.

"I just solved a riddle, is all."

And then Flam does something I never expect, something I've never witnessed. He walks up to Jupiter and kneels down in front of her. She takes a hesitant step back but otherwise, holds her ground. Me, on the other hand, I stumble backwards and gasp so loudly it echoes in the room. Clara looks at me in confusion, but I can't tell her that I've never seen the Flamingo on his knees for anyone besides Doe, not right now.

Flam drops his head and exposes the column of his neck.

"I am in your debt, Dream Walker. I've come to join your fight."

My gasp, this time, brings a chuckle to Clara's lips, and it distracts me. I suddenly want to kiss her. This is a monumental occasion. We should celebrate!

Doe looks down in adoration at her husband. When Flam stands again, I can see the gears turning in Jupiter's head.

"Do you shift into a giant flamingo?" That's the first question she asks him after he's just sworn to fight at her side. White's mate is an odd one.

Flam grins in answer, before his eyes dart over to Doe.

"Big enough to ride."

None of us miss the double meaning there, and Clara snorts in amusement.

"Well, this should be interesting," she says.

Indeed, it will be. Indeed, it will.

Chapter 12

I open the car door and offer my arm to my mom. Attie comes around and helps her up, before pulling her oxygen tank out behind her. We'd thought it best to take mom to her favorite restaurant for dinner. She hadn't been able to eat much, claiming she wasn't hungry, but we all know that she hasn't eaten properly in months. Dr. Frank said it's from the decline. I say it's my mom's way of helping things along unconsciously.

Either way, it sucks.

Bad things happen to good people. I know that. My dad had been an honest person; caring and kind. He'd volunteered on the weekends at the local soup kitchen. He didn't even curse. And yet he was taken far too young by a drunk driver.

Mom's the same. She used to make clothes for the kids in the foster home down the street, taking notice that their foster parents spent the money on anything but them. That was the kind of people my parents were.

Now, one's dead, and the other might as well be.

Tonight, she's catatonic. Attie has to place her in her wheelchair and adjust her. She doesn't even twitch or take notice. She just stares blissfully at the moon above us. I can't blame her. The moon is full tonight and shines so brightly, it washes everything with its paleness. Combined with the sound of the frogs croaking and the summer bugs, it's a nice evening. For some reason, it immediately puts me on edge.

"Calypso."

I turn at the sound of my name, the voice definitely not belonging to my mom or brother. Attie turns with me, and we both stare at the man behind us. I sigh.

"Do I even want to know how you found out my address?" There's no anger in my words. At this point, it just feels like White is some kind of magical creature following me around. I'm tempted to run inside and hide like I do if the Jehovah's Witness come knocking on my door. Last time I opened for them, I got a strong lecture on my life choices that lasted an hour. Never again.

White shrugs at my question, but otherwise doesn't give an answer.

"Attie, can you take mom inside?"

He nods and pushes her a few feet towards the door, but he moves slowly. I don't chide him for it. White's eyes flick over to Attie before coming back to hold my gaze. His silver eyes almost seem to glow in the moonlight, and it's almost enchanting. It would be if there wasn't this heavy feeling hanging over everything.

"What can I help you with, White?"

He glances at the watch around his wrist. I can hear the ticking of its hands which is odd. I shouldn't be able to hear that.

"Remember what I told you, about Wonderland?"

"Are you still going on about this?" I ask, rubbing my temple. "I've already told you I'm not interested."

"You may not have a choice," White answers, his voice solemn.

I glare at him.

"I always have a choice, White. And I don't know what freaky shit you're trying to pull, but I'm not interested."

I turn to go inside the door only to run right into Attie's back where he'd paused with mom.

"What the fuck are you doing here?"

I turn at the new voice, searching until I find Cheshire. Where the hell had he come from? White just stares at Cheshire, neither seeming to breathe, as they each fight for the upper hand. I watch in confusion.

"What are they doing?" Attie whispers.

"Fuck if I know." Louder, I ask, "What the fuck are you two doing?"

In answer, White moves so fast, I can barely follow. His hand twists against his waistcoat, and he pulls a card from his pocket. Cheshire growls.

"Don't you fucking dare, Rabbit."

My brows skyrocket, looking between the two. I push Attie a little more behind me, making sure my back protects both him and my mom. White throws the small white card at the ground, and all the summer noises stop. The crickets stop chirping. The frogs stop croaking. The trees stop rustling with the wind.

I watch as a bright light flashes, and I blink hard to clear the sudden blindness, before some force begins to pull me forward. I don't scream. I don't think I can. I just turn, and press against Attie hard, attempting to push them away. It doesn't work. We all slide a little closer, and real fear spreads throughout my body.

I don't know what's behind me, or what's trying to eat us, but I want no part of it.

"If she won't go willingly," I hear White scream over the sounds of the bright spinning hole, "then she's going against her will. I can't let Wonderland die. Not when Jupiter is a part of it."

"You asshole!" Cheshire snarls, and I turn just in time to see Cheshire take a step towards him and get sucked towards the . . . *I should call it a portal.* That thought crosses my mind so confidently that I have no choice but to accept it. "I told you no!"

"One day, you'll thank me," White replies, adjusting his waistcoat and glancing over towards us. I can see the alarm spring to his eyes when he sees me pushing against Attie and mom's wheelchair. I don't know what the panic is for.

"I'm going to rip you to shreds," Cheshire promises, just before he's yanked towards the portal.

At the same time, I feel a hard pull on my body, as if there's a string attached to me, and someone is pulling it. I try to fight against it, to at least shove Attie and mom out of harm's way, but the same force grabs onto them, and I'm suddenly falling through open air, my little brother and sick mom right behind me.

White follows us in as I scream, and the rage that spreads through my body almost tears me apart.

The snarl that rips through my throat startles even me, and I know, whatever just happened, it's not going to be pretty when we land.

♠

IT TAKES ME A SECOND, BUT I REALIZE PRETTY QUICKLY THAT WHITE just took us down his rabbit hole, just like in the story books. I'd known he'd been adamant about Wonderland and being the White Rabbit, but I hadn't believed. Hell, I still don't. Maybe I've been drugged, and this is some extreme hallucination.

I grind my teeth against the pressure falling puts on my body. It feels like I'm being squeezed mercilessly, and the pressure threatens to force my eyes closed and my body limp, but my anger keeps me from blacking out completely. It doesn't get rid of the fuzziness around the edges of my eyes though, as if I'm struggling hard to remain awake.

I can make out Attie and mom above me. Mom's wheelchair is gone, but her oxygen tank trails behind her. Both of their bodies are completely limp as they fall, their clothing whipping around them. Above them, I see White lounging backwards as if he's on a couch, completely unfazed. I wiggle in an attempt to move higher up, to strangle him maybe, but it doesn't seem to work, so I relax again and focus on remaining awake.

I try not to focus too hard on the things in the walls reaching out for us, the skulls embedded in flashes of dirt. I'm starting to get the feeling that Wonderland won't be anything like the happy stories from home. They certainly never mentioned the White Rabbit and the Cheshire Cat kidnapping people.

I watch the swirling lights for what feels like hours, the green, white, and silver colors blurring together into a kaleidoscope of dizziness. I repeatedly feel my head loll back only to jerk back awake. When the colors start to spin faster, I think it's just me finally losing the battle, but then a bright light spreads, and I'm suddenly free falling through open air.

I slam into the ground, hard, and I hiss as all my breath leaves my body. If I didn't break my tailbone, it's certainly bruised. I panic when I see Attie start to fall above me, my mother right behind him, but Cheshire swoops in out of nowhere and catches first Attie and my mom as if it's no big deal to hold their weight. I try to ignore how sexy that is and instead, watch as he sets them gently on the tile away from us.

I pull myself from the floor, grimacing as pain tingles in my spine, and face Cheshire. He turns at the same moment, his face serious, and meets my eyes.

"What the fuck did you do?" I whisper, my voice deadly. I take a step towards him. "Where the hell are we?"

Cheshire scowls, but before he can answer, White slams to the ground behind me in a crouch. I whirl in time to see him stand tall and brush his hair from his eyes.

"It wasn't Cheshire. It was me."

"How dare you?" I shout, the fury coming right back. I storm up to him and get right in his face. "Take us back."

"I can't." White's ear twitches with his words, and my fingers ache for my wrench.

"I said," I growl, "take us back." My lips are pulled back from my teeth, so I can feel the literal snarl on my face. White doesn't seem to react to it. Instead, his eyes dart to Cheshire's, and they seem to have a silent conversation.

"It's a one-way trip, Calypso. I'm sorry, but Wonderland needs you."

"I told you I don't have time for your nonsense fairytales! I have people who depend on me." I turn and point at my still unconscious family. "They depend on me. And my mom is sick. She needs medicine. She needs care. And Attie has school on Monday."

"It's too late," White shrugs. "You've just dropped right into the fairytale you refused to believe. And your family being here is unfortunate. I only meant to take you."

"Unfortunate?" I mimic. "As if this is just a walk in the park. You brought us to some other world, which I'm not sure I believe yet, and expect me to accept that?"

"You don't have a choice," White growls, finally getting fed up with me, it seems. "You're here now. There's no way back until you fulfill your destiny. So, wise up, and direct your anger somewhere else, Calypso."

I turn away from White, glaring at the black-and-white tiled room, tempted to kick anything I possibly can in my anger.

"Fucking rabbit," I snarl.

Cheshire laughs, and if I would have grabbed my wrench before we fell down the rabbit hole, I would have thrown it as hard as possible at his face.

Chapter 13

Attie and mom are still unconscious. I have no idea how long it'll take them to wake up. I'd already checked on them to make sure they're still breathing, and both seem completely okay besides ending up in a magical world after coming through a portal.

I start to pace up and down the room, the tiles making me dizzy because they don't seem to be square. If I look at it too long, it's like someone stuck their finger in the room and swirled it around. It trips me up so much that I come to a stop.

"What the hell is wrong with this room?" I wrinkle my nose. "And what's that smell?"

"Just ignore it," Cheshire answers, a wicked glint in his eyes. I don't know if it's amusement or something else. "You don't want to know what the smell is."

As if in answer, my eyes flick over to the table in the center of the room. I'd been ignoring it, an overwhelming sense of 'DO NOT TOUCH' eating at my skin every time I even look at it. The tablecloth has the coloring of flesh, and it sends a race of goosebumps down my arms.

"This isn't where y'all flay my skin from my body and wear it like a suit, is it?" I gulp. "I'm claustrophobic. Putting me in a hole and lowering lotion down in a bucket won't do a damn thing."

I eye both White and Cheshire warily. White has the decency to look disgusted. Cheshire, on the other hand, takes that moment to look me up and down as if imagining that very thing.

"I don't think you'd fit as a suit," he says, that slow grin spreading across his lips. "Much too small. But there are other ways I'd like to wear you."

I can feel my hysteria wrap around me at his words, and it comes bubbling up my throat. I start laughing so hard, that I have to bend over and brace myself on my knees before falling to the floor, clutching my stomach. Tears run down my face as I laugh and laugh. I can't stop, and I can't even breathe anymore.

"This doesn't seem normal," I hear Cheshire say. I take in great gasps of air in an attempt to calm myself, but then it just turns into sobs.

"Actually, this is the most normal any of the women have acted. Clara compartmentalized her freak out. Jupiter was excited." He pauses, and I can feel his eyes on me where I sit on the floor. "It seems Calypso is the first to actually lose it when she comes to another world."

A harsh sob breaks free, loud enough to echo, and White squats down in front of me, before placing his hand on my shoulder. Cheshire growls, but I ignore him, focusing on the silver eyes in front of me, even if they're blurred from my tears.

"Breathe, Calypso," he urges me. "There's no use panicking now. You're here."

With his words, my panic morphs to anger, and I slap his hand from my shoulder.

"You're the reason I'm here." White doesn't look worried as I stand, just following suit, and I take a step closer to him. He watches in fascination as I swell with rage. "If anything, and I mean anything, happens to my mom or Attie, I will skewer you with a spoon."

"A spoon?" He smiles.

"A dull edge hurts worse than a sharp one. And I plan to scoop out your insides and feed them to you."

Cheshire perks up. "You're blood-thirsty. I like it."

"Shut up, Pussy Cat. You're not out of this, either. If one hair on their heads is hurt, I will do so much worse to you than I will White."

"Why me?" he growls. "I told him not to bring you."

I look him up and down, the sneer still on my face.

"Because you think this is funny. Even now, you're holding back a laugh. My family's safety is not funny."

Cheshire straightens up at my words, the twinkle in his eye instantly extinguished. He's completely different, standing there as if he wasn't just teasing me a second ago.

"You're right," he says. He bends at the waist, bowing before me, and it catches me so off-guard that I take a step backwards. He looks up at me from his position and meets my eyes. I try my hardest not to let the sight affect me, to not imagine him doing something else while looking up at me. It's a losing battle. "I vow that no harm will come to your brother or your mother from Wonderland while I'm alive."

The air seems to swell in the room and then contract, buzzing with energy until the hairs on my arms stand on end.

"What the fuck was that?" I breathe, my eyes still locked on Cheshire's.

White's voice is solemn when he says, "Cheshire just swore an unbreakable vow."

Chapter 14

I'm staring at Attie and mom deep in thought when Attie opens his eyes and sits up. I watch as he looks around the trippy room.

"Where are we?" he asks, pushing his hair out of his eyes. I'd been telling him to cut it for weeks, but he insists on keeping it longer. I think the girl he likes prefers the length. God, what if we don't make it home? What if he never gets to worry about talking to the girl he likes at school again? The panic threatens to overtake me, so I focus on my words.

"Wonderland, apparently."

"Well, not yet," White corrects. "We have to go through one of the doors before we're officially in Wonderland. Think of this just as a train station, or like a purgatory."

"Fantastic," I grumble.

Attie stands up and immediately starts walking towards the table.

"No. Don't touch the table, Attie," I tell him before he can get too close. "I'm pretty sure it's wearing rotten skin."

"What the hell?"

"Don't ask," I say. "Apparently, it's not a pleasant story. And watch your language."

"We drop into a fictional world, and I still can't cuss?" He grins. "Where are your priorities, Sis?"

"Probably left on the other side of the rabbit hole to be honest." I smile at him. If anyone can bring me out of the panic, it's Attie. He's always so level-headed.

Mom blinks open her eyes then, and both of us rush over to her side. Her eyes are clear for a moment, her dark-grey irises duplicates of my own. We help her sit up, and she touches her hand to my cheek.

"Calypso?" she says, and I smile.

"Yes, mom. It's me."

"Everything is going to be okay. Take care of your brother."

"What?" I don't get an answer. Her eyes glaze over, and she slips away again. I blink at the tears in my eyes. I seem to be doing that a lot lately. Normally not one to cry at all, my emotions are all out of whack. Add in all the stress of falling through a portal, and well, it's thrown my hormones into chaos.

"The memory thing," Cheshire says, a frown on his lips. "Is it a disease?"

I sniff quietly and leave Attie with mom to keep her company. She's looking around the room now in curiosity, but there's so familiarity in her eyes. Everyone in this room is a stranger to her.

"The doctors says it's dementia, even though not all of the symptoms line up."

"So, her memories just flit away like that?" He seems to be in thought, going over what I told him. "There could be someone here in Wonderland that could help."

"What do you mean?"

"The Keeper of Memories. I don't think he can cure her, but maybe he could allow her to remember? I'm not certain," he says when he sees the hope in my eyes. "I don't know if it's possible. But I just wanted to tell you that there could be something."

"Thank you for telling me." I nod my head and glance back over to my mom and Attie.

"You worry."

"Of course, I do. I'm raising my little brother, and my mom is on her deathbed," I whisper.

"You're handling it pretty well."

I glance at Cheshire in confusion. "This is the first time we've talked without you making any snide comments."

He snorts. "It's coming, I'm sure. Kind of like you could be." He wiggles his brow.

I just roll my eyes and look away. I refuse to entertain him.

White comes over then and looks between us.

"Now that everyone is awake, we should get moving. We're late."

"Late for what?" I ask, curious.

"Everything." White glances at his watch. "We're literally late for everything."

"Okay, so let's go through the door." Cheshire moves over to a pretty door, but White shakes his head.

"No. The Bandersnatch are guarding that one. And we can't go through the Dark Lands. There's too many of us. If a Chimera storm hits, I can't carry you all, and you can't fade everyone away." White runs his hand through his hair. "I think we should go through the white one."

I glance at the only white door in the room. It has a pearlescent sheen to it, and painted on it in bright-red paint is a giant X. It's like whoever painted it, didn't care if it dripped. The red runs down the door in little rivers.

Cheshire shakes his head. "We can't. We have too many weak variables."

He gestures in my direction, making it clear that he thinks I'm one of the weak variables. I try not to take offense at it. I really don't know what I'm getting into here, or what waits behind the white door. I take it that it's not a good door to go through, if Cheshire's reaction is any indication.

"We have to go through the white door, anyways, at some point. Calypso will need the Vorpal Blade," White argues.

"She isn't ready. She doesn't even know why she's here."

"How about y'all tell me what you're talking about, so I can weigh in with my two cents?" I interrupt, raising my brow. I have no idea what the Vorpal blade is or why they think I need it, but it would be nice to at least know what's going on.

"You tell her," White tells Cheshire when they stare at each other for too long. Cheshire sighs, clearly annoyed, but he still opens his mouth.

"There's a prophecy of a triad of women destined to bring about the fall of the Red Queen and save Wonderland. Clara Bee was the first. Jupiter is the second." Cheshire pauses, and then meets my eyes. "And you're the third."

"That's ridiculous." I frown.

White answers my proclamation with his own. "Whether it is or not, doesn't matter. You're here. You're the third. And you're destined to save Wonderland and become Cheshire's—"

"Ally," Cheshire interrupts White. "To become my ally."

White gives Cheshire a look, and I wrinkle my nose. "An ally in what? War?"

"Well, yes. You're the one destined to win the war. And to do that you'll need the Vorpal Blade. Which is behind the white door." White growls the last part at Cheshire. Cheshire's ears lay down on his head, and his tail swishes side to side.

"I'm not some savior," I sputter. "I'm just a mechanic."

White shakes his head. "You're so much more than that, Calypso. You're the last chance we have to save Wonderland. You're prophesied to complete the triad and bring down the Red Queen."

Attie grins. He'd been listening intently to the conversation, looking back and forth between them. "Wow, sis. You're like the Chosen One. Guess that makes me your sidekick."

His words bring me out of the shock I'd been in, the confusion about why I'd be chosen and not someone else more capable. Surely, I'm not the best fit for saving an entire world.

"Absolutely not. Whatever we're in, you're not a part of it. I'm going to find you somewhere safe, and then you're going to stay there until I convince these idiots that I'm not their Chosen one."

Attie frowns at me, pouting out his lip jokingly. "Aw, man. I thought we were gonna be like Batman and Robin." I don't smile. I just cross my arms and look at him. "Scooby Doo and Scrappy?" My lip twitches. "Macaroni and Cheese?" I can't help the laugh that bursts out this time. I reach out and ruffle his hair.

"You're still not doing anything dangerous," I remind him. Just because I laughed doesn't mean he can get himself killed. Any place that uses skin as a tablecloth is not somewhere I'd bet money on being nice and friendly.

"Well, then, you'd better save the world, so we can go home." Attie looks over at mom. She's staring at the table in the middle of the room, contemplation on her face. At least her face isn't blank this time, but I don't know how long until she zones out again. "We need to get mom out of here."

I can hear the rasp in her breath, see the shaking in her hands. I nod my head. We need to get mom out of here.

Chapter 15

"What's behind the white door?" I ask, staring at the giant red X as if it'll give me all the answers.

"The White Queen." Cheshire answers me with a flick of his tail. "You're hot, but I doubt you'll be able to survive more than a few seconds with her."

I scowl at the cat and dismiss him completely. He's no help, so I turn to White. I can see Cheshire grin out of the corner of my eyes, and I know he's goading me rather than being serious. He'd been nothing but kind so far to Attie and my mom, but as soon as his eyes turn to me, he becomes an asshole. I'm tempted to throw something at him, that or kiss him. But one of those options isn't a good idea, obviously.

"Tell me what I need to know."

"You're the final prophecy," White replies, crossing his arms across his chest. "You're supposed to bring down the Red Queen but to do that, you'll also need to take out the Jabberwocky."

"Okay, that sounds like the stories from home. The Jabberwocky in the books looks like a dragon thing. Is that the case here?"

White's ear twitches. "Not quite. But we can talk about that later. The first problem is that there's only one sword that can kill a Jabberwocky, and overcome a Jabberwocky's powers."

"The Vorpal Blade," mom interrupts with a smile. "I used to read this book for my daughter, Calypso, when she was a baby. She's older now and doesn't care for such things. Teenagers."

There's an overwhelming feeling of sadness that creeps around the room at that statement. I fight hard not to show the hurt in my eyes.

"Very good, Diana," White continues, knowing that pondering on her condition does no one any good. I'm grateful for it. "The Vorpal Blade is, indeed, what I'm talking about."

"And the White Queen has this blade?" I ask, pressing my hair from my face. "So, we just go ask her for it."

"Not exactly," Cheshire says from his position against the wall. "The White Queen doesn't have the Vorpal Blade. She guards it. She's also not the White Queen any more. Not exactly."

"What does that mean?"

"She's fast, venomous, and about the ugliest thing you'll ever set your eyes on." Cheshire's lip curls at the statement, as if something he said is funny. I don't see the humor in it.

"That's still your Queen," White hisses.

Cheshire doesn't comment, that smug look on his face fixed, a mask, I'm sure.

"And what about my mom and Attie? Someone needs to protect them."

"I'll take care of them. Cheshire will help you with the White Queen." Cheshire scoffs, and White growls. "It's your duty, Cheshire. Protect Calypso at all costs."

"I can protect myself," I interrupt, scowling at Cheshire. "I'm sure the cat would sooner let me die than protect me."

"You're right," Cheshire agrees. "I care for no one."

White sighs. "I'll protect Diana and Atlas with my life. You have to only worry about getting the blade from the White Queen, Calypso. The sooner you fulfill your destiny, the sooner you can go home."

I nod my head. "What does the blade look like?" I'm not certain if it should be a sword or a dagger. The stories back home seem to have it interchangeable. I'm hoping it's a sword. How cool would that be?

"You'll know it when you see it. It'll sing to you."

Cheshire straightens and steps towards the door. "Well, come on, Cupcake," he says. "Let's see what you're made of."

Fed up with his shit, I step up to Cheshire. I have the dagger he'd been wearing at his waist out of the sheath and at his throat quicker than he can react. Surprise passes his eyes as the steel kisses his skin, but he quickly hides it behind his signature look. He doesn't hide the lust, though. He lets me see every bit of that.

"Call me Cupcake again, Pussy Cat, and I'll neuter you." I press the dagger a little harder, not breaking skin, just enough to warn him.

Fire ignites in his eyes, and his grin widens. "Why would you do that, when we could have so much fun?" he asks, his voice rough with desire.

"Oh, it would be fun for me to neuter you," I promise. "Don't push me."

His eyes sparkle as he reaches up and pushes the dagger away from his neck. His finger presses against the blade, bringing blood to the surface to drip down his fingers, but he doesn't seem to notice.

"But it's so much fun to push your buttons," he whispers, leaning down and almost rubbing against my neck. He takes a deep breath, inhaling my scent, and my stomach clenches.

Someone behind us clears their throat. I don't know if it's White, Attie, or my mom, but my face flames either way. I step away from the tempting cat, and Cheshire's grin widens impossibly further as he turns towards the White door. The red X seems to mock me as I stare at it, preparing for what's on the other side. Cheshire makes way for White to step forward.

"Do your thing, Rabbit."

Chapter 16

WHITE

I watch the banter between Cheshire and Calypso, my eyes following them as if they're actually throwing a ball back and forth. Neither seems to be aware of the rest of us, standing to the side. Calypso's mother stands right next to me, a happy smile on her face. Attie stands a few steps away, a scowl stretching his lips.

Diana leans closer to me as Cheshire says something that makes Calypso bristle. "Those two are gonna be an item soon," Diana whispers, good humor in every word.

"What makes you think that?" I ask, keeping my voice low.

"The way they look at each other when the other isn't looking. Cheshire looks at her with longing so deep, it almost hurts. And the girl, poor girl, has already fallen. She just doesn't know it yet."

I meet Diana's eyes, searching for the mother in there. When I find none, I simply grin devilishly.

"I'll tell you a secret, Diana."

"Hmm?"

"Those two, there's a prophecy written about them. They're destined for each other, even if they have no idea."

"Yes," she comments. "Calypso is a stubborn child. Always was. She will fight it until the end."

My eyes sharpen, but just as quickly as the recognition came, it flits away like a hummingbird, Diana's eyes once again glazed.

"What are you two talking about?" Atlas asks, stepping closer.

"Nothing," both Diana and I say at the same time, which sends Diana into a fit of giggles.

"I do believe this is the best dream I've ever had," she says, clapping her hands together.

I frown, the action reminding me of March. Perhaps, we really should take her to the Keeper of Memories. Perhaps, there's some reason Calypso wasn't brought to Wonderland alone.

Chapter 17

Jupiter

"They're in Wonderland."

"How do you know?" Clara asks, glancing at me in confusion.

"I can feel it." I rub my chest, where it feels like a string is pulling at my heart, pulling me towards my White Rabbit.

"I can feel it, too," Hatter adds, tilting his head, his eyes glazed as if he's looking inside himself. "They're certainly here. I can feel both White and Cheshire."

Flam and Doe sit across from me, their fingers intertwined as if they're afraid to part. I can't blame them. Doe had been stuck in her dodo bird form for over a hundred years before I'd come along and broken the enchantment. At the time, I didn't know the significance of what I'd done. Now, watching the two revolve around each other, as if one can't exist if the other doesn't, it makes me happy in a way I never expected. The dodo bird and the flamingo. I really want to hear their love story one day.

"Have you been practicing your powers?" Flam picks up his tea cup and takes a delicate sip completely at odds with his appearance. I keep expecting him to tip the table and storm out while flicking the finger at us. Instead, he's a complete gentleman, pinky in the air while he drinks his lemon-yellow tea and everything.

"You know about those?" I didn't realized it's common knowledge.

He motions towards Doe, and I nod in understanding. Of course, the two love birds would talk. "Dream Walkers need to work their muscles in order to grow stronger."

"I've been practicing. I think I might have discovered a new aspect of it." Every night when I go to sleep, I've been practicing sending myself around Wonderland, sitting in the forests and trying to project my powers outward. I'd been successful, and I've been stretching that muscle since I discovered it.

When I'd first started sending myself out, I thought it was wise to follow Alice, to look for the Jabberwocky, things that could help us. I quickly found out I couldn't see the Jabberwocky at all, no matter if I knew he was there or not. My powers almost seemed to ignore him completely. When I'd mentioned it to Clara, she'd hadn't known why. I'd stopped following Alice after I couldn't stomach the massacres any more and instead, went around Wonderland to look for allies.

"She's already strong." Hatter stirs his tea, his eyes affixed to the swirling liquid. "She was able to protect White while she dream walked. She kept Alice from hurting him."

Flam blinks at the words.

"Really?" When I nod, his face turns contemplative. "I've only heard of one other person who had the power that strong."

"Who?" Clara and I speak at the same time. We meet each other's eyes and smile. Curiosity seems to be a common thread in the triad. I wonder if Cheshire's mate will be the same.

Flam meets each of our eyes, almost like he's confused we don't already know.

"Well, Danica was a Dream Walker."

Clara gasps, and Hatter finally looks up from his tea, his brows wrinkled.

"Of course. I'd forgotten she'd had that power," he mumbles, before turning to study me. I shift in my seat.

"Who's Danica?" I ask. I haven't heard the name before.

"Danica is–" he begins, but pauses. "Danica was the Hope Bringer." He glances at Clara as she worries her lip. "And she was Cheshire's little sister."

Chapter 18

White kneels in front of the pearlescent door, a small black case open and showcasing lock-picking tools. I hadn't asked why he needs to pick the locks rather than having the key. I also don't mention that there's a key on the skin table. Obviously, it doesn't work if White hadn't grabbed it. Besides, I'm not going anywhere near the thing. Even now, the smell of rancid meat threatens to crinkle my nose. I can almost taste it on my tongue, and I'm sure I won't be able to scrape it clean even if I try.

"I'm going to need to be able to move." Cheshire shrugs the leather jacket from his shoulders and passes it to Attie. "Protect that with your life, kid. It's my pride and joy." Attie rolls his eyes but takes the jacket. I suspect he's having way too much fun with this, ignoring the obvious danger we're walking into. "The White Queen is fast. Don't let her touch you. She's venomous."

"Of course, she is," I mumble, because why not? Why wouldn't the White Queen be fast and venomous? Now all I keep imagining is a spider with a crown. Surely, that's not what we're walking into. The White Queen is supposed to be the sister to the original Red Queen, magnanimous and kind. Of course, this isn't the story book. "Do I need a weapon?" I don't really want to walk in there with nothing in my hands.

Cheshire pulls a wicked-looking dagger from his waist and passes it to me hilt first. "This won't do that much good, but it's something. Once you get the Vorpal Sword, use it."

"Do you have a weapon?" I only ask because I can't see any on him. If he gave me his only weapon, he might make better use of it than me.

Cheshire holds up his hands, and on the tips of his fingers, curve wicked-looking claws that hadn't been there before. I raise my brows. "I have a sword, too, if I need it."

I don't ask. I can't see a sword, but I'm not going to question it.

Cheshire takes that moment to pull his shirt over his head, revealing a tantalizing view of skin. My eyes dip low, taking in the washboard abs, the Adonis belt peeking over the edge of leather pants, the well-defined muscles everywhere. I hadn't let myself look at him when he was shirtless in my shop. Now, I ogle away. He's sin and chocolate all wrapped into an asshole personality, and it's a mixture I'm somehow still drawn to.

"You can touch them if you want," Cheshire teases when he catches me looking.

I don't look away or blush. I'm allowed to admire him. Doesn't mean I have to take his shit. I meet his eyes, unflinching, as my fingers grab the hem of my shirt and pull it up to reveal my own stomach. They aren't nearly as defined, but I have the outlines of a six pack. I haven't been able to give up the burgers to take it any further. Still, I know they're decent. Cheshire's eyes immediately drop and absorb the skin I reveal, hunger in his eyes.

"No thanks," I say, a teasing lilt in the words. "I have my own."

A smile curves Cheshire's lips as he meets my eyes again, the electric blue almost brighter as he straightens and studies me. He's standing in nothing more than leather pants and boots. When he turns, I get a good look at his back, and the thick muscles there. I school my features when he looks back at me, but I must have made a sound. Gorgeous isn't a word I would use to describe him.

Maybe brutally beautiful is a better description.

The lock clicks, and White stands from his position, tucking the small black case back inside his waist coat.

"You two will go in first and distract the White Queen." He points to Cheshire and me, his eyes lingering a bit longer on Cheshire, as if imploring him to listen to whatever silent words he's saying. "Once she's watching you, I'll take Diana and Atlas past and out of the cave.

It'll be up to you to retrieve the Vorpal Blade, Calypso. That's your destiny, and yours alone."

I almost tell him I'm not sure any of this is my destiny. Jesus, I'm not meant to be anyone's savior. It's a struggle just to make sure Attie is okay. I don't say any of that, however. I feel the weight in White's words, as if I can feel the prophecy he speaks of. With that feeling, I turn towards the deceivingly pretty door and take a deep breath.

"Will that be enough for you to be able to get them through?" Attie and my mother are my first priority. Even now, I'm glaringly aware of the oxygen tank my mother needs, it's little wheels crooked from the fall. White reaches down and grabs it, taking any burden from my mom.

"I'm fast," he nods. "I can carry them both if I have to. Watch your back, Calypso. Stay away from her teeth."

I clench my jaw in answer and roll my shoulders. Avoid the venomous White Queen's teeth?

Easy peasy.

Chapter 19

CHESHIRE

I watch Cal with intense eyes, as she stares at the door in front of us, waiting for the it be thrown open, so we can barge inside and step into a nightmare. It's been years since I've had to deal with the White Queen, far longer than I can really recall. She was one of our greatest failures when Alice came back to Wonderland, and she haunts my dreams. I can still remember the look on her face as Alice had drained her completely before our eyes, starting her transformation. It hadn't been anger, or agony, or any other emotion you would expect from someone in her situation. No, it had been acceptance, and strength. She'd known it would happen, and I always had the feeling that Absalom had slipped another one of his prophecies inside her mind.

Cal is beyond what I imagined when searching her world. I'd been almost afraid of what I would find, if my mate would be destined to be a soft creature that couldn't handle my darkness. And yet, here Cal stands, tall, strong, beautiful, and so full of fire that I want to wrap myself in it and go up in flames. I want to fan the inferno, until she overflows and takes me out with her.

But no temptation, no prophecy will force us together.

I can tell she's not on board with the prophecy, either. She doesn't want to be the savior, and yet, she steels her spine, and prepares for battle against something she has no idea about. I can only imagine how she would react if she found out the second half of the prophecy, that she's my mate.

No, best to keep that part hidden for now. Until I'm unable, I'll protect her and her family, help her save Wonderland, and then I'll send her home to live her life.

No matter how much I long to keep her.

Chapter 20

White doesn't throw open the door like I expect. Instead, he twists the knob slowly, silently and pushes the door open just a crack. Immediately, the scent of must and stale air hit me in the face. A chill only found in caves runs over me, and I shiver. White's ears twitch, and I listen with him, picking up only the sounds of dripping water and a constant thrumming echo of enclosed spaces.

White turns to look at us, nodding his head and pushing the door open on silent hinges, the full force of the chilly air and must hitting me. I wrinkle my nose but take a step forward, before Cheshire grabs my arm. He shakes his head and moves in front of me. I'm tempted to scowl, but I don't really know what I'm walking into, so I move behind and put my trust in him.

White moves to the side for us to pass, pulling a sword from his back I'd never seen, and holding it at the ready. I glance back at my mom and Attie one more time. Attie looks worried, his shoulders tense, but he attempts a smile and a thumbs up for me. My mother simply nods her head at me, her little oxygen tank beside her, ready for White to grab it once we slip inside.

I take a deep breath and focus on Cheshire's back, the scars almost comforting. I place my hand on his shoulder as he peers inside the cavern to make sure we don't get separated. It's dark, only a soft glow coming from somewhere, and I don't have any special eyesight like I suspect Cheshire does. A slight tensing of his muscle is the only sign that he even feels it.

When we step over the threshold, the only thing I note is that the glow is brighter deeper inside, and it flickers like a flame. A soft scuttling sound reaches my ears, and I tense, but Cheshire doesn't pause, leading us closer to the glow.

The first torch comes into view pretty quickly, the flames dim by normal standards but enough to spread light a short distance. That's when I see the webs, thick as silk, spread along the walls. My heart gives a hard throb, and Cheshire's ear twitches in answer. I wonder how he would react if he knew I'm an arachnophobe? Already, I can feel my skin crawling, and I pray to whatever god is listening that there aren't actual spiders in this cavern.

Something scrapes along the stone in front of us, and I press myself to Cheshire's back. To his benefit, he doesn't push me away. Instead, he reaches back with a clawed hand and gently touches my hip. I don't know if it's in comfort or something else, but it makes me feel better either way.

We move forward as one unit, taking tiny steps forward. I twist my head to look behind us but the torch doesn't penetrate into the darkness enough. When I feel eyes on me, I prepare my dagger. I don't know what I'm about to be up against, but it's stalking us, waiting for the right moment to strike.

I almost breathe a sigh of relief when the torches grow more frequent along the walls, and their combined glow spreads outward, slowly chasing some of the darkness away. For the first time, I'm able to see the ceiling, and I cringe.

Webs. There are webs hanging from everything. And there's nice thick sacs that scream of a spider's prey cocooned inside. When one twitches, I practically wrap myself around Cheshire's back. Fuck this. This is not what I signed up for.

I'm ready to climb Cheshire like a tree and make him take me out of this place when a brightly lit area appears, and something sings inside of me to move towards it. I lift my hand and point over his shoulder, right at the center where what appears to be a sarcophagus lays. The closer we get, the more details I can pick out, and the louder the singing gets in my blood. It's carved into the shape of a woman, and I wonder if it's meant to be the White Queen. She's beautiful even in carving, delicate, a tiny smile curling her lips.

I don't believe in prophecies, or destiny, but the draw I feel towards that sarcophagus makes me think otherwise. Whatever is in there, it's meant for me.

The scuttling sounds again, above us, and I whip my head in that direction, but there's nothing there. Cheshire tenses, and we take a step closer together. His ears twist on his head, listening, hearing more than I ever could. He must be following the stalker, waiting for it to attack. I'm afraid what it'll be. I'm afraid of whatever the White Queen has become.

When we get within ten feet from the sarcophagus, that's when every nightmare I've ever had forms into a ball and then becomes even worse. The scuttling stops, and for a moment, I think it has disappeared, deemed us unworthy of dinner, anything really. It's not because the creature has given up on us.

It's because she chooses that moment to show herself.

The White Queen drops from the ceiling with a quiet thump, her feet light as she lands on the depiction of who she used to be. You wouldn't be able to tell they are one and the same. I freeze and clench hard against Cheshire. I peer over his shoulder, but the urge to run flows through my body. I suppress it. It's obvious that's what she wants, and she would pick me off in seconds. She waited for us to get deeper inside before she appeared. She knows she has us at a disadvantage.

"Your Highness," Cheshire says, bowing his head the slightest bit.

If he expects me to curtsey, I'm going to bash his head in.

The White Queen no longer looks Queenly. She wears no clothing, her skin gray and sunken deep, until she appears as skinny as a skeleton. Her legs are bent at an unnatural angle, making her walk on all fours. There's no meat on her body at all, as if she's been sucked dry. Her hair, once white, hangs in thin strings around her face, where thick pinchers clack together. Each time they touch, my body grows more tense. When those pinchers open and reveal the fangs inside her mouth, I flinch. Her eyes, as dark as I've ever seen, catch the light and suck it inside their inky blackness. On her head sits a dainty silver crown, so delicate, it makes me hurt.

We're going to die.

The thought flits through my head before I can stop it. I have too much to live for, so I shove that thought aside, and clench my dagger harder. My hand is shaking violently, but still I step to the side of Cheshire and raise it. My breaths come in small pants, but I ignore everything unnatural about the woman in front of me, and attempt to talk to the Queen she once was.

"Your Majesty," I whisper, and her eyes dart to me. Her head twists to the side like a predator sizing up its prey. Her eyes don't linger on the dagger at all, dismissing it as no threat. "We've come for the Vorpal Blade."

Her pinchers clack together again, and she moves a little closer. I tense, but don't back down. Cheshire keeps his eyes trained on the threat in front of us, not daring to look away.

"You thinkkkk that you cann come into my hommme," she hisses, "and takeee what is minnnnee."

Goosebumps race up and down my arms, the sound of her voice is husky and raw, as if she hasn't spoken in a long time.

"We need the blade to save Wonderland, Your Highness," Cheshire speaks.

"Ssssave Wonderland?" She focuses on Cheshire. "Wonderland is alreadyyyyy dead."

She doesn't give us any warning. One moment she's talking to us, the next, she springs from the sarcophagus, her fangs bared, and Cheshire has just enough time to shove me to the side and away. I land against the wall, the webs closing around me like silk, and I start to hyperventilate. I rip myself away, but they come with me. I have the urge to do the spider dance, the one where you walk into a web and freak before waving your arms around, but I don't have the chance.

I barely have time to raise my dagger and leap out of the way as the White Queen scurries for me, her legs moving far faster than I would expect. I barely avoid her before Cheshire has his arms around me and is hauling me towards the sarcophagus.

"Get the sword!" he yells, shoving me toward the light. "Now!"

I scramble towards the stone woman and push against the lid. It doesn't move. I grunt and push harder.

"Watch out!" Cheshire's warning almost comes too late. I throw myself to the side just in time for the White Queen to speed past, her fangs centimeters from my shoulder. She turns, but Cheshire is there to meet her, teasing her away from me, tempting fate.

"Come on, you blood-sucker," Cheshire goads her. "Here's dinner."

If I wasn't shoving with all my might to open the sarcophagus, I might have laughed. Instead, sweat breaks out along my skin as I push as hard as I can. Still, the lid doesn't move.

"It won't open!" I shout, just as Cheshire dives out of the way of the White Queen's outstretched claws. He taps her on the shoulder as he goes, pissing her off even more.

"Try your blood!"

"What the fuck?"

The White Queen screeches in anger and moves faster towards Cheshire. He barely avoids her, her pinchers narrowly missing his shoulder.

"It could be locked with blood. Put a drop of blood on her mouth."

Because, of course. Why didn't I think of that?

I prick my finger with the dagger. The moment a drop of blood wells out, the White Queen stops what she's doing and turns to me, the hunger in her eyes freezing my heart.

"Unlock it!" Cheshire screams just as she darts for me. I smear my thumb across the mouth of the stone lady and duck just in time, her movement making my hair swirl, she was so close. I don't wait for the lid to open. Frantically, I move around the side, away from the blood-crazed creature that now only has eyes for me.

I focus only on getting away, even if I can hear the lid of the sarcophagus open and whatever is inside pulls me towards it. If I'm dead, I can't grab it.

Cheshire sprints to my side and pulls me with him much quicker than I can move, the White Queen's movements growing faster and more determined.

"You have to get the blade. The longer we're in here, the more danger we're in."

"Easier said than done," I growl, leaping towards the open container as she scuttles closer. I get a good look at a shining sword inside just before I have to move again to avoid fangs. The sword isn't the only thing inside. There's a body of a man, too. I don't ask who it is. It doesn't matter at the moment. I throw myself towards the sarcophagus again and reach inside.

The moment my hand wraps around the hilt of the sword, a sharp prickling runs down my arm all the way down to my toes. The White Queen stops and looks at me, the sword glowing bright as I lift it and hold it above my head.

"Enough." My voice is hard, and I hold the Vorpal Blade, as it sings to me songs of victory and battle. "Enough."

If I expected the White Queen to actually back down, I'd have been stupid. My command only throws her into a fit of anger, and I dive out of the way just in the nick of time. Cheshire is there to catch me, and he pulls me back into the darkness, towards the way out. The scuttling follows us, her screeching angry and intent on catching us. The harder we run, the more webs that catch on our bodies, dragging us down. Cheshire slashes through them with his claws, growling with every swing, pushing us harder. The screech comes from above us again, and I realize she's following us on the ceiling. Fucking spiders.

In front of us, a doorway stands open, not the one we came through. This door is stone, but the light that filters in from the other side is bright, lighting up the whole area. The scuttling gets closer, and I realize we're not going to make it. We're not fast enough.

Not today, bitch!

I release Cheshire just in time to spin and hold the Vorpal Blade up, ready to impale her. But Cheshire grabs me and throws me to the side. I watch in horror as the White Queen sinks her fangs into his shoulder and he grunts in pain, before ripping away. The White Queen chitters and scuttles backwards, giving us enough time to stumble towards the door and into the light.

I push the door closed on the White Queen's angry screeches and turn to where Cheshire lays on the ground.

"Why would you stop me? I had her," I snarl even though blood drips down Cheshire's shoulder.

"I can't kill her. Wonderland won't let me. She's still my Queen."

My anger deflates at that, and I kneel down next to him. I set the Vorpal Blade on the grass and study the wound.

"What do you mean Wonderland won't let you?"

Cheshire sighs and shifts, grunting in pain.

"My role in Wonderland is to be the Hand of Justice, the Punisher of the Damned. I can't harm her because Wonderland hasn't deemed me to do so."

When Cheshire shifts again, I notice for the first time that black veins spread from the wound, the flesh gaping and shredded. It's relatively small compared to the White Queen's pinchers at least, but red blood streams from the hole. The skin around it is a little green. They'd said the White Queen was venomous. And Cheshire has been bitten. It takes a moment for that fact to sink in but when it does, panic officially sets in.

My eyes widen in alarm, and I meet his eyes.

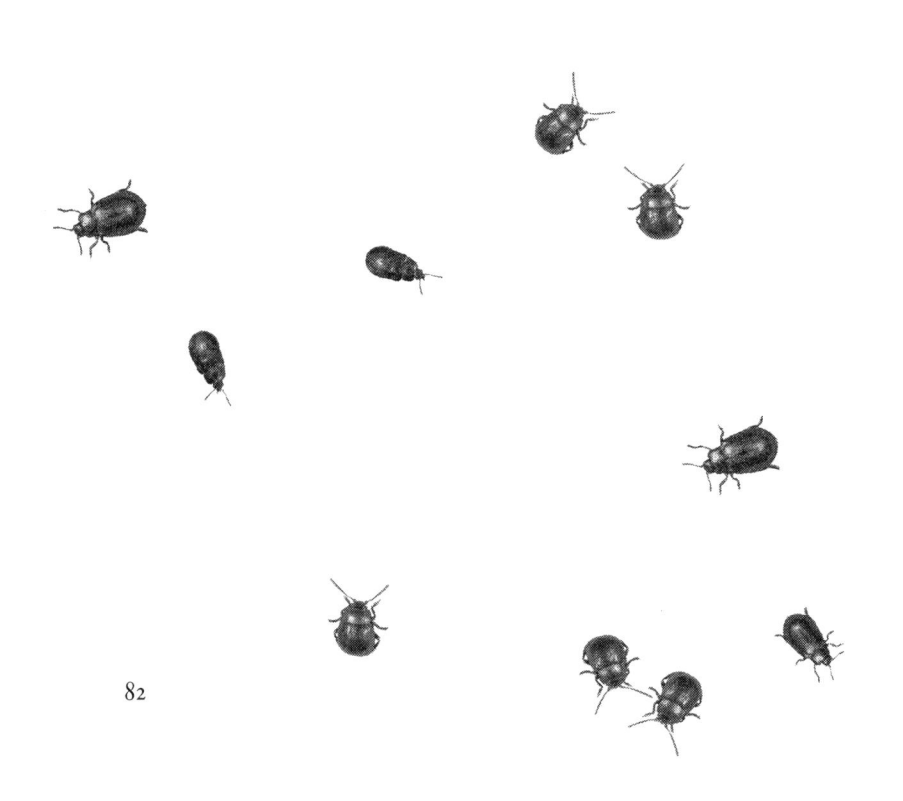

Chapter 21

CHESHIRE

I can see the moment Cal realizes how bad the bite looks. My first instinct is to tell her it's fine, that I'll survive. It hurts like hell, and my shoulder feels like it was run through a meat grinder, but after a few minutes, I'll be good as new.

Cal doesn't know that, though, and the urge to play with her crosses my mind. How far can I push her if she thinks I'm dying?

I groan and let my elbows collapse underneath me, like my body can't hold itself up anymore.

"Fuck! She bit you. You said she was venomous," Cal says, panic threaded through every single word.

"Oh, Wonder. I can see the light." I reach my hand up towards the sky and let my eyes go unfocused. "I'm coming home, mom."

Cal scowls. Maybe I put that on a little too strong. I need to bring it back down.

"How can I help? Is there an antidote? An anti-venom? What do I do?"

Cal hovers over me where I lay, her hair falling around her face. Even though there's panic in her face, she's still beautiful. Her eyes are wide, and when I see the fear there, it makes me stumble. But I can't help but to keep the ruse going. It's far too fun to tease.

"There's only one solution to the White Queen's bite," I say, my voice purposely weaker sounding. Can't have her thinking I'm healing already. So far, she hasn't noticed the black veins receding, but Cal is smart. If she focuses on them, she'll see.

"What is it?" she asks, leaning closer.

I meet her eyes, my face solemn.

"You have to suck the venom out."

Her brows go up and she glances at the wound. I wait for her to notice that it's closed, but either it doesn't register or she isn't really seeing it. The blood probably helps with that.

"You're serious?" She looks at me skeptically, and a tiny smile threatens to curl my lips.

"Dead serious." I enunciate the word 'dead.' She doesn't even roll her eyes at my joke.

"How do I do that?" She leans just a hint closer.

"Well, you put your mouth over the wound," I say, heat filling my body. When we meet eyes again, I continue. "Then you suck." Fire ignites in Cal's eyes despite the situation. I hum low in my throat. "I'm so cold." I really lay on the act. "We don't have much time. You have to hurry."

"Fuck my life," Cal mumbles, before leaning down, excruciatingly slowly.

I hold my breath, anticipating the moment her lips land on my skin, tense for the moment those feather-light touches tease my shoulder. She places one of her hands on my chest to brace herself and the muscle jumps in answer. I lean my head back and wait.

The first touch of her lips is hesitant, unsure of exactly how to go about sucking venom from my veins. But she seems to come to her senses and remember the "direness" of the situation because her lips close around the now closed wound, and she sucks hard against my skin.

There's a bite of pleasure-pain, the burning of the venom completely forgotten for the pull of her mouth. My cock immediately springs to attention, and I reach up and thread my hand through her hair, cradling the back of her head. My chest rumbles at the feeling, my eyes closing as the sensation washes over me.

She releases my skin far to soon and turns her head to the side to spit. I'm ready for her to lean down again, contemplating bringing her lips to mine and giving up the ruse, when a throat clears behind us.

I groan as Cal jerks away and turns.

"What are you doing?" White asks, amusement clear on his face.

"Cheshire was bitten. I was sucking the venom out," Cal rushes to explain.

My lips curl up as White's brows raise, his eyes dancing with laughter.

"Why would you do that?"

"He was going to die," Cal points out, confusion on her face.

White doesn't hold back his laughter this time. He throws his head back, and his laughter fills the air. Attie and Diana step up behind him, their eyes taking in my sprawling position on the ground, and Cal kneeling beside me.

"What so funny?" Cal growls, looking between us. I can't help it. My grin grows before I start chuckling with White.

"He's pulled a fast one on you," White says when he can catch his breath. "A Son of Wonderland can't die."

"What?"

"We can't die." She turns at my words and meets my eyes. "But if you want to keep going, I have something else you can suck the venom from."

Cal scowls, but I don't miss the glance at my cock. It gives a hard jerk in response, and I'm so tempted to wrap my hands in her hair and drag her to me.

She stands, grabbing the Vorpal Blade from where she's laid it, and glares at me.

"If you're done playing games, Pussy Cat, I'd like to get on with this."

She storms towards Attie and Diana, holding the sword in her hand. *I need to make a sheath for it,* I think, just as she whirls on me. I'm still stretched out on the ground, my tail twitching beside me.

She growls deep enough that it impresses me. I wonder how she'd feel about my growl against sensitive skin.

"Get your ass up, Chesh. Let's go."

When she brushes by Attie, I hear him ask, "Did you get the

venom out?" There's obvious laughter on his face, and I'm pleased that he seems happy with the situation rather than angry. I could always use the little brother on my side.

"Shut up, Attie," she tells him.

I'm rewarded with the sight of a brilliant blush spreading across Cal's cheeks.

My chest rumbles with laughter again.

Chapter 22

As we're walking through the trees, I study the sword in my hand. Even in the darkness of the forest, it seems to glow, it's power tingling through my arm. I don't know why, but the sword feels right in my hands, it's weight not too heavy that my arm aches. The entire sword looks made of silver, intricate vines etched along the blade. The hilt follows the same pattern, beautiful vines carved into the metal, not so much that it cuts into my hand; rather, it seems to cradle my hand gently. There's a glistening blue jewel in the pommel, catching on whatever light there is and sending little sparkles around the forest. It's mesmerizing, and if I didn't know any better, I would think it's nothing more than a decorative show piece. But even I can sense the power that resides in the sword, not something I understand, but I feel it nonetheless.

In the distance, some kind of creature shrieks, and I jerk my head up to scan the trees. It's followed by an answering chortle, and I frown.

"How safe are we right now?" I ask, keeping my voice down. I don't know what kind of creatures I can attract if I talk too loudly. Cheshire doesn't think the same thing.

"Not at all." He answers at a normal level, and I grimace as it echoes a little around us. "I'd offer to carry the Vorpal Blade, but I doubt it will let me."

"What do you mean?" I turn my head to meet his eyes just as a root I'd been stepping over lifts off the ground and trips me. I'm about to eat shit, the ground rising too fast for me to catch myself, when

Cheshire wraps his hand around my arm and lifts me back up. He continues as if nothing happened, as if I can't still feel his hand on my skin.

"The Vorpal Blade only sings for a warrior chosen by Wonderland." He shrugs. "It would probably give me a nasty bite if I touch it."

I eye the sword again. "That's interesting."

"It just proves that you are the final piece of the prophecy," White comments, helping my mom over a particularly large root. He's been supporting her the entire time, keeping the oxygen tank close, and I'm grateful for it. He hasn't left her side at all. She's been leaning heavily against him, her legs growing weak from so much walking. She hasn't responded to any talking since before the cave, her eyes glazed like she's apt to do. She's locked inside her mind, and no one can ever reach her when she's there.

When she stumbles over a smaller root, White bends down and scoops her into his arms, taking the burden from her completely.

"Thank you," I whisper, touching him on the shoulder.

"It's my pleasure, Calypso."

Attie watches, worry clear on his face, and I can't blame him. Our mother shouldn't be here. Hell, none of us should, but my mother is draining before our eyes, and there's nothing we can do about it.

There's an abnormal screech that comes from in front of us. It brings us all to a halt.

"What was that?" I whisper, scanning the tree line. I can't see anything, the trees too thick and the forest too dark to reveal its secrets.

"It sounded like a Chimera." White scans the trees with me, squatting closer to the ground, my mom still cradled in his arms. He doesn't struggle with her weight. I follow suit, pulling Attie down beside me. Cheshire stays standing and sniffs the air.

"What's a Chimera?" I've heard the legends from home, but somehow, I doubt this is going to be anything like that. No doubt, this will be ten times worse. Everything always is here.

"Nasty creature," Cheshire mumbles. "It usually travels in packs."

"Fantastic."

White meets Cheshire's eyes above my head. "Can you take care of it?" he asks, and Cheshire nods.

"Chimeras are always punishable."

"Okay. Here's what's gonna happen." White meets my eyes. "We're close to the Hatter's house. I'll go ahead of you and take your mother out of harm's way. Once inside the Hatter's house, we'll be safe."

"Can you take Attie, too?"

"I can only run so fast carrying one person, and a Chimera is fast. There will no doubt be Bandersnatch patrolling the woods. Cheshire will keep you both safe. Don't worry, Calypso."

"Can I trust you?" I ask, because he's running off with my sick mom, and leaving me behind with a cat who likes to play games more often than not.

"You can trust us both," White answers. "Our goal is to protect you, and therefore, that stretches to your mother and Atlas. We won't let anything happen to you."

I glance at Cheshire, as if I'm expecting him to contest that vow. Instead, he nods his head to me, agreeing. "I've got you."

I lean over and touch my mom's hand. She doesn't react, doesn't give any sign that she can even hear me. "We're gonna split up, mom, but it's only for a little bit. We'll be back in a jiffy."

White shifts her in his arms and stands. He nods his head to us once more and then takes off through the trees so fast, I gasp.

"Show off," Cheshire mumbles. "Stay behind me. Chimeras have a nasty bite."

I do as he says, pulling Attie behind me. Cheshire may like to play games, but if he says to watch out for whatever this is, then I trust him.

The screech sounds again, closer, and Attie presses into to me. I can feel his reluctance to keep moving forward. I reach back and touch his hand gently, letting him know it's okay. "Whatever that is, I'd prefer not to meet it," he grumbles behind me, one hand clenched in my leather jacket.

"Too late," Cheshire says. "Prepare yourselves. This is gonna get ugly."

The trees in front of us begin to shake, small little hisses sounding as whatever the creature is steps on the hissing flowers we've been passing. We'd encountered them every so often, and I always given them a wide berth. I don't take any chances with something that hisses "food" as we pass by. When the creature presses through the undergrowth and steps from the trees in front of us, I tense.

Ugly doesn't even begin to describe it.

It's humanoid for the most part, or at least in the general shape of a human. It walks upright, it's body hidden by a tattered black cloak. Cracked and Grey skin covers the hands, which peek through the sleeves. I can see three-inch long claws tipping the fingers. Its face looks like a skull, although certainly not a human one. W I would think a dragon skull would look like, that's how it appears. A hood is pulled up over its head.

"What the fuck?" I whisper, moving behind Cheshire just a little more and wrapping my hand around Attie. With the other, I raise the Vorpal Blade.

"Pretty much," Cheshire comments. "The skull isn't its face. Wait until you see that."

"No thanks."

Cheshire actually chuckles before looking at me over his shoulder. "I have to take care of it. Protect yourself with the blade. It's a far greater weapon than anything else you could use."

I nod my head and watch as Cheshire steps towards the creature. It screeches in answer, and I grimace at the feeling in my ears.

"I am the Hands of Justice," Cheshire growls, stopping out of reach of the creature. "You have committed sins against Wonderland, and acted on the Red Queen's orders. Your verdict has been decided by the land. Have you any words for it?"

The Chimera screeches again. I watch as it reaches up and pushes the hood back, followed by the skull lifting. My fingers tighten around the hilt of the blade, tense. Whatever the fuck this thing is, I hope I don't have to fight it. A mouth dripping with yellowing razor-sharp teeth opens and grins at us. Goosebumps scatter along my arms.

Nope. That's a big fat nope.

I push Attie back a step, and the creature focuses on us.

"Don't look at them," Cheshire growls. "If you have no last words, then you will be executed with swift hands."

I blink, hard, as Cheshire's skin seems to shimmer and grey fur sprouts along his body, until he's covered in it. Electric-blue stripes matching his ears and hair, slice through the grey, bringing pops of color into the dark trees. When he glances back at me, his eyes are full electric blue and slit like a cat's. That grin spreads, and I see exactly how he resembles the Cheshire cat from our stories at home. I'm pretty sure my mouth is hanging open as his tail swings from side to side. He winks–the cheeky bastard–before returning his attention to the Chimera waiting patiently in front of him. I don't understand why it's just standing there, but I don't question it. Who cares why?

Cheshire drops into a ready position, his fingers tipped with razor-sharp claws. The Chimera takes that opportunity to charge, faster than I could have ever expected. Both Attie and I stumble back as the Chimera screeches a god-awful battle cry and reaches out with those talons.

Cheshire dances out of the way, flowing around the creature as if he's dancing. His claws rake across the chimera's shoulder, thick red blood squirting out across his chest. The creature bellows and swings its arm around, catching Cheshire on the forearm, blood welling out with the slight cut.

"We have to help him!" Attie yells, trying to be heard over the screeches and growls.

"I don't think we can, buddy. We have to sit this one out."

I say those words, but I don't feel them. Even now, I itch to join the fray, to drive the Vorpal Blade between the creature's ribs. But Attie needs protection, too, so I stand vigilant in front of him, and watch the deadly dance between a Cheshire cat I'm starting to care what happens to and a creature from nightmares.

"Is that all you got?" Cheshire laughs, dancing away and raking his claws down the chimera's back. More blood. "I expected better from a Chimera."

Those words only serve to piss off the creature more. It whirls, the cloak flying around it, and goes for Cheshire's throat. Cheshire disappears before my eyes, and I blink just as he reappears behind the creature. The chimera doesn't even get a chance to react as Cheshire shoves his hand through its back, and through his chest. In his claws, is the creature's heart, bright-red blood welling around the still beating organ. My heart freezes as he rips his hand back through and free. The chimera collapses to the ground with hardly a sound, and Cheshire drops the heart on the ground with a squelch I'll never be able to unhear.

"Your fate has been decided. May Wonderland have mercy on your soul," Cheshire mumbles.

He turns and looks at us. Slowly, he transforms back to human, his skin replacing fur. The cat eyes are the last to go, and he blinks to clear the change. He's coated in blood, his arm completely covered up to his bicep, and it still drips from the tips of his fingers. A few droplets splatter his face, giving him a terrifying appearance.

I don't shy away from the sight. In my mind, somehow, I knew Cheshire was capable of brutality, of danger. Here he is, fresh from battle, coated in the life force of a creature he executed, and instead of running away, I pull the shop towel I keep in my back pocket free; it somehow hadn't been lost throughout our journey so far. He watches me warily as I step forward, taking slow measured steps, and stop in front of the man who makes my heart race, who's the worst decision I can make, and I give him a tiny smile.

"I think you missed a spot. There isn't any blood on your forehead."

His shoulders loosen at my remark, his ears twisting to take me in, and his lip curls the tiniest bit.

When he reaches his hand to wipe his face, I shake my head.

"Here, let me."

I touch the towel against his skin, wiping away the droplets from his face. I can't do much for the rest of his body, but at least I can clean the red from his face. I wipe slowly, cleaning away the blood, making sure to soak up as much as possible. When his face is clean, I wipe some of his chest, his muscles jumping at my touch. My towel grows damp quickly, until it no longer wipes up the red, and instead smears it around.

I hum in disappointment and meet his eyes.

There's a fire there that draws me in, and regardless that he's still covered in blood, I'm tempted to lean forward and meet his lips. His hand raises, the one covered in blood, and tips my chin up. Just when I think he's going to kiss me, Attie clears his throat behind us and breaks the moment.

I turn towards him, wiping the blood from my chin, and stare at Attie as he looks off innocently into the trees.

"I'd walk off," he says, a teasing smile on his face, "But I really don't want to be eaten." His eyes flick between us two before he stares off into the trees again, his face displaying a slight blush.

I clear my throat. "We should probably catch up with White."

"I have a better idea." Cheshire grins. "Now that there's only two of you, I can Fade us to the Hatter's house."

I'm almost afraid to ask.

"'Fade us' there?"

Cheshire's grin widens.

Chapter 23

HATTER

"There are Bandersnatch prowling around the border," I remark, watching from the front porch. The trees shake with a phantom wind, and every now and then, I catch a glimpse of the creatures between them. Almost in answer, one of them shrieks, and I feel the warm wetness trickle from my ears and run down my neck. I don't flinch even as Flam snarls back at the beasts. They grow silent.

Neither one of us moves to wipe away the blood dripping.

"Do you want me to clear them out?" Flam asks. I don't look at him, keeping my eyes trained on the trees. Jupiter has been growing anxious, watching the forest. Clara only convinced her to leave when I told her I would watch for them.

"Would you take that risk?"

Flam isn't normally willing to risk anything unless he gets something in return. It's a bit difficult having him here, on our side, knowing that he has no allies besides Doe, and now Jupiter.

"Doe would want me to."

I nod in understanding. Yes, Doe would want him to, because she is unabashedly on the side of good.

"Not yet. We just need to watch for the others. White and Cheshire will come with the third, and she's the most important member of the triad. She completes the prophecy." The third holds so much weight on her shoulders, and she probably doesn't even know it yet.

We fall into silence again, our eyes both focused on the trees. I'm tempted to ask the Flamingo about his powers, if they're still completely locked inside his body, but I hold my tongue. Best not to anger him while he's on our side.

"When I was on my way here," Flam begins, glancing over briefly, "I passed by the Caterpillar's home."

I turn fully and meet Flam's gaze. "He's done purging?"

He nods. "I have a feeling he'll make his appearance when we most need it. Most likely when the third arrives. He never comes before he's ready."

I breathe a sigh of relief. "Thank Wonder. I was beginning to worry he would never finish purging. Did you see his appearance this time?"

Flam shakes his head. "No. I only caught his voice. He wouldn't allow me to climb. It sounded softer than before."

"This time was the longest it's ever been for a purging. And at the worst imaginable time." I shake my head. "I never understood the Caterpillar, but Absalom has been an invaluable asset."

"He would say that it's the perfect amount of time," Flam chuckles, no humor in the sound.

"Absalom sometimes leaves us to wonder, have we done wrong and gone asunder?" I grimace a bit when the rhyme slips out, and Flam looks at me. Those fuchsia-colored eyes glow and threaten to hypnotize. I have no doubt he could do far more than that.

"That's the first time I've heard your madness since I've arrived," he comments.

I pull my hat off and run my hand through my hair in agitation.

"With Clara Bee by my side, I've come to understand, with her, the madness is held at bay, without, it slips back in."

Flam looks away first and nods. "I understand.

I touch my hand gently to his shoulder, removing it far quicker. The Flamingo isn't safe, no matter who's side he's on.

"I know you do, Flam. Let's hope Cheshire and White arrive soon. I feel it in the air. Don't you?"

"What?" Flam turns his face to the wind and closes his eyes, taking a deep breath.

I do the same, letting the tingling wash over my skin as the phantom wind pushes past me. There's something so sinister about it, like Wonderland isn't just dying, she's disappearing. When I open my mouth again, I can't help the word that slips out, the feeling too strong to ignore. I glance over at the Flamingo, waiting until his eyes meet mine to answer. When they do, I finally speak.

"War." I frown. "It feels like war."

Chapter 24

"So, explain to me who you are to Wonderland," I say, stepping over another tree root. Cheshire had said we could fade, but we have to be within a certain distance from the Hatter's house to do so. I have no idea what he means, something about a new enchantment to keep the Red Queen away. I don't question that part. I'm not an expert on Fading.

Cheshire's lip curls up, and he turns away from me, pushing aside more trees.

"I'd rather not. It's not something I like to dwell on."

"You said something when you took out the chimera," I push. "A saying. What did that all mean?"

"Are you going to stop asking questions if I don't answer?" he asks, irritation in every word.

Attie just watches the whole exchange, staying silent and trailing behind us. I have a feeling he likes Cheshire, but the damn cat is so stand-offish, it's hard to tell anything.

"No, so you might as well tell me."

Cheshire sighs and looks off into the trees. "We only have a short distance to go before I can Fade us into the clearing. There will no doubt be Bandersnatch."

A shriek echoes through the trees again, and both Attie and I clamp our hands over our ears, the sound sending sharp needles of pain through them. Cheshire doesn't even move to cover his ears, and I watch as blood begins to drip down his hair. His ears twitch at the feeling.

"That one was far away. We're safe at the moment."

"What the fuck was that?" Attie asks. I don't even scold him for the curse word. It's definitely warranted. The fear in his voice brings me over to wrap my arm around his shoulder and hold him closer.

"It was a Bandersnatch." Cheshire glances over at us before wiping the blood from his ears. It's pointless really. He's still completely coated in the chimera blood. Kind of silly to wipe away a little bit more. "And it's no doubt the sign that White made it to the Hatter's." When he sees the panic that spring to my eyes, he adds, "Don't worry. If they were captured, there would have been more shrieks. The beasts like to howl their victory."

"That doesn't really make me feel better," Attie mumbles.

I stop our movement forward and turn Attie in my arms. "I won't let anything happen to you, Attie," I tell him. "And Cheshire is protecting us, too." I drop my voice even though I'm sure Cheshire can still hear. He has cat ears, after all. "And between you and me, he's one scary-ass motherfucker. Did you see him shred the Chernobyl?"

"Chimera," Attie corrects and smiles. I grin right back, knowing all along what it was called.

"Right, the chimera. I think we're safe."

Attie nods, and I stand tall again, my eyes finding Cheshire's where he stands, looking completely serious, and there's so much pain in his eyes that it throws me before he can hide it. I'm tempted to reach out, to comfort him the same way I did for Attie, but he turns away and looks back through the trees.

"Just a little further," he repeats as we stumble through the undergrowth.

Cheshire's ears turn and twist on his head, taking in the sounds of the forest, the movements of the creatures. There's less of the hissing flowers here, and I'm thankful for that. When we reach a tiny little clearing, Cheshire stops us and holds out his hands. I take the one coated in blood without hesitation. Attie takes his other.

"Okay, we're far enough."

A Bandersnatch shriek sounds so close that I grimace. A tingling travels up my arm, and I glance over at Cheshire, his eyes closed in concentration. When I look down, my arm is turning opaque.

"Attie, close your eyes," I tell him, and he listens immediately. The shriek sounds again, and I feel wetness trickle down my neck.

As the tingling spreads throughout my body, I watch as a massive terrifying beast bursts through the trees just as we Fade away completely. Still, my heart gives a hard kick in my chest, and I just barely swallow my scream.

Chapter 25

When we reappear, I double over in pain, gasping for air with lungs that feel far too small. On Cheshire's other side, Attie does the same, clutching his chest as if he's in pain. My organs feel like they've been stirred and wrung out, my head fuzzy. Hell, even the tips of my fingers feel like I pricked them. Whatever Fading is, I'm not a fan.

Cheshire watches us with intelligent eyes, glancing over our bodies as if to make sure we really are okay. I can't say if we are or not. At the moment, I feel like I'm dying.

"You could have warned us," I grit between the pain as he grabs my, and Attie's, arm and leads us onto a porch.

"Where would the fun in that be?" he teases, but I don't miss the scrutinizing he does over our appearances. He pretends like he doesn't care, but it's all a mask. I'm starting to realize that's all it is.

"I'm dying," Attie groans, wrapping his arms around his middle. "Have mercy and kill me now."

I look over at him in alarm.

"He's not dying," Cheshire reassures me. "It's a side effect of Fading when you're not used to it. It'll pass."

"Tell Bethany I love her," Attie adds, and I smile at that, even though the pain is still echoing through my body.

"I'll make sure to tell her," I mumble, holding my own middle.

"No, wait, don't do that," Attie corrects, looking over at me.

"Too late. We already made a deal."

"Nooooo," Attie howls. A shriek in the distance answers, and we both look warily towards the trees.

"Don't worry. We're safe in the Hatter's house. They can't even come in the clearing anymore. We had an," Cheshire pauses, thinking on the word, "Let's say an incident when Jupiter arrived."

"Reassuring," I mumble.

"You have blood dripping down your neck," Attie points out, already stretching. The pain is receding quickly now. I can only assume that his is as well.

I lift my hand and wipe at my neck. My fingers come away smeared with red, and I frown. I'm definitely not a fan of the Bandersnatch. Not to mention the brief sight I'd seen before we Faded. I'll be happy if I never have to see them again.

"Welcome," a new voice says, and we turn to look.

A man sits in a rocking chair, shirtless, wearing similar leather pants and boots to Cheshire. He's pale, his eyes rimmed in black. On his head, sits a prominent top hat, and I know instantly who he is.

"Dude, that's the Mad Hatter," Attie beats me to the recognition.

The Hatter stands from his seat, stretching to his full height, and I raise my brows at him. He's not what I expected, although, I suppose nothing is here in Wonderland.

"You must be Calypso," the Hatter says, reaching forward to take my hand. "White told us to expect you. I'm so glad you're here."

"It's just Cal. And well, we weren't really given a choice."

"I'm Atlas! The Hatter is always my favorite in the stories at home." I grin over at Attie. He's acting like he's meeting a rock star, and I can't blame him. This is pretty cool.

Cheshire growls. "How come I didn't get this reaction when you met me?"

I shrug. "Easy. You'd already pissed me off before I found out who you were."

Hatter chuckles. "I like her."

Cheshire rolls his eyes and gestures to the door. "Are we going to go inside or stand out here like idiots?"

"Yes, please, please come in, come inside and meet our friends." I notice the slight wince Hatter tries to hide after the rhyme, and I look at him curiously. Does the Hatter not like to rhyme?

"Cal," Attie whispers, moving closer. "We're about to go inside the Hatter's house. What if he invites us for tea?"

"Only drink the tea that Clara tells you is safe," Cheshire comments. He meets my eyes. "Some of it can get you drunk. Others can make you sick if they're not made for you."

"Because, of course." I shrug my shoulders. "Who's Clara again?"

"Clara Bee is my mate," Hatter answers with a grin. "And the first of the triad."

"Ah, right. I'd forgotten that bit."

Hatter crinkles his brow but turns and leads us inside. As soon as we step into the entryway, I realize that there's something off about the house. It's like the whole thing is crooked, but when I walk across the tiles, it doesn't feel like it. It's almost like the whole thing has been shifted on the foundation.

There are odd statues and busts decorating the area, not all human in their appearance. The tiles are black and white, mimicking those from the room we landed in after the rabbit hole. When I look up, there's a beautiful painting of the Hatter's tea party on the ceiling.

"I think you're the first one to ever notice that," Hatter mumbles, watching the awe on my face.

"It's beautiful." I study the colors, how they pop off the painting. It's almost like I'm there in the scene, like I can hear the tea that the Hatter is pouring from a teapot.

"What are you looking at?" Attie asks, following my gaze. "I don't see anything."

"You don't see the painting?" I crinkle my brow at him in confusion.

"It's just purple. There's literally no painting."

I meet the Hatter's eyes, and he smiles, but he doesn't answer the burning question. Why can I see a painting and my brother can't? Before I can open my mouth to ask, another voice interrupts and draws my attention.

"Oh, there you are. I was so worried." My mom's voice echoes around the entryway, and we all turn towards the hunched woman dragging an oxygen tank.

"Mom," I sigh in relief. "I was so worried."

Attie goes to step towards her but stops at her next words.

"Mom?" She glances between us. "My children are young'uns."

I thread my fingers through Attie's and squeeze.

"Of course, Mrs. Diana. I'm sorry," I correct.

She eyes us a little more and turns around. "They're handing out tea. You have to try the yellow one. It tastes like lemons."

We watch sadly as our mother turns away, none the wiser of the pain she's caused her children.

"Has it always been like that?" Hatter asks, a frown on his face.

I shake my head. "No. She used to remember us more often. Now, if she remembers us at all, it's a good day, and those are far and few between."

"I'm sorry," Hatter mumbles.

"It is what it is," I shrug and move towards where my mother disappeared, my hand still intertwined with Attie's. It's more for my benefit than it is his. I feel suddenly overwhelmed, like everything that's happening is starting to crash down on me. My heart beats a little faster than normal, and I can feel it stealing my breath as they grow shallower. I focus only on taking one step after the other, but when we get to the doorway and see the long tea table, full to capacity with various creatures and people, I release Attie's hand and turn away.

"Are you okay, sis?" I feel Attie draw closer, and I wave him away.

"I'm fine, Attie. Go have your tea with the Hatter. Make sure to ask Clara what's safe."

Just as quickly, I feel him move away and go inside the room. I step away from the door and lean against the wall, tuning out the world. I look up at the ceiling and focus on the painting and on taking deep breaths. Inhale, exhale, repeat.

"You're not going to faint, are you?"

If I wasn't so focusing on not doing exactly that, I would have rolled my eyes at Cheshire. Instead, I ignore him, and focus harder on the elaborate painting above me. Finally, my heart slows, my shoulders loosen, and I close my eyes.

"Feel better?"

I peek open my eyes and glance at Cheshire where he stands on the opposite side of the doors, leaning against the wall and mimicking my position.

"A little," I mumble, scrubbing my hand down my face.

"You know what helps me when it all feels like too much?" Cheshire asks. When I look over at him, he's staring up at the painting, as if he sees it, too. "I have to get away from everyone and focus on one good thing. And then I tell everyone else to fuck off. That usually helps."

I can't help the smile that curls my lips. An answering one curls the barest corner of his.

"Yeah, I can see how that would help." I pause a moment before gathering my courage. "What's the last good thing you focused on?"

His smile straightens, and he looks away towards the front door, hiding.

"There aren't too many good things left," he admits. "But Clara and Jupiter were probably the last ones. Jupiter managed to place an enchantment on the Red Queen, but in order for her to do it, I had to leave her and Clara, Hatter, and White, at the mercy of the Red Queen's whims. I wasn't able to leave completely, I couldn't just leave them there, and I felt like my chest was bursting apart."

I don't interrupt him, afraid he'll stop talking if I do. This all seems like way more information than he meant to give, or that he ever willingly tells. But he just keeps staring at the front door, as if he's not dropping such emotion at my feet.

"So, I focused on Clara and Jupiter, because they represent something larger than I ever thought I would be a part of." Finally he turns and meets my eyes. "And now you're here to complete the triad. So, I suppose I can focus on you."

We stare at each other for a moment, and there are so many things I'd like to say, and yet, nothing comes to mind. In classic Wonderland fashion, nothing makes sense, and I can't even catch onto a thought. But we don't look away from each other's eyes; I can't. This moment feels strung with possibility, and before I know what I'm doing, I push away from the wall and walk forward. I don't stop until I'm right in front of him, and I move close enough that there's hardly any space between our chests.

Finally, my words come, and I look up into his eyes. For once, there's no sarcasm there, no scowl or agitation. He just watches me, his eyes looking so deeply into mine that I feel as if he's memorizing them.

"Next time, when I'm feeling completely overwhelmed," I whisper, placing my hand over his heart; his skin still splattered with blood, but I don't even notice anymore. "I'll find you and tell you that your one of my good things, even if you have an infuriating knack for being an asshole."

His lips quirk up again just the tiniest amount.

"I can be pretty distracting," he purrs, and his hands lift to cup my waist.

"I have no doubts about that," I breathe, smiling. "Just remember, Pussy Cat, you're not the only one with claws."

Fire ignites in his eyes, and he tugs me closer, until I'm pressed against his body, and I can feel his warmth straight to my core. He leans down, his lips at my ear, and I close my eyes at the feeling of his breath there. My own hands thread around his neck without thinking about it, digging into the hair at the base of his neck.

"I look forward to your claws," he purrs in my ear.

My entire body clenches, the words going straight to my core and setting it on fire. I clench my hands hard in the hair at the base of his neck, and he growls in answer. His fingers squeeze harder against my waist and slip down, down, until they cup my ass. He grinds me against him, and his hardness presses against me through his leathers, tempting, so tempting.

"You two done fucking against the door?"

I jerk away from Cheshire at the voice, stepping away and putting distance between us. Cheshire doesn't move. He keeps leaning against the door, his hair a little wild from my fingers, his cock straining against his zipper, and a grin spreading across his face.

"Flam, I'm surprised you're here," Cheshire says, as if we weren't just caught with our hands in the cookie jar.

I turn towards the new voice and meet fuchsia-colored eyes. I raise my brow as I take in his appearance, the tattoos running along every bit of skin exposed, the piercings on his face, the hot pink leather pants and jacket. He's completely drool-worthy, and gives Cheshire's 'bad boy' aura a run for its money, if it wasn't for the pink. But it looks anything but feminine. I'm really uncertain what to think of him.

"Seems you two are already pretty cozy," Flam comments, and I tilt my head.

"Can't help it if he's hot," I shrug, trying to play it off.

Flam smiles. "And yet, you didn't do the same thing with White, or Hatter, or me, even though you've been checking me out since the moment you noticed me."

"Well, I'm not going to just wrap myself around every hot guy," I scowl. Flam actually laughs at my words, and I wrinkle my brow in confusion.

"It's funny, that you pick the one man to 'wrap around' as you say, that has no interest in a mate."

"I never said a thing about mates." I meet his eyes. "Just because I want to fuck someone doesn't mean I'm proposing."

For the first time, I feel Cheshire shift, and I glance over at him. The grin is gone, replaced with a scowl. He straightens from his position and curls his lip up at us.

"I'm tired of this bullshit," he says. "See you inside."

He enters the room, leaving me alone with Flam.

"If I didn't know any better, I'd think you hurt his feelings, Calypso," Flam says, staring after Cheshire. "That one has a heart of stone, though."

"Right. So, that's impossible." I stare after Cheshire, too.

Flam laughs.

"This is Wonderland, dear girl. Nothing is impossible." He straightens his leather jacket. "And if anyone can break through the stone, it would be you."

I want to ask him what he means, why I have a better chance of that, but instead, I ask, "What are you?"

Flam turns towards the open doorway, before grinning at me. "Haven't you guessed, love?" He winks. "I'm the Flamingo."

And then he disappears inside, leaving me in the entryway alone. I stand there for a moment, confused, before I decide to follow him.

This time, when I enter the room, many of the people and creatures sitting at the table stop talking and look at me. There's only one open seat, clear on the other end, and I realize I'll have to walk in front of all of them in order to reach the chair. That overwhelming feeling crashes down on me, and my heart speeds up, the pressure of my role here really settling in at the looks on their faces.

Down at the other end of the table, Hatter and who I imagine must be Clara, sit in throne-like chairs. White sits next to a woman with bright red-orange hair. She smiles at me, and I try to return it, but my lips don't respond to my command. Flam winks at me from where he sits next to a woman with rainbow-colored feathers. The empty seat is right next to Cheshire, who meets my eyes for a moment. He doesn't blink, and I lock onto his gaze, on a good thing, before taking a deep breath and making my way forward. I completely ignore the eyes on me, the hushed whispers as I pass, and keep my eyes locked on the electric-blue beacons. When I finally reach the chair, I sit down in it hurriedly, and set the Vorpal Blade near my feet.

Cheshire looks away from me to sip his tea again, the color of it like ripe blueberries. Attie leans over to me, from where he sits on the other side.

"Hey, Chosen One."

"Shut up," I mumble.

On Attie's other side, sits our mother, delicately sipping yellow-colored tea and making happy noises under her breath. At least she's enjoying herself. Somehow, her oxygen tank doesn't seem to be running low, and I chalk it up to the weird Wonderland magic that seems to be in everything.

"Hi, I'm Clara," the woman beside the Hatter says, giving me a little wave. She seems pretty normal, even if she's dressed in some sort of military-style coat that mimics the Hatters. "We've all been so excited to meet you."

"And I'm Jupiter," the redhead adds. Her arm is intertwined with White's, clear love in her eyes when she looks up at him. Odd, that the members of the triad, ended up pairing off with the Hatter and White.

"Cal," I say, nodding my head to them. "You can call me Cal."

"It's so nice to finally meet you, Cal," Clara replies. "All of the food in front of you is safe to eat. The tea is safe, too. If you want something a little stronger, the teapot Cheshire has is a bit like whisky."

I'm so tempted to try it, but the thought of getting drunk and leaving Attie with these people stops me. He's still my responsibility, and my mom needs constant care. For the first time, I realize we don't have any of her medicine. I glance over at her, but she seems fine, even without the fifteen pills they prescribed her.

"I'll pass," I say, going for the safe food instead. Now isn't the time to start losing my head.

Clara nods. "Today, let's just let you three rest, and then we can discuss the prophecy and the story of Wonderland later."

"Sounds like a plan to me," I mumble, biting into a croissant when I realize how hungry I actually am.

Something brushes against my leg under the table, and I twitch the slightest bit. I'm almost afraid to look what's under the table, but I do it anyways. When I lean over, it's to see Cheshire's tail twitching back and forth, brushing against my ankle each time it moves. I straighten and look over at him, but he doesn't meet my eyes, just continues to look down at his teacup.

Instead of ignoring it, or calling him out, I reach over under the table and squeeze his knee gently, letting him know I'm there. He doesn't react, and I start thinking I've overstepped. I start to draw my hand away, but his fingers curl around mine, holding them in place. I don't react outwardly, not wanting to draw attention to the movement, but it feels good to have his fingers curled around mine.

As I take a sip of my tea and listen to the quiet murmur of the tea party guests, I feel something soft and comforting wrap around my ankle rather than brush against it. It stays there. My lips curl up as the flavor of the tea hits my tongue.

It tastes like woodsmoke and wild honeysuckles.

Chapter 26

Two days later, we still haven't discussed the prophecy, not really. It's been mentioned and hinted at, but not a single person has actually told me what the prophecy is, besides that I have a role to save Wonderland. It would be frustrating if I wasn't so preoccupied with taking care of my mom and Attie.

My mom seems to be moving slower, her energy lower than when we first arrived. I tell myself that it's just the stress of the environment and the events that have happened. I refuse to think it's because of something else, or that her time is drawing near.

Attie has embraced Wonderland with a vengeance, and it's been difficult convincing him that this isn't just some fun adventure. I still don't think it's sunk in. He's taken to training with the Hatter and White, with a sword. I'd about killed them when I realized they'd given him a real sword to practice with until they pointed out that it's enchanted, so it doesn't break skin. It still didn't make me feel any better to see my fifteen-year-old brother swinging around a gleaming silver sword as if it's a baseball bat, but it helped a little bit.

I've never seen the kid so interested in the history of anything, preferring math and science in school, but he's taken to learning the history of Wonderland as best as he can. Not everyone wants to talk about it, but the Hatter always looks at him fondly and answers if he's able to. It seems they've all taken a liking to my little brother. Clara and Jupiter have been doting on him like mothers, Jupiter especially when she realized he likes science. Now they've been laughing like nerds over some pop culture reference. Turns out they both like the same nerdy things. It's made for some interesting moments where I stare at them completely lost while they chuckle over some joke.

The tea party is going strong again today, the table full as always. The people at the table are always different save for us and a few others. The Tweedles, who I've been warned away from by pretty much everyone, never change out. They just sit in their seats in the middle of the table, making everyone uncomfortable as they drink black tar-like tea. They look at me a lot, and it unnerves me so much, I've taken to pretending they aren't even there. Creepy motherfuckers.

"Where do all the people come from?" I ask Attie softly, wondering if he's already figured out this answer in his history search.

"Remember when Cheshire told us he's the Hands of Justice, like the Punisher?" I nod. "Well, the Hatter is the Soul Escort. Kind of like the Grim Reaper. He escorts the dead to the Here After."

"What does that have to do with the people at the table?"

"They're the ones he's escorting. The Hatter's Tea Party is the last stop before the Here After."

"They're all dead?" My voice is a little too loud, and some of the others look over at me.

Attie nods. "Isn't it trippy? They don't look dead. They seem just as whole as you and me."

"It's an enchantment," Hatter comments. "Placed on my home by Wonderland herself. Those that have died can walk into my home and can partake in the food and drink on the table one last time, before we cross through the portal to the Here After."

"So, the Here After is like Heaven?"

"Yes," Hatter nods. "It would be what you call Heaven in your world. All souls go to one place. The Here After looks different for each person."

"So," I start, looking between them all, "Hatter is the Grim Reaper. White is the Time Keeper. And Cheshire is the Punisher."

"Exactly," Jupiter answers, smiling. "We all have our roles to play here."

"What's your role if you don't mind me asking?"

"Of course, not. I was the second, so my role was to strip Alice of her immortality, or of her ability to draw power from the Jabberwocky. Past that, we haven't figured it out yet." She looks over at White. "Coming to Wonderland awakened powers I never knew I had, so we've been practicing with those, to see their full extent."

"My role was the first of the triad," Clara continues. "I was prophesied to take out Alice's Knave, and now I sit beside Hatter for every tea party."

"Y'all keep saying Alice . . .," I trail off.

"Ah, yes. An important bit of information, the Red Queen is also Alice," Hatter adds, as if that's not the biggest bomb dropped.

"Is she still a little girl?"

Jupiter snorts and shakes her head. "No, she's definitely not a little girl, not at all."

"She came to Wonderland as a child," Clara adds. "But she left. When she came back, she was a woman full of scorn and revenge."

"She's a monster," Jupiter clarifies. "And as the third, your role is to bring her down completely."

I stare at all of them, shifting on my seat, before my eyes land on Flam and Doe.

"What are y'alls roles?" I ask.

Flam shrugs. "I have no role in Wonderland. Not a specific one. I am just one of her many creatures." He looks over at Doe. "I doubt we would have been allowed to be together if I'd had an official role."

"What do you mean? Wonderland deems who can be together and who isn't?"

"Not exactly." Doe meets my eyes. "But those who have prophecies written about them rarely get to choose their fate."

"That's not true," Clara interrupts. "Sure, a prophecy encourages you into your role, but any one of us could have chosen to walk away. It's simply a matter of if Wonderland chose right. The prophecies have known what they're talking about, and Absalom is always there to give us further direction."

"There may be a prophecy, but it isn't set in stone. It could have turned out vastly different." Jupiter stirs her tea, and everyone falls silent.

"It doesn't really seem like anyone has tried to fight the prophecy," I say quietly. "So, how do you know for certain?"

Clara meets my eyes, and I tilt my head, waiting. "Have you heard the full prophecy yet, Cal?" I shake my head no. "Once you've heard it, and get to think on everything that happened, and we get to the end of that war, and it's time for you to go home, ask the question again." She smiles. "You will know."

I shrug and look at the table. "Which of these teapots is like the whiskey again?"

Cheshire slides a blue teapot towards me, and I pour it into a cup.

"If I'm going to be led around like a puppet, at least I can have a good time doing it," I mumble.

I take a sip, and fire burns through my veins. Cheshire leans over towards me as I throw the whole teacup back and pushes a plate of cupcakes in front of me.

"If it's a good time you're wanting, try these." He winks at me.

Taking the challenge for what it is, I pick up the cupcake and take a bite. His lips curl as he watches me.

Someone clears their throat. "Perhaps, slow down a bit."

"Why?" I ask. "Am I going to war today?"

"No." Clara answered. "But if you keep eating the food like that, you're gonna feel pretty intense."

"Good." I take another bite.

♠

WONDERLAND FOOD IS NOT LIKE GETTING DRUNK. IT'S A completely different feeling than anything I've ever had before. At first, I thought it was like the time I tried a joint in high school, but it completely surpassed that. Music started funneling into the room, and I wasn't sure if it was real or imagined. Still, I felt like I wanted to sway. Attie kept looking at me funny, so I became convinced that I had something on my face, and I constantly tried to wipe it away.

Now, I'm sitting in my chair, chuckling under my breath, all because one of the creatures down the table sneezed, and it sounded like a trumpet. "A fucking trumpet," I say under my breath, but I'm actually doubled over from laughter. The alligator creature looks incredibly offended, and I don't know how to apologize even if I could.

Cheshire just lounges beside me, enjoying the show. I'm tempted to give him a real show, but there are too many people in the room. I stand up from my seat, swaying a bit. Flam and Doe watch with amusement as I brush my hair out of my eyes.

I try to think of something to say, some grand gesture to tell them I'm leaving. Instead, I turn into a school child leaving the dinner table.

"May I be excused?"

Clara snorts and gestures to the door. "Go right ahead."

Then I salute her. Like, actually salute her. Wow. Wonderland food is weird.

I leave them all behind in the tea room and think really hard about where I want to go. Somehow, I end up at a window that leads right out to the roof, and I smile. I'm pushing it open and climbing outside before I even realize what I'm doing.

I don't go far. My feet are a little unsteady for walking along the whole roof. I just scoot over enough that I can sit comfortably without falling and lay back against the warm shingles.

The sky is dark like it always is. There never seems to be any sun here, even when it's supposed to be daylight. Jupiter said it was something to do with the Red Queen, that it never used to be bright here, but not so dark. I don't know if I believe that or not. The darkness seems to fit the world.

There are a few stars that dance around and move, beautiful to watch, but a little trippy when you're drunk on Wonderland food. In the distance, the sounds of creatures reach my ears, quiet for the most part. If I squint my eyes a bit and pretend, I can imagine I'm back at home, listening to the cicadas and the bullfrogs. But this isn't home. And I'm reminded of that fact when something knocks on the roof beside me.

I turn my head and meet electric-blue eyes, walking along the roof as if it's as easy as a trapeze. I suppose for a cat, it probably is. For someone who seems incredibly annoyed by my existence, he never seems too far away. My heart gives a little throb at that, but I ignore it.

"Stalker much?" I ask, turning back to the sky.

"Can't have you falling off the roof in your drunken condition. You're important to Wonderland, remember?"

That's a lame excuse, I think. When he snorts, I realize I said it out loud. Wow. I've never done that before while drinking. Granted, I haven't been wasted in a very long time.

"Just to Wonderland?" I don't turn and look at him, waiting for his answer. I focus on one particular star that's going in circles.

There's a heavy pause before he finally speaks. "Yes."

I nod my head. A second passes, before Cheshire sits down next to me and follows my gaze. "My mom used to say that the stars are fireflies that got stuck in the sky, so they put on a show rather than burn out."

I smile. "That's actually quite a nice thought."

I turn my head to look at him and realize he's much closer than I expected, but I don't move away. I meet his eyes completely, letting him see whatever is on my face.

"I don't believe in such fairytales anymore," Cheshire says, his tail curling around behind me.

"You literally are living a fairy tale. You have cat ears. There are books written about you."

"But for me, this is normal." He shrugs. "You're the odd one out in this world."

"You're not wrong." I bite my lip, and Cheshire watches the movement. "Am I going to die here?"

His eyes jerk back up to mine. "What makes you ask that?"

"This prophecy says I have to take out the Red Queen. What if I'm not that person? I don't know the first thing about war or killing someone. What if I fail?"

Cheshire studies my eyes for a moment. "The prophecy speaks of you succeeding."

"And yet, prophecies don't always come true. There could be a million alternate prophecies, and in only one, I might succeed. What if I'm not strong enough?"

Cheshire lifts his hand and cups my cheek, the touch so gentle, I turn my head into it, even though I know the tender touch won't last.

Cheshire is made of iron and steel, of anger and pain. A tender touch is not something he's used to.

"You're plenty strong enough, Little Goddess. All you have to do is believe."

I snort. "Easier said than done."

"It's always easier said than done. Always."

The air grows still, and my eyes drop to Cheshire's lips, where they sit tempting me. How easy would it be to give in, to say it was the food that did it and claim a kiss? How easy would it be to taste danger?

"What is it you want, Little Goddess?" Cheshire whispers.

His tail curls around my bicep where I lean up on my elbows against the roof.

"Right now, It's a kiss."

Cheshire leans forward and for a moment, I think he'll listen to me. I should have known. There's a few inches between us before his lips curl up in a wicked grin.

"Not yet, Cal."

I growl, but before I can grab him and slam my lips to his anyway, he pulls away and stands up. He walks to the edge of the roof and looks back at me.

"Tonight, I hope your brain runs over this scenario a million times, and each time you imagine the kiss a little different, so when it really does happen, it'll blow away even your wildest imagination."

He steps off of the roof, and my heart gives a hard throb before I remember the saying about cats, that they'll always land on their feet.

"I hope you land on your ass," I call down, not even sure if he can still hear me.

A tiny smile curls my lips when a husky chuckle meets my ears.

Fucking Cat.

Chapter 27

"Someone needs to fetch Absalom," Hatter mumbles a week later. "He's taking entirely too long. We can't wait anymore. We need his guidance."

"Can't we just call him?" Attie asks.

I snort and cock my brow at him. "You got a Wonderland phone, little bro?"

"No but they might." He crosses his arms defensively, and I chuckle.

"Unfortunately, we don't have phones. Wonderland doesn't like that kind of technology."

"But you have electricity," Attie points out, ever the obvious. There's a chandelier hanging above us, indeed with electric bulbs.

"She doesn't like certain types of technology. We've had what you call electricity for as long as I can remember. In fact, I think it was our technology that was stolen to power your world."

Attie shrugs.

"They don't teach us that in history class."

Hatter smiles at him, clear affection on his face. In the two weeks we've been here, the Hatter has started to dote on Attie, showing him all sorts of things, teaching him how to fight with a sword. The others have taken it upon themselves to teach him whatever they can, too. My mom has been mostly distant, almost catatonic half the time. She hasn't recognized us since we arrived at the Hatter's house. I'm afraid she never will again.

"No, I doubt they would," Hatter tells Attie, smiling at him.

"Who can go get Absalom?" Clara asks, worrying her lip.

It's almost like the entire room shifts to look at me as I have my mouth open around a croissant.

"Really?" Exasperation coats my answer, and I glare at them all.

"Well, you and Cheshire are the next part of the prophecy," Jupiter points out.

"Why me and Cheshire? I thought it was just me being part of the triad."

Jupiter and Clara both look at Cheshire. He's sitting beside me, sipping his tea, as if he doesn't have any connection to this conversation. Both of them frown before Clara sighs. Cheshire glances up at the sound and meets her eyes.

"Oh, Cheshire," she breathes.

Cheshire growls and looks away. "Drop it."

"What?" I ask. "Drop what?"

"It doesn't matter." Cheshire drops his spoon a little too hard on the table, making the dishes clatter. Down the table, the Tweedles perk up, but I look away from them. I have no desire to deal with those weirdos. They give me a serious case of 'run away' vibes. There's something about them that screams of harming, hurting, and destroying, and I get the feeling that they don't belong to this world any more than they belong to mine.

Jupiter and Clara have been nothing but kind to me since I've been here, but I've been sticking to my mom and Attie's side. Mom, for all her dementia and health issues in the nursing home, seems far more content here even if she doesn't seem to be remembering us. When she's not locked inside her mind, she's talking with everyone as if she's happy to be on this adventure. She grows weaker and weaker every day. The doctor had warned that she's deteriorating, and that it would be her choice when she's ready to go. It could take a while or it could be suddenly. Either way, it's only a matter of her being called away.

My mom sits beside me right now, happily sipping Chamomile tea and eating a cupcake. She never questions the creatures, the odd people we sit with. She just pretends as if nothing is there, or as if she's dreaming. It makes me unbearably sad, to think that she won't at least recognize the oddness.

"You two will have to go get Absalom," Clara says, nodding her head. "Flam said he's finished purging."

My eyes flick over to Flam. He winks at me when he sees me looking, but I don't accept it as anything other than him being funny. His arm is around Doe as she sips her tea, her rainbow-colored feathers making them an even odder pair, and yet it's obvious they're completely in love.

"We'll leave first thing tomorrow." Cheshire is wearing his signature tiny smirk. "That is, if we can get you up from your beauty sleep," he teases. "Although, you do have such a cute snore."

"Shut up," I grumble, taking another vicious bite of a sweet bread.

I'm so agitated, I don't think to ask how he knows I snore.

Chapter 28

I step over a tree root thicker than my arm, and it rises with me, trying to catch my toes. I step high enough to avoid it, but it still pisses me off.

"Why do we have to walk through the forest? Why can't you Fade in?" I go to step over another root, but this one rises higher than I expect, and it catches my toe. I trip, and nearly fall on my face. Luckily, I catch myself. The tree laughs at me, it's woodsy sound grating on my nerves. "Fucking trees," I grumble, kicking the root for good measure. It sends a sharp pain up through my toe, and I growl. "Someone should take a chainsaw to your ass."

"Now, now," Cheshire teases. "They can't help it if you can't handle your wood."

I have yet to see a single tree branch rise up to trip Cheshire, and that only serves to piss me off more. I snort.

"That was a lame line, Cat. Does that impress the ladies?"

"Oh, I can assure you, they're happy with my wood."

I roll my eyes. I'd walked right into that one. "That's what you think," I mumble under my breath, but I completely forgot about Cheshire's super duper gee wizz hearing.

He turns on the spot, his eyes looking me up and down, taking in the sight of my shirt stuck to my chest from sweat, and my jeans uncomfortable with all the walking.

"Is that a challenge?" He purrs.

"It's a statement of a fact." I stop and push my hair out of my eyes. "You tell yourself they're happy because you're an asshole, but I doubt you've ever stuck around long enough to ask."

He shrugs. "No point in sticking around when we get what we came for." I shake my head and start walking again. I go to pass Cheshire, but he grabs my wrist, locking me in place. "Does that bother you, little goddess?"

I look into his electric eyes, that always somehow seem brighter when filled with emotion. Right now, it's amusement. I amuse him, and it fills me with such anger, I don't know where to direct it. So, I don't comment on it.

"I've learned my lesson with men like you," I say instead. "You're a good fuck, perhaps, a nice story to tell the girls, but nothing else. Because you refuse to be anything else, choosing to conquer one before moving on. So, no, it doesn't bother me, Cheshire, because I expect you to act like that. You're a bad boy, and the kind that will never change. I'm not jaded. I'm not ignorant. I know exactly what you are."

"You know nothing about me," he growls, his voice going straight through my body. I love when he gets all grumbly, but I'll never tell him that. It would give him too much leverage.

"I know all I need to." I jerk my arm from his grip, and I know he lets me go rather than my strength giving me freedom. If Cheshire hadn't wanted me to move, he wouldn't have let me. The fact that he did, speaks to his character more than anything else.

I start walking through the forest again, weaving through the trees. I don't look behind me to see if Cheshire is following; I can feel him, moving as quietly as a panther. I don't know why I'm so aware of him, but I can practically feel his life force, and it sets my nerves on fire.

"You're right," Cheshire says from behind me, and I pause but don't look back.

"About what?"

"I am a good fuck."

I should have known it wouldn't be some in-depth recognition of his attitude, or some grand gesture. I forgot for a moment that this isn't really a fairy tale, and Cheshire certainly is no prince.

"No sex is worth you being an asshole," I say. I still don't turn around. I can't, because I might just accept it for the challenge it is.

"Are you sure about that?" I can feel him move closer, just a little, like a shift in the air. "Aren't you a little curious what it's like to be wild, to be free, to let someone else take charge?"

"I don't need a man to take charge. I'm perfectly capable of taking care of myself." My fingers twitch at my side, his energy pushing against my own, stroking my fires.

"But why should you take care of yourself when I can do it for you? I can have you screaming your ecstasy to the trees, little goddess. Just let go." He pauses. "I'd say it would be a good story to tell, but I get the feeling you don't have any women you actually talk to about such things."

And then my anger just disappears. I'm no longer pissed. I'm no longer angry. Because he's right. Raising Attie and taking care of my mom has left me with no friends besides Rob, and he doesn't really count. The girlfriends I'd had didn't understand why I couldn't have lunch or hang out on the weekends, and so we'd lost touch. It doesn't bother me, but Cheshire poking fun at it, well, it brings a tiny pinch into my chest. I start walking again, but his presence is so close behind me that I can practically feel his heartbeat. How, I don't know, but it's slowly stroking my anger again, just a little bit.

"No response to that?" Cheshire goads. I don't reply, even though I can literally feel the grin he's sporting. He's poking the bear, and I try my hardest not to respond. "Come on, Calypso. That must burn. No friends, all this responsibility. Have a little fun. What can it hurt? Pretty sure I'll be the best you've ever had."

"Why don't you just fuck off, Pussy Cat?" I toss the words over my shoulder, annoyed with the smug bastard behind me. I'm trudging through a forest that's literally trying to kill me, on a mission that I have no choice in, and he has the absolute audacity to keep that shit-eating grin on his face.

"I'd rather just fuck you," he drawls, not even reacting to the nickname.

And just like that, the urge to fight with him, to give him a run for his money, fills my body, and I come to an abrupt halt right there in the middle of the forest. There are the sounds of birds and creatures in the distance that I probably have no interest in coming into contact with, not after the ones I've already seen. I have no idea how much further we have to go, or even if we're going in the right direction. Jupiter and Clara said I would know where to go because I could feel it, but to be honest, all I feel at the moment is a mix of annoyance and lust that I seriously want to take out on the cat behind me.

I'd had the feelings before—the Cheshire Cat is too sexy for his own good—but I'd shrugged it off. Not anymore. This time, the urge is far too strong to ignore.

"What's the matter?" Cheshire teases behind me. "Cat got your tongue?"

I whirl around, a snarl on my face but stumble when I realize just how close he had stopped behind me. I'm tall, tall enough to tower over a lot of the men at home, but Cheshire is still a few inches taller than me, enough that I have to turn my head up a little bit to meet his electric-blue eyes.

"What the fuck is your problem?" I hiss, curling my lip. "I'm here, aren't I? I'm fulfilling some goddamn prophecy for people I don't even know! Do you have to be such an annoying ass the entire time?"

His lip curls up the smallest amount at my outburst, as if I amuse him, and it sends me over the edge. I reach up and shove him as hard as possible. I'm not surprised when he barely moves; the small amount that he actually does is most likely from surprise rather than my strength. I'm strong from lifting car parts and weights, but I'm not Wonderland strong. In my mind, Cheshire becomes every man who's walked into my mechanic shop and looked down on me because I'm a woman. He becomes every man who hits on me, and when I don't agree and smile, calls me a "bitch" and walks away. He becomes the ones who felt threatened by the fact that I'm making my own way, that I'm successful on my own. And I want to take out my anger on him. I want to be the one who takes control. I want to be the one in charge.

Cheshire's face changes from the smug curl of his lips to a snarl.

"What the fuck—?"

I don't let him finish. I grab a fistful of his shirt and yank him back towards me, slamming my lips against his. He doesn't respond immediately, perhaps too shocked to realize what's happening, but it doesn't last long. He growls beneath my lips and threads a hand through my hair, yanking me even closer against him with his other. I feel the briefest pinch, his claws scraping through the material of my shirt, even though I know he didn't have claws a second ago.

Cheshire tastes like everything I never expected, like the wild honeysuckle he smells like, as if he's so much a part of the earth, that he leaks its flavors. The feel of him against me is even better, his warmth wrapping around me like a caress.

Our kiss feels like a wrestling match, both trying to one-up the other. Our teeth clack together in the aggression, and I flinch under the sudden pain. It doesn't slow us down. The anger, the lust, still flows through me, and I realize I'm tired of fighting it. I'm not worried about being wholesome. Hell, the mission I'm on could kill me. Why resist what will no doubt be a good fuck with those odds? Why not enjoy it while I can?

Cheshire doesn't have to be a gentleman. I don't have to be a lady. I only have one thing in mind, and for once, I don't feel like I'm being judged because of my aggression. Instead, it only seems to fuel Cheshire even more, low rumbles in his chest letting me know he's just as angry, just as turned on.

I loop one hand around his back, trailing down low enough to brush against the base of his tail. He tenses against me but doesn't slow, not until I trail my other hand up his chest to wrap around his neck. The touch is gentle, just enough to sit there, but he breaks the kiss anyways and meets my eyes. We're both panting heavily, sucking great lungfuls of air. It feels like I can't breathe, and yet, at the same time, it feels like I have too much air in my body.

Cheshire's eyes slit like a cat's when my fingers twitch against his corded neck, and his fingers tighten in my hair until I feel his claws scrape my scalp.

"Would you choke the life from me if you could?" he purrs. "Would you watch the light leave my eyes?"

I frown, unsure how to answer. Am I a killer? No, but I would kill to protect those I love. Cheshire poses no threat to Attie or my mom, but he does pose a threat to me. Cheshire is the bad boy mothers always warn about, the ones they tell you you'll want to change, but it's hopeless because they're too far gone. My mother's words whisper in my mind.

Eventually, Calypso, you're gonna have to let go and live a little. You'll find your soulmate in someone completely unexpected, in someone you think isn't right for you. That you'll almost fight against wanting. That's how you know.

Those words she spoke to me after my first big heartbreak in high school, when Steven Turner broke up with me, and I cried my eyes out. I'd been moping in my room for weeks, determined that it was the end of the world, and she'd come in with those words. I was too young, she'd said, I'd barely tasted life. When it was meant to be, it's meant to be. She'd told me that she and dad hadn't seemed meant for each other, that they'd hated each other at first. I'd taken her words to heart.

I try not to focus too hard on those words now as I stare into those eyes slitted like a cat's, that tiny curl of lip mocking me, the tail my fingers brush against flicking back and forth, but I can't. Cheshire is going to be the end of me.

The only thing I can do in retaliation is to be the end of him, in return.

"No," I whisper, answering his question. His ears twitch with the single word, his tail coming around his body to curl around my thigh. "I'd rather watch the fire there as I make you scream out my name."

In answer, the flames I speak of spring to life in his gaze, that smile widening until he looks like the Cheshire from the storybooks, that grin temptation and sin.

"What makes you think I'll be the one screaming?" he teases, a single claw scraping down my spine.

Goosebumps break out along my skin in answer, but I don't change my expression. I squeeze my fingers around his neck, just enough to put pressure there. His eyes narrow the slightest bit, and those claws digs in just a little more at my spine.

"You'd best be careful how you proceed, Cal." Cheshire's hand tightens in my hair.

"Where's the fun in that?" I ask and squeeze tighter. I feel the corded muscles in his neck flex beneath my fingers, his Adam's apple bobbing as he swallows with the gentle restriction.

"Last chance," he growls, and I feel it in my hand as it vibrates in his throat. "You want to go to war, little goddess, we'll go to war."

A tiny smile is my only answer.

Chapter 29

For a moment, neither one of us moves, locked in an intimate, rough embrace, my fingers curled around Cheshire's neck, his threaded through my hair and at my back. Now that the gauntlet has been dropped, it seems neither one of us wants to move.

Cheshire swallows against my fingers again, and I'm tempted to squeeze a little harder. What would he do if I did?

Our eyes are locked, a silent dance for dominance that I know won't end even when our clothes are removed. Neither one of us wants to give up control, for different reasons, and yet, probably the same. We both fear what happens if we give up that control, even if neither of us admits it.

"Are we just going to stand here and look at each other?" I whisper, my voice already husky. I'm not embarrassed by it. Cheshire is hotter than any man I've ever seen, and being around him these past few weeks has only served to draw me closer. I know he's bad. I know he's all wrong for me. That doesn't stop me from wanting him, from wanting to keep him.

"I'm thinking," Cheshire murmurs, the vibration felt in my hand. I do squeeze then, and his eyes narrow on me.

"What's the matter?" I ask. "Cat got your tongue?"

I smirk at my own joke, of throwing his own words back at him, but Cheshire certainly doesn't find it funny. Those cat eyes narrow even more, and I roll my own. "Fine. If you're too afraid to act," I throw the words away, teasing, the smirk still on my face. I loosen my hold on his throat, intending to step away, but Cheshire's deep growl stops me.

"I didn't say to fucking move." His claws tighten against the base of my spine where they rest.

I scoff. "Well, you seem pretty uncertain to me. I was all ready to fuck you, and here you are, hesitating. It's not that big of a decision."

"Isn't it?" Cheshire asks, his hand slipping down from my hair to curl around my neck. No pressure. I can barely feel his touch, but it's enough. My heart rate speeds up. "Isn't it a decision that will change everything?"

He leans down and nuzzles against my cheek, his tail coming around and gently caressing down my arm where it lays wrapped around his hip. It's so light, it feels like a feather, sending goosebumps along my skin.

"No," I answer, a little breathless. Teasing, always teasing.

"Then, you're lying to yourself," he purrs, just before his teeth nip my ear. I hiss out a breath but don't respond. "If we do this, things will change, fundamentally, irrevocably. Are you prepared for that?"

"I'm prepared for you," I moan, digging in my nails at the base of his spine. Control, I need the control back. I move my hand from the back to the front and rub against the hardness in his leather pants. A hiss is my answer.

"Remember you said that," he growls just before he squeezes my neck, restricting my air supply just the tiniest amount. A bolt of panic shoots through me that's immediately replaced with excitement as he backs me against a tree and hikes my leg around his waist. "You're so fucking perfect." The words are a husky snarl, as if it almost pisses him off to say it.

I shove the leather jacket on his shoulders, trying to push it free. He shrugs out of it quickly, dropping it to the forest floor without a care. I don't blame him. I don't even look as I rip the shirt over my head and toss it to the side, before going to the button of his pants.

"This doesn't mean anything," I say out loud, more to myself than Cheshire. Neither of us comments on the lie that is. I can feel it, the change Cheshire talked about, but I don't focus on it. Control. I'm in control.

"Fuck!" Cheshire leans forward and runs his tongue along my ear just as I get the snaps undone on his pants and thrust my hand inside to wrap around his length. He's velvet steel in my hand, hot as a brand.

I jerk away from him when he goes to nip my ear again. The sound that comes from his throat is animalistic, a warning, but I'm not some piece of ass to be conquered. I won't give up my control.

I move my hand from his neck to his hair and jerk his head down, my lips crashing against his as I stroke him in his leathers. He jerks against me and squeezes harder against my neck. Liquid fire moves down to my core.

The kiss is just like before, a battle for dominance with neither willing to give up. It's violent, our teeth clacking in our fight. Against my back, the bark scrapes my skin, probably shredding it to ribbons, but I don't care. The pain mixes in with the pleasure, until I'm kissing him harder, my lungs running out of air.

When we finally break apart, we're both gasping, but Cheshire doesn't give me a chance to catch my bearings. He drops my leg and spins me until my chest is to the tree, my back against his chest.

"You think you can gain the upper hand?" he hisses in my ear, that hand at my throat still clutching, looser to allow me to breathe, but still a pressure. "You think you can conquer me, little goddess?"

A husky chuckle slips from my lips. "I'm not so easily conquered, either, Pussy Cat." In answer, I grind my ass against his hardness, and he groans, his free hand clutching my hip and pressing me back harder.

His teeth go right to my shoulder and clamp down. I cry out, growing wet enough to soak my underwear. He releases the skin and runs his tongue up the curve of my neck.

"All women want to be conquered," he whispers, slipping his hand down the front of my jeans. When his fingers touch my wetness, he purrs. "Even now, the thought of it excites you. You want to kneel before me, little goddess. Let me conquer you."

"No," I moan, grinding back into him until he hisses. "I will not."

"You will," he promises. "You'll be screaming my name in worship when I'm done with you."

I chuckle again.

"Which of us is actually named after a goddess, Pussy Cat? I think it will be you worshiping me."

I reach down and wrap my hand around his wrist, pressing his fingers against myself tighter, coaxing him to move.

Another bite on my shoulder, more juices flowing. Fuck, this is the hottest sex I've ever had, and we haven't even done anything yet. I reach back with my free hand and thread my fingers through his hair as he sucks and bites at my skin. I touch his ears and rub one, arching my back as his hand strokes my clit a little harder. His other hand leaves my neck to roughly caress my breast.

"Say my name," he orders. I smile but keep my lips clamped shut. "Say it!" he growls. He unsnaps my jeans faster than I can follow and shoves them down over my hips, leaving me in nothing but my underwear. I kick my shoes and the pants free from my legs and grind a little harder as his fingers go back to my clit.

"How about you say mine?" I moan, clutching his ear harder. He jerks against my backside, a snarl my answer. Neither one of us speaks the other's name.

His finger slips inside me, and my breath stutters just in time for him to add another digit. His lips move along the back of my neck, kissing, nipping, teasing.

"I'm going to enjoy breaking you, little goddess." A husky whisper in my ear. "You'll say my name."

I would have snorted if his tail didn't join the fray, senses overloading as it feathers over my nipples, his free hand jerking my head back and crashing his lips against mine. My neck is twisted at an odd angle, but I don't even notice it as he kisses me hard and deep, seeking that control. I bite his lip in answer, his chest rumbling at the little pain.

When his lips release mine, he spins me again, but I don't give him a chance to put me in another position. I practically tackle him to the ground, hoping the surprise is enough. We end up in a tangled mess of limbs on the forest floor, my body on top of his. A grin spreads on his lips.

I straddle Cheshire's waist, grinding down on his hardness that's still inside his leathers. I reach down and free his erection, pumping it twice for good measure. His hips jerk up into my hand, and I grin at the tiny victory. I notice he doesn't flip us over, though he could easily. He's humoring me, making me think I'm in control. He doesn't realize I actually am. I lean down and run my tongue along the side of his neck as his hands come up to clutch my waist. His claws are back, but they don't harm me. I bite the Adam's apple at his throat and feel a satisfying jerk of his hips.

"Where are your sweet spots, Pussy Cat?" I whisper. "Is it behind your ears?" I run a hand along one with the question, and his hips jerk again. "Is it your throat?" I bite the skin there again before moving down to kiss and lick the tiny tattoo on his shoulder I'd never noticed before. It's in the shape of a spade, black ink against his golden skin. I keep going, sucking at the skin on his chest, running my teeth over his nipples. "Is it here?" I chuckle when his muscles tense but keep going, until I slide down and his cock is in front of my face. "I bet this is a sweet spot." I glance up and meet his electric-blue eyes. They're hooded but there's a grin on his face.

"Why don't you taste it and see, little goddess?"

I snort, tempted to bypass the area but it was my goal all along. He thinks he's in control. I flick out my tongue and run it over the head, his breath hissing from between his teeth. I don't give him any warning before I close my lips around him and take in as much as possible.

"Fuck," he growls, his claws threading through my hair and holding me there, but he doesn't restrict me when I come back to the tip and swirl my tongue.

"Say my name," I tease, throwing his words back.

He snarls in answer, and I drop down his length again, caressing the side with my tongue, scraping my teeth gently against the head as I come up. He throws his chin back, and I do a few fast bobs of my head, going as deep as I can.

He sits up so suddenly that it startles me. Before I can figure out what he's doing, he grabs my hips and spins me around until my legs are parted around his face, and I'm laying on top of him.

"You want to tease, little goddess? Let's tease."

When his lips press against my underwear, I gasp. He eats me through the material, my hips grinding down. I almost forget I'm supposed to be in charge. When I remember, I circle my lips around his length again and hollow out my cheeks, sucking hard. In answer, he pushes my underwear to the side and finally presses his lips against me. I buck hard when his teeth gently nip my clit, before his tongue soothes the tiny pinprick of pain. His finger presses inside of me again, and my abs clench. Fuck, I'm going to lose it. I bob faster, my rhythm off as my thighs begin to quiver. He adds a second finger and pumps them inside me, curling his fingers, touching a spot inside of me that threatens to collapse my legs. I try to squeeze them closed, but his shoulders hold me open. I give up the pretense of trying to suck him and clutch his leather-clad thighs.

"Fuck," I growl, grinding down harder on him. My orgasm hits me hard, and I cry out, my body pulsing with the pleasure, my thighs shaking. Angry that he won this round, I bite his thigh hard through his leathers. He bites my ass cheek in answer, and I groan.

He's moving us before I'm ready, flipping me onto my back onto the forest floor. His hands grab my wrists and lock them over my head as he comes over me, his eyes glowing so brightly, they light up the area.

"Submit," he growls.

I laugh, hooking my legs around his waist. "No."

He lets go of my wrists, but I don't move my arms. Appreciation flashes in his eyes until I pillow them under my head, lounging on the floor, always teasing. His chest rumbles, but he doesn't fight the move, moving down to strip my underwear from my legs so that I'm lying beneath him completely nude. I eye his boots and pants, and he gets the point, standing up to kick his boots free. He does it methodically, as if he doesn't realize how sexy it is to see him in the act, pressing his leathers down his legs, revealing golden skin that I hungrily take in. When he catches me looking, he reaches down and strokes himself. My core tightens, and I raise my brow at him, a challenge.

"Turn over," he commands. I grin, but I don't move. That would be too easy. He growls and crouches down at my feet, before stalking up my body like the cat he is. "I will conquer you, little goddess."

"Keep telling yourself that," I whisper, keeping my eyes on his.

His shoulders roll with power, with barely contained strength, as he comes over me, hooking my legs around his hips. His cock nudges against my entrance but doesn't push inside, barely touching. That tail strokes up my thighs, and I shiver, before hooking one arm around his neck. My other hand wraps around his throat, a gentle touch.

"Think you can worship at this temple?" I smile. It's a cheesy line, one I've never felt comfortable using before, but the words slip out before I can stop them. A grin spreads across Cheshire's face, and a husky chuckle rumbles out.

"Only so I can conquer a goddess," he purrs. When his lips capture mine, It's not as hard as before, a slow dance rather than a battle. I start to think I've won, but I should have known. I'm so invested in the kiss, how sweet it is, that I'm caught off guard when he slams inside of me. I clutch my fingers around his throat and throw my head back with a gasp, my heart kicking hard in my chest. "And conquer you, I will." A growl as he lifts my ass higher from the ground, pulls out, and slams back in again.

My fingers clench hard around his neck, and I can feel his snarl in his throat. It only serves to fuel him on more as he starts to piston inside me at a punishing pace. I can't catch my bearings, can't catch my breath, as my body seems to short circuit on pleasure. His own fingers circle my throat, gently squeezing, until my hips begin to thrust with his, keeping his pace as he pounds inside of me. My eyes slide closed, but when he growls, they pop back open again to crash against his.

"Keep them open," he snarls.

I obey, if only to keep my eyes on him as he turns far more animalistic than I've ever seen him. He seems to be fighting control of his own wild side, fighting a shift, fur trying to sprout along his shoulders only to be pushed back. He's trying so hard to keep himself in check that it hurts me. I can feel his fear, afraid of what I will think, but it's part of who he is. I'm not afraid of Cheshire. I'm afraid of what he'll do to my heart, but I'm not afraid of his wild.

"Turn me over," I whisper. His rhythm stutters, but he keeps up the punishing pace. "Turn me over," I say again, louder. I'll give him this, let him feel comfortable to be who he is.

He jerks out of me, and I have a moment of emptiness before he lifts me and places me on my knees. I get a whole second to adjust before he thrusts inside me again. My back arches, his claws clenching hard at my hips, pricking, and for the first time, I feel a tiny drop of blood well from one. He's being careful, but losing control. His thrusting halts, and I look at him over my shoulder to see him staring at the blood.

"It's okay, Pussy Cat." His eyes jerk to mine. "It's okay." I lift up and wrap my arm around his neck, twisting to nip his jaw. "Don't stop." He twitches inside me, and I grind back against him. I reach between my legs and touch the base of his cock, pressing back against him, moaning. "Say my name." It's not a command as much as a reminder of the game we're playing.

It works.

One hand leaves my hip to thread into my hair, yanking my head to the side to give him better access as his teeth close around the muscle between my shoulder and my neck. At the same moment, he thrusts inside me hard enough to sting, and I cry out in pleasure.

"I'm a monster," he growls in my ear. "A beast. You've invited a beast in, little goddess," he groans, biting me again. I'll, no doubt, be marked up by the end of this, from his scratches and bites, but I don't care. I relish when he bites me again, my core pulsing with the pleasure as he continues to wind me tighter and tighter.

"Every goddess needs a monster," I groan between breaths, my chest rising and falling in rapid rhythm.

I'm not sure what I expected from those words. Maybe nothing at all. His hand releases my hair to wrap around my neck and clench tightly enough to seriously restrict my air flow. My heart kicks in my chest, a little panicked, as Cheshire pounds inside me harder, punishing, showing me exactly what he's capable of. From out of the corner of my eyes, I see fur spread along his shoulders and down along his arm to his hand where it brutally caresses my breast.

I'm completely at his mercy, drawing in air as best as I can with his hand around my throat, one arm looped around his neck. When he bites me this time on my neck, I scream, both pleasure and pain mixing together until I explode around him. My fingers claw at the hand around my throat, spots swimming in my vision, trying to gain purchase. They loosen just the tiniest amount as I ride my orgasm, those spots dancing as Cheshire keeps up his pace, the sound of his skin slapping against mine sending me over the edge again before I come down from the first one. He slams inside me once, twice, my body shaking with the force, before I feel warmth spurt inside me, his teeth clamping down a little harder on my skin, a growl rumbling in his chest where it's plastered against my back. Sweat drips down my face, my body so liquid, that if Cheshire lets me go, I would, no doubt, slide to the ground like a wet noodle. My thighs are shaking, the aftershocks from my orgasms making my body tingle.

Cheshire releases my neck, his tongue running along the bite mark, soothing the pain that's only now starting to filter in. He kisses the spot with such tenderness, it almost brings tears to my eyes, but I hold them at bay. His next kiss is on my throat, then my jaw, until he tilts my head towards him, and captures my lips. He's no longer covered in fur. He looks just like normal Cheshire, with a fire in his eyes that hadn't been there before.

This kiss is slow, tender, although still dominating. He's still pressed inside me, locking us together so intimately, I don't want to pull away.

Cheshire's other hand runs down my body in soft touches, his claws put away.

"You didn't say my name," he whispers when he pulls away and looks into mine.

"You didn't say mine," I toss back, my voice hoarse.

A tiny smile curls his lips, and my own match.

"A draw, perhaps," he purrs. "Next time, I'll conquer the goddess."

I don't respond, my heart throbbing in my chest as my words come back to me. No, oh no. My breathing starts to pick up again, panic shooting through my body. Cheshire frowns and gently pulls out of me before slowly laying me down. I immediately feel the loss, but don't comment on it. I'm too wrapped up my head.

"Are you okay?" His eyes roam over my body, taking in the red skin, the tiny pricks from his claws at my hips, the bruising where he bit me.

"I'm fine, Pussy Cat." But I'm not. Not really.

His eyes say he realizes I'm not fine, but he doesn't push, perhaps understanding where the panic comes from. Cheshire was right. Everything has changed.

My mom's words come back to me, and the words during the intimacy.

You'll find your soulmate in someone completely unexpected, in someone you think isn't right for you. That you'll almost fight against wanting. That's how you know.

Every goddess needs a monster. . . .

Chapter 30

We haven't talked since we got dressed and started walking through the forest again. Cheshire seems to be annoyed by that fact, attempting to say something to me, but I'd only shaken my head. I couldn't handle the inevitable conversation. I still can't. I'm not sure what I can say, or if I even want to say it.

I sneak another glance at him from underneath my eyelashes and end up tripping on another damn root. The tree laughs as I launch forward and slam into the ground. I hit it so hard that I swear I feel my brain rattle, and I snarl at the offending thing.

"Fucking trees," I growl as I push myself back up. Cheshire doesn't step forward to help me, and I don't expect him to. He just watches me with crossed arms. "How much further until we reach it?"

I'm fed up with this tension. I'm fed up with this forest. I just want to tell Absalom that we need him and get back to Attie and Mom.

"We're here."

"What?" I look around. There's nothing but trees. "Where?"

Cheshire doesn't answer. Instead, he points to a large tree, thick with age. For the first time, I notice little holes carved up the side, made specifically for feet and hands.

"Absalom," he calls.

A bit of smoke trickles down from the top and almost seems to beckons us to follow it. I'm sure it actually does, if I go by the other weirdness around Wonderland. Cheshire gestures for me to start climbing, and I oblige him, if only because I don't want to be on the ground by myself longer than I have to be. I hate this forest with a passion .

When I get to the top and peer over the edge into a doorway carved from the wood, I crinkle my brow. The inside of the tree is hollow, allowing a spacious area. I heave myself the rest of the way into the room and look around as Cheshire fluidly joins me. Cheshire seems completely at home this high. Me? I move further away from the opening. I'm too close and don't want to have to worry about falling out.

The inside is carved from the wood, smooth from years of use rather than it being made that way. The wood is a light color, making the area seem more inviting than the trees outside are. I wonder if this one used to be alive before it was carved, or if it was a regular old tree. It would be absolutely Metal if it used to be alive. I wish I could carve one of the blasted things up.

Cushions and pillows cover the floor around a table set with a hookah, and I smile in recognition. At least that part of the stories are correct.

From an open doorway, a woman saunters in, and I crinkle my brow. Her skin is slightly blue, darker blue spots peppering her skin like freckles. Her hair looks like moss, small bugs and creatures threading through the locks. She's completely naked, strolling in without a care in the world that I can see her junk. I glance at Cheshire in confusion who only seems amused.

"I'm sorry," I say. "We're looking for the Caterpillar."

Cheshire snorts when the woman glances up at me, a small smile on her face.

"You found me. I'm the Caterpillar."

"What? No, I'm certain Hatter said you were a man."

"I was," she nods, but she doesn't elaborate. Well, okay then.

"This is the first time I've seen you as a woman," Cheshire says as she moves around the hollowed-out tree. She grabs a mug of something from the kitchen area and strides back towards us. I try not to notice too hard that her breasts don't seem to move with the action. As if she hardly moves at all. "It must have been a big purge."

"I felt it was time," Absalom replies. "This is the body most necessary."

My eyes drift over towards the hookah for some reason, and I study it, the pull towards it both confusing and intriguing. Something about it calls to me, but I don't know what.

"It's because you're the third," Absalom interrupts my thoughts.

"Excuse me?"

"Why the smoke calls to you. You're the final piece of the prophecy. Of course, it will call to you."

"What exactly is the prophecy?" I ask, taking a step closer. "No one has even told me what it is."

Absalom's eyes flick to Cheshire before quickly meeting my own again.

"No one has told you the prophecy?"

"What it's about, yes. I know that Clara, Jupiter, and I are part of the prophecy. The triad to bring down Alice. Is there more?"

"Yes. Come, child." She gestures towards the pillows around the hookah, and I take a seat across from her. "You, too, Cheshire."

"I don't need to see your dancing visions," he replies, looking away.

"I need you to sit, Hands of Justice."

When Cheshire hears his formal title, he frowns and takes a seat reluctantly. He seems completely uninterested in whatever Absalom is about to show us. Why he's so stand-offish, I'm not sure.

Absalom takes a pull from the hookah, longer than necessary if you ask me, before blowing the smoke in between us. It swirls in circles, the rest of the home fading away, growing darker, as I focus on nothing but the smoke. It curls into shapes, three of them women. The other three, I know instantly. One wears a top hat, one has rabbit ears, and one has cat ears and a tail.

And then Absalom begins to speak, her voice melodic and dancing the same way the smoke shapes do, as if they're one and the same.

"The first of three is Clara Bee
Who will come to set Wonderland free,
She'll tame the Hatter and down the Knave
Because Clara Bee fights for the brave.
A triad begins to destroy the Queen
Though nothing is ever easy it seems,

She must lose her heart while taking a stand
To the first son of Wonderland."

Absalom pauses as the smoke Hatter and one of the women dance around each other and morph into one for a moment before breaking apart, and dancing around in circles.

"The second comes in the dead of night
After saving the life of Wonderland's White,
She'll befriend the creatures of the day
And strip the Red Queen's immortality away.
Destined for the second Son of Wonderland,
She'll conquer his heart and take his hand,
The triad will be two strong
And right the things that have been wronged."

Smoke White dances over towards the second smoke woman and scoops her into his arms before dancing away. My eyes focus on the last woman, and the smoke Cheshire who stands a little close, and a little far away at the same time.

"To complete the triangle, one must ask
How the third son wears his mask,
He'll fight the hold, but best be quick
Or he'll lose his chance with each tick, tock, tick.
The third completes the triad of three
That will bring about the fall of the Red Queen,
Stronger together as they take their stand
To save the Sons of Wonderland."

The last two smoke shapes push together, and I watch enraptured as their arms stretch out. Before their fingers can touch, the smoke stirs and fades away, leaving the final part of the prophecy hanging in the air.

My heart beats a staccato rhythm in my chest as I stare at the spot they used to be, and I replay the entire scene in my head again, the smoke characters pairing up, meant to be.

I look over at Cheshire who's staring at where the smoke was, his face solemn.

"Why didn't you tell me?" I whisper, realizing the gravity of the situation. Yes, I'm the third that helps bring down the Red Queen once and for all. But I'm also prophesied to be with Cheshire.

Suddenly, our tryst in the woods makes so much more sense, and the pull I've felt towards Cheshire since the beginning. His avoidance on the subject becomes so clear. He purposely kept the information away from me, as if it wasn't important to know.

I wait for him to answer, his ears lying flat on his head, his tail doing a constant twitch. When he finally turns to look at me, those agonizingly blue eyes crashing with my own, they're so haunted that it makes my chest squeeze hard. I ache to reach out to him. Instead, I thread my fingers together and will them to stay in my lap.

"Because it doesn't matter," he says, and the words hit me like a slap in the face. "Because no prophecy is going to dictate how I live my life."

I school my features, hiding the pain those words cause even though he's right. I don't want my life decided by a rhyme from a smoking caterpillar, but even Cheshire must feel the connection we had, even before I knew we were destined for each other. Didn't he feel it?

I immediately chase the thoughts away. It doesn't matter, because Cheshire is obviously not interested in that sort of thing. In my need to take the pain away, my mouth opens before I can stop it.

"You're right. I'm taking my mom and Attie back home, anyways.

He needs to finish school, and mom needs some normalcy in her last days. It was smart to keep this from me."

My voice feels hollow to my own ears, unconvincing even on the best days, but Cheshire buys it. He may pretend there's nothing here, that the prophecy is wrong, but he knows there's something. He growls at my words and stands, shoving the pillows around him away. He doesn't say a word as he moves to the opening and leaps from the tree, away from any talk of prophecies and mates. Because that's what I am; I'm the Cheshire Cat's mate.

Absalom and I watch Cheshire go, staring at the spot where he disappears, before she turns back to me. Carefully, she offers me the mouthpiece of the hookah. I shake my head. I really don't want to get high off of prophecies today.

"No, thank you."

Absalom shakes her head. "No, child. You're going to want to see this."

I bite my lip before gingerly taking the mouthpiece from her blue hands, studying the intricately carved metal. Small symbols I have no meaning for surround it, the gold gleaming as it catches on what little light is in the room.

"Will it hurt me?"

She shakes her head, so I lean forward and place my lips on the mouthpiece. When I pull in, the smell of vanilla and flowers assaults my senses, the smoke filling me. I pop the mouthpiece free, and blow the smoke into the center between us like I'd watched her do. Somehow, I don't collapse into a coughing fit as the smoke leaves my body. Something about it makes it seem as if it doesn't even touch my body, more like a tickle than smoking anything.

The smoke cloud swirls in front of me, twisting and weaving, until it drops to form into shapes.

Two this time.

The shape with cat ears scoops the woman shape into his arms and spins around the circle, dancing around to a silent waltz, holding each other close.

> *"Child of metal, fire in your soul,*
> *You'll take out Alice and save us all.*
> *Open your heart and love complete,*
> *The journey won't be easy, and you'll know defeat.*
> *Wonderland asks for everything you have,*
> *She'll demand your heart, and that you take the Cat's mask.*
> *You must surrender it all to succeed in this war,*
> *The third, the mate, the chosen liberator.*
> *Your love will be deep, which will help you succeed,*
> *Love Justice and Wonderland, but then you must leave."*

THE WORDS FEEL LIKE THEY MANIFEST FROM DEEP INSIDE ME, AND even though it's Absalom that speaks, I feel the words ring in my mind as if they came from my lips instead.

In front of me, the smoke characters release each other and back away, before the smoke swirls, and they disappear forever. I'm so tense, I can hardly think, and I certainly can't find my voice for a few minutes. Absalom seems content to remain in silence, watching me in curiosity.

"Is that true?" I breathe, my eyes meeting hers. I squeeze the material of my jeans between my fingers in an attempt to stop the shaking that starts up. It doesn't help. I feel as if a chill goes down to my bones. My teeth begin to chatter.

Absalom nods her head, her lips tugged down into a frown.

"Wonderland is seldom wrong. In order to defeat Alice, you must commit to Wonderland completely."

"And that means opening my heart?" I ask, pained, looking after where Cheshire disappeared.

"You must accept all of your roles to be successful." Absalom follows my gaze. "Cheshire is a special part of Wonderland, but he's been a victim to her, as well."

"A victim how?"

"It's best he tells you that story," she answers, blinking pitch-black eyes at me. "But don't give up on him. You may wish to leave Wonderland, but in order to do so, you have to save it. You have to give her everything."

"And then leave it all behind," I whisper, clutching my chest.

Tears mist my eyes, but I don't let them fall. Not yet. A savior shouldn't cry . . .

. . . No matter how much she may want to.

Chapter 31

Cheshire returns hours later, after I had been staring at the wall lost in thought. Dancing smoke people swirled around my mind, and words spoken so deeply they make my chest ache. At some point, Absalom had given me a cup of tea. It only served to remind me how much I miss my mom. She used to make the best sweet iced tea. It's been years since I've had some so I'm not sure why it pops up now, why I'm suddenly plagued by memories and responsibilities. Always haunted by the same things.

Cheshire doesn't speak to me. Instead, he lays down on the mats that Absalom set out for us to sleep on and closes his eyes, as if there's not a whole forest outside, howling, and begging to kill to us. I stare at the ceiling for hours after I lay down, listening to the hissing trees and the distant shrieks. At some point, I finally close my eyes and surrender to sleep.

♠

I'M STANDING IN A ROOM THAT LOOKS VAGUELY LIKE THE HATTER'S tea room, but it looks all wrong. Black seeps down the walls, the plants are withered and dead. The table and chairs are missing save for one in the center of the room. It seems to be spotlighted.

"Something is coming."

I whirl, looking for the source of the voice. There's no one behind me. When I turn back around, a brilliant flash of red draws my eyes to the chairs again.

"Jupiter," I breathe a sigh of relief. "What's going on? Where am I?"

"There's no time for that. You need to go," she urges. She stands from her seat and rushes towards me. "Something is coming for you."

"Who?" I meet her eyes, the fear in them causing panic to thread through my chest.

"I don't know." She looks behind her into the darkness. There's nothing there besides dripping walls. "But it's bad. I can hold them off, but I don't know how long my powers can last yet. They're still new. I can give you a few minutes, tops. But you have to hurry. You're running out of time."

"But where am I?" I look around me in panic. "How do I get out?"

"You just have to wake up," Jupiter urges. "Now!"

And I'm thrown out of the dream.

※ ♠ ※

I SHOOT UP FROM THE MAT, MY ADRENALINE ALREADY SO HIGH, I practically trip over myself in my haste to slap Cheshire's shoulder. He springs up, alert, as if he hasn't just been in a deep sleep. He climbs to his feet with a fluidity I'd attribute to a snake rather than a cat and looks around, tense, and ready for whatever is coming.

I scramble to my own feet, far more awkward and so tense that I start to shake with the sheer force of it.

Absalom sits at the entrance to her home, looking out of the doorway and into the trees. Distantly, I can hear something crashing through the forest, so massive, it sounds like the trunks are being broken and thrown aside. Terror freezes my arms for a moment as the thought of some new threat becomes apparent.

"It's time to leave," Absalom comments, no panic in her voice. She seems so calm, it almost puts me at ease, until I notice a hazy shape of Jupiter standing beside me.

Her eyes are closed in concentration as she lifts her arms up and out. Slowly, a golden dome begins to drop around us. Cheshire looks at it in confusion, before flicking his eyes at Jupiter.

"This won't last long," he says, scooping me into his arms without a complaint.

He strides towards the entrance with me cradled in front of him. I thread my arms around his neck, making me feel more comfortable with the position. The golden dome follows us as we move, Jupiter's ghost staying as close to me as possible. She seems to float, mentally attaching herself to the sphere. I'm so in awe while also freaking out. What the fuck is going on?

Cheshire leaps from the tree without warning, and we drop to the forest floor. He lands in a crouch, completely unaware that he has the added weight of me in his arms. And then he begins to run in the opposite direction of the crash.

"You can't fade?" Jupiter asks through grit teeth.

"Not until I'm outside of Absalom's circle." Cheshire barely seems aware of the golden dome encasing us, protecting us, as he weaves through the trees. Something roars behind us, and I shakily look over Cheshire's shoulder, afraid of what I'll find.

"What is it?" he asks, not stopping his run.

"Whatever it is, it's gaining on us."

The crack of a tree trunk makes my point, so much closer than before. Whatever is chasing us is fast, faster than anything I know of. It sounds like the creature is tearing through the forest as completely as a tornado. The roar sounds again, and this time, it's joined by a series of Shrieks that can belong to only one type of creature.

"Bandersnatch!" I shout as blood trickles from my ear.

"Fuck. Just a little further. How are you holding up, Jupiter?"

"Just keep going," she growls, her voice strained. Every so often, the dome shimmers, as if she loses focus.

And then the creature behind us comes into focus as it crashes through the trees, toppling them like dominos. My eyes widen, my fingers clenching to Cheshire hard.

"What? What is it?" Cheshire asks, not daring to look backwards. He keeps his eyes focused ahead, knowing we're running out of time.

"Fuck if I know but don't stop."

It's as big as a fucking dragon, whatever it is. Black in color, covered in spikes down the ridges of its back. When it opens its mouth to roar again, giant dripping teeth rim its gums, yellowed and so pungent, that I can smell its breath from here.

"Here, kitty, kitty, kitty," it hisses, and I stare in horror as the beast smiles, flowing through the forest like a giant snake. Its wings snap out to push aside more trees, so strong, it barely stops them. "Come to the Jabberwocky."

Double fuck. That can't be good.

At the Jabberwocky's sides, Bandersnatch leap beside him, fighting to be in front.

Cheshire is fast, but he's not as fast as White. The beasts gain ground quicker than we can move, and Jupiter begins to sweat as she holds the dome.

"Just a little further."

We don't get any more time. The first Bandersnatch slams into the force field, and Jupiter cries out. The dome flickers. Two more slam against the sides. Cheshire stumbles when one skids to a stop in front of us but keeps going. The dome acts as a sort of battering ram, pushing the Bandersnatch out of the way, but it only works for one. Three more jump in front of us. This time, when we hit them, we bounce back, right into more of the vile creatures. Cheshire spins in panic, trying to find a way out, just as the Jabberwocky moves closer, and looks at us with one bright-blue beady eye.

"What is this fancy protection sphere you got, Cheshire?" he hums. "How much pressure can it take before it breaks?"

As if to test the theory, the Jabberwocky places one sharply-clawed foot on top of us and begins to push. Jupiter screams out in agony, her arms beginning to shake as she uses all the energy she has to keep us protected. The Bandersnatch start attacking the sides, pushing against the golden dome in an attempt to get in.

Cheshire squats down with me when the dome collapses a small amount, becoming smaller around us. He wraps himself around my body, and I reach out a hand for the ghost of Jupiter, where she starts to fade.

"I'm sorry!" she cries, a scream leaving her throat as she fights the force of the Jabberwocky.

"It's okay," I reply, because what else do you tell someone when you're about to die? When my hand passes through her ankle, she glows brighter for a moment, the dome stretching just a tiny bit wider, but the damage has already been done. There's no way out. I look up at Cheshire, knowing that he can't die bringing a little peace to my soul. But these people, this creature will destroy him, and it's that thought that makes me scream.

"Absalom!" I don't know why I scream for her, why I think she can save us, but something tells me it's meant to be, that she will be the reason we leave today.

As if by magic, she appears next to us, crouching in the golden dome, just as it begins to flicker faster. Time slows as the Jabberwocky presses down with all his might. Jupiter's scream pierces my ears as her image flickers, and fades. The golden dome begins to drop, and Cheshire squeezes me against him.

Absalom chooses that moment to blow smoke from her mouth, taking the place of Jupiter's trick, and it holds the creatures at bay.

"Go!" she shouts at us. "Two steps to your right, and you'll be able to Fade."

Cheshire practically drags me to the spot we were so close to but had been out of reach of in the dome. As we move, the smoke spreads around us, licking our skin, until we step on a piece of dirt that somehow feels less restrictive.

Cheshire reaches towards Absalom after he wraps his fingers around mine, but she shakes her head.

"My place is here."

"But they'll tear you to shreds!" Cheshire reaches for her again, and she backs away. The Jabberwocky laughs above us, the Bandersnatch slamming into the sides of the protection more frequently. The smoke keeps them at bay, but just barely. A paw swipes through on one side and withdraws with a yip, but it still manages to leave a nasty scratch on Absalom's leg.

"Come on, Absalom!" I reach my hand out for her, too, my terror of leaving her behind forcing me to take a step forward, but Cheshire keeps me held to his side, refusing to let me move. "They'll kill you!"

"I know." Her words hit me, and I start to scream, fighting Cheshire's hold to grab her arm.

As hard as I shove, as much as I claw at his arm, he doesn't release me. He stares at Absalom, his jaw clenched hard. I meet her eyes as the smoke begins to swirl and fade. Another paw swipes in, the claw of the Jabberwocky pierces.

"Come with us!" I scream. "Come with us!"

Absalom smiles sadly at me, before lifting her arms at her sides.

"I'm meant to die here," she says with no fear. "Now, go!"

I scream again, and Cheshire's hold tightens, before I feel the creeping sensation of his powers start to crawl up my arm.

"Absalom! Come with us! Absalom!" The power crawls up to my chest, slowly taking over.

The smoke starts to fade at a rapid rate, and the Bandersnatch howl in victory. The first snout pokes through.

"Remember, child," Absalom says. "Everything. It must be everything."

I scream bloody murder as the Fade takes us over, my voice going hoarse with my fight to grab her, to save her, to fight whatever destiny dictates this. Fate is not always right. It can't always be right.

Just before the world disappears around us, I watch the smoke scatter, and the Bandersnatch and Jabberwocky descend on the Blue Caterpillar.

My screams fade away to nothing.

Chapter 32

I stumble as we hit the ground faster than I expect. Cheshire lets me go, and I collapse to my knees on unsteady feet, my voice hoarse as a sob wracks my throat. In the distance, I can hear the howls of the Bandersnatch, telling me that we didn't go very far.

The urge to threaten Wonderland, to let it die, eats at me. What kind of power is okay with letting its creatures die, the need to fulfill prophecies greater than the need to keep people alive.

"We can't stay on the ground," Cheshire whispers, scooping me up. I feel his powers wash over me, but nothing happens, and he growls. "Climb onto my back."

I don't know what he has planned, or why he suddenly doesn't want to Fade, but I loop my arms around his neck, and he lifts my legs to wrap around his waist. Then he begins to climb the stalk of the giant mushroom in front of us. It's larger than any redwood tree I've seen on the Discovery channel at home, bigger around than anything I've seen ever. Cheshire uses his claws to start the climb, doing some fancy maneuver that puts us on top.

Gingerly, I slide to my feet, and wipe at my face, getting rid of the tears that had escaped. I'd barely known Absalom, but it feels like I've lost a friend. Cheshire sits down in the center of the mushroom, and I follow suit, unsure of exactly what we're doing. A roar sounds in the distance, and I flinch, but neither of us move. I trust Cheshire to bring us to safety if we need to be.

The phosphorescent glow from the mushroom casts everything in a green light, making Cheshire look even more otherworldly than normal. I'm tempted to reach forward and hold his hand, but I'm not sure if he will appreciate that.

"Absalom has been a constant in my life since I was a child," he says, breaking out of whatever trance he's sunken into. "And she died because a prophecy told her to." He turns to look at me. "I could have saved her, if she'd only taken my hand."

This time, I don't hesitate to thread my fingers through his, his warmth comforting me as much as I hope mine does for him.

"I'm sorry about Absalom," I whisper. "I know that doesn't help to say that. It never does. But I'm here if you need to talk."

We sit there in silence until the sounds of the Bandersnatch fade, until the roars of the Jabberwocky no longer reach our ears. And still we don't move, content to sit on to top of a giant mushroom, in a make-believe world that's come to life.

"I used to have a sister," he says, so quietly, I almost miss it. We've been sitting for hours, listening to the sounds of the forest. I don't particularly like the hissing trees or the flowers that try to nip you when you get too close, but the sounds are a little relaxing.

"Used to?"

"She died, when Alice first came back to Wonderland. We were both chosen by Wonderland to fulfill roles. We were a team. I'm the Hands of Justice. Danica was the Hope Bringer. Together, we came when we were called. Where my role is to be the axe, Danica was the negotiator. Before blood was spilled, she would attempt to remedy the situation. If there was no hope, then justice was served. But she made a mistake."

I wait a moment for him to continue, listening intently. When he doesn't continue, I ask, "What was the mistake?"

He looks over at me, such sadness in his eyes that I automatically lean forward, and the urge to smooth the hurt away takes over me. But I don't reach towards him; I wait.

"She fell in love with the prince, and he fell in love with her."

"Why was that a mistake?"

"When Alice came as a small child to Wonderland, Prince Alexander and she were inseparable. Young love, that wasn't love at all.

Alice was twisted, even as a child. And the prince just saw something different. But Alice focused on young Alex, fixated on him, as if he was the answer to all her problems. When she returned, one of her first goals was to enslave the prince, and he became her Knave.

We were called to the castle one day, the powers inside us screaming at us to go. When we arrived, it was a bloodbath. Justice demanded I act, but even then, I couldn't touch Alice. I didn't even know it yet. There would be no negotiations. The Hope Bringer joined with the Hands of Justice, and we sought to enact our duties."

He pauses, such anger crossing his face that I have the urge to move away.

"Danica thought she could get through to her prince, thought that love would be stronger. In the end, she stood there and refused to raise her sword while the Knave skewered her. She died in my arms."

I give into the impulse and pull Cheshire closer to me, holding him against me as he spills his heart.

"In Wonderland's cruel fashion, it turns out that Justice cannot die, but Hope can. All hope dies." He takes a deep breath, as if to clear his head. "And because of the Jabberwocky, I can't touch Alice, even though my very being calls for her death."

"What do you mean, that you can't touch her?" I ask. My heart hurts for this man, who's been left alone, and lost so much, who's embraced his anger rather than let it all go. I wish I could take some of the pain away, but I have my own. We're just two sad creatures, swapping stories.

"For years, I've wondered why I have the call to justice, and yet I never seem to be able to raise my sword to Alice to complete it. I thought it was just some sort of fluke, some Wonderland twist that Alice knew about. But then Jupiter revealed that Alice had a Jabberwocky." He chuckles, no humor in the sound. "Or rather, the Jabberwocky has Alice."

He nuzzles into my neck, seeking comfort that I willingly give. Slowly, I open my heart to him, accepting whatever I need to. Destinies will hurt, and fate is a bitch, but the least I can do is try my hardest for a world begging me to help. And it all starts with the Cheshire Cat beside me.

"Jabberwockies have a strange power. They need a host to feed their power into to survive. Like some sort of reverse leech. He feeds Alice power, and he takes it at the same time, in a never-ending cycle of growth. Jabberwockies aren't Wonderland creatures. No one knows where they come from, and as far as we knew, they were extinct. So, my power doesn't work on him, since he isn't a creature of Wonderland. But Alice was accepted into her folds as a child, because this world wrapped her in its greedy hands, and claimed her."

"Then why can't you touch her?"

"Because she also has the jabberwocky's power flowing through her, threaded into her very makeup."

I nod in understanding, my hand slowly rubbing Cheshire's back.

"You feel the call, but you can't touch her, because she's not completely of Wonderland anymore."

Cheshire nods. "And it has eaten me alive ever since. She's the reason my sister is dead, why my parents are dead, why my friends die every day. And Wonderland does nothing about it. She sits dormant and expects us to just fulfill her prophecies, as if she's planned it all."

The anger tenses his body again, but I continue to stroke his back until he relaxes. He shared some of his deepest feelings with me, and I want to do the same.

"I can understand anger, and wanting to get revenge," I mumble. His chest rumbles, almost a purr, as I continue. "At least you have someone to direct that anger at." I look up at the trees above us, my chest tight. "My mom is wasting away in front of me, and she doesn't even recognize me when I tell her I love her."

"How long has she been like this?"

"Too long. I had to raise Attie since he was ten, when it was no longer safe for her to live in the house with us. She drew a gun on us one night, thinking we were strangers in her home. Nothing prepares you for that, for the light to leave their eyes."

"It must have been hard, raising him all by yourself."

"I had to learn a lot of things, had to figure out how to make enough money to keep us fed. We had some hard times, where I didn't get to eat dinner because I only had enough money to buy Attie something small. And teenage boys eat a lot. I'll never forget the moment he understood what we were going through. He was thirteen, and I handed him an apple, and I told him I had to go find something else, because the cabinets were empty. I was planning on not eating—skipping meals isn't so bad when you drink a lot of water–but he took a knife and cut the apple in half." Cheshire looks at me where I've wrapped myself around him. "That thirteen-year-old boy looked at me and said, 'Sis, I know you've been skipping meals. You need someone to take care of you, too, like you do for me.' I barely managed not to cry that he'd grown up too fast, that because of me, he lost his childhood. But we made a deal. We were each other's rocks, and we made it work." I smile at the memory now. "We never skipped another meal again, and I hustled until I knew we would never have to."

Cheshire holds me like I'd done for him, and I can admit that it feels nice, to have someone warm comforting me. I breathe in the scent of woodsmoke and wild honeysuckle, curling around him as if it's so comfortable, even though we fight most of the time.

"When we get back, maybe March can help your mom," he finally says, his fingers stroking my hip.

"The March Hare?"

"He's the Keeper of Memories. He would know about a memory sickness more than anyone else. He can't cure her, but maybe, he could help her remember."

"Thank you," I whisper, drawing myself tighter against him and into his lap, getting comfortable.

"What are you doing?"

"Just accept it, Cat." I squish my face into his chest. "Don't get used to it, though."

"I won't," he says, even as he draws me closer, his warmth surrounding me. "What did Absalom mean, about it has to be everything?"

I don't answer, clenching against him so hard, there's no space left between us. I feel that if I can just push harder, I can disappear for a little while, and pretend there isn't a hurricane coming, that war isn't just around the corner.

We stay that way until the glow of the mushroom dims, before Cheshire Fades us back home.

Chapter 33

CHESHIRE

I feel something is wrong as soon as we Fade near the Hatter's house. There's an energy around the house I haven't felt in a while. Something is very wrong.

Cal must feel it, too, because she releases my hand and takes the stairs two at a time before throwing open the door and barreling inside. I watch her for a moment, sadness prickling my senses, before I follow.

"Hello?" Cal yells when no one comes to greet us. The house is silent, as if in waiting. My hackles rise immediately.

No one comes running. No one appears. But I can sense them all in the house.

"They're here," I say out loud, tilting my head. "Upstairs."

We both move towards the stairs, and I focus on that link between Hatter, White, and me. I follow it like a tether. When we stop outside of the door to Cal's room, I tense. I can smell it.

Death.

Or the beginnings of it.

I look over at Cal in worry, but she shoves me aside and pushed open the door. The smell gets stronger when the door swings open. Every eye turns to look at us. I don't move from the doorway, not even when Cal rushes towards the woman lying prone on the bed.

"What happened?" There's panic in her voice, so slight, I'm not sure anyone else picks up on it.

Attie is standing beside the bed, adjusting the pillows around Diana. Diana doesn't answer, doesn't move. Her eyes are closed, and her breath is wheezing in and out as if it's a struggle to even do that.

"She wouldn't answer when it was time for tea," Attie chokes out, and I focus on him. His eyes are glassy, but he holds in his anguish for his sister. He doesn't realize that Cal is doing the exact same thing, holding it all in for her brother. "I came and checked on her. She was staring at the ceiling, unresponsive. She closed her eyes a little bit ago."

Cal looks up and meets my eyes, and I see the torment there as she realizes that her mother won't make it back home, that her journey will end in a foreign world, surrounded by strangers. I feel her sob, rather than hear it, the dam breaking loose before she can stop it. She curls her arms around her little brother and holds him close as his emotions join hers. Everyone else files out of the room, giving them their privacy, letting them mourn in solitude, but I linger by the door. Diana is sleeping, but her memories are locked away inside her mind somewhere. Her body might be failing her, but the least I can do is find a way for her to remember her children in her last moments. The least I can give Cal is a final moment with her mom looking at her in love.

"March can help," I whisper, but Cal hears. The sight of her red eyes, of the tears tracking down her cheeks kills me, but I don't look away from her pain. I can't. I'd take it away if I could, if she'd let me.

"We can't move her," she croaks, and my chest squeezes. So much agony in those words. March can't leave his cabin. And her mother can't leave the bed.

Flam leans close to me from the hallway as I watch Cal wrap her fingers through her mother's. Her mother doesn't even twitch, as if she's already gone.

"I might have a way that we can get March here," Flam whispers, low enough that Cal can't hear. Getting anyone's hope up would be a very bad thing. "Follow me."

"I'll be just outside," I say quietly, but Cal doesn't even look up as I close the door behind me and give them space. Once I step away further from the room, I turn to meet Flam's eyes. "What do you mean? March is tethered to his cabin. If he leaves, he dies."

There's a tick in Flam's jaw, belying his calm.

"I have a sort of charm that if March wears it around his neck, he should be able to Fade with you from his cabin to here, but it'll only last a short amount of time. You'll have to move fast."

"And where did you get such a charm?" I ask, curiosity killing me. I've never heard of such a thing.

"Does it matter?" Flam looks towards the closed door, a frown on his face. He pulls a necklace from his coat pocket and presses it into my hand.

"No, it doesn't." The charm could have come from the depths of evil, and I wouldn't care, not as long as it helps Cal.

"Remember, it won't last long once it's around his neck."

"Understood." I turn to head to the porch, ready to go get March right away, but Flam stops me with a hand on my shoulder. I glance back at him, furrowing my brows. "What?"

His eyes are serious, intense, as he looks into mine.

"Don't let fate decide for you, Cheshire," he whispers. "But don't let your stubbornness ruin your chance at happiness."

"Whatever do you mean?" I ask, a hint of sarcasm in my voice, my tail flicking in agitation. I keep my mask in place, not giving anything away, but Flam sees through it anyways. I would expect nothing less from the Flamingo.

"You know what I mean."

He releases my shoulder and walks away. I stand in the hallway for a minute longer, the necklace hanging from my fingers, my chest tight, before I turn away.

I throw one last glance towards the blue door, wishing I could take the pain leaking inside away.

Chapter 34

Attie and I stay with mom. She hasn't moved, no change in her appearance. Her breath still wheezes from her chest, even though the oxygen is on. I can feel her slipping away, sense her body giving in. I try to stay strong for Attie, but I'm dying inside. I don't know if I can handle this. Not here. Mom was supposed to be comfortable at home when she went, not stuck in some fantasy world because of me.

"It's gonna be okay," Attie whispers. He's been saying it over and over again. His warmth, as we hug each other, helps, but both of us are just barely keeping ourselves whole. I don't know where everyone else went. I don't even know where Cheshire is after he said he would be outside. I focus only on my family, and on the constant wheeze of my mother's breaths.

"What do we do now?"

I look over at Attie where he holds mom's hand, his eyes just as red as I'm sure mine are. "I don't know."

I have no idea what happens from here, if there's even anything we can do for mom while we're in Wonderland. The best I can think is to make her comfortable in this strange world.

There's a soft knock on the door, so faint, I barely hear it. I look up in confusion.

"Come in." I don't answer very loud, not wanting to disturb mom as she sleeps, but whoever it is hears me just fine. The knob twists, and the door opens on silent hinges before Cheshire pokes his head in. "Cheshire," I breathe, gesturing for him to some inside.

He opens the door fully, and I get a good look at who's behind him. I stand up, pushing Attie behind me.

"No, it's okay." Cheshire holds his hands out like he's approaching a skittish animal, and I suppose he is. I step forward to block my mom from the eyes of the man, thing, behind him.

"Who the hell is that?" I ask, taking in the sight before me.

The man was probably once attractive. Now, he's covered in gaping wounds and sores, more like what I expect a zombie to look like. The coat and pants he wears are in tatters. Half of a rabbit ear is missing on his head, the other riddled with holes. His eyes, bright-toxic green, meet mine and the anguish, the depth, in them almost brings me to my knees.

"This is March." Cheshire speaks slowly, making sure I understand.

"The March Hare?" Who else could it be with a name like March? Still, I eye him warily. "You said he can help, but you said he can't leave his cabin."

"Flam helped." Cheshire points to a vial hanging from a chain around March's neck. For the first time, I realize it's glowing a faint pink color. "He doesn't have long, but I thought maybe he can help your mom with her memories."

"Can you do that?" I ask the rabbit.

A tiny giggle escapes when he opens his mouth, and he clamps his hand over it as if he can catch it. He doesn't succeed, and another one trickles out right after.

"Memories are my specialty," he whispers as if it's some great secret.

"March is the Keeper of Memories," Cheshire clarifies. "He might be able to unlock the part of your mom's brain that keeps her memories at bay."

March giggles again. "It's far more in depth than that, Kitty Cat. Yes, it is, oh, yes, it is. . . . "

I stare at him for a second, squinting my eyes. "Are you sure he can help?" I glance at Cheshire, uncertain about the man now staring at the chandelier with starry eyes.

"If anyone can, it's March. I wouldn't have brought him here if I thought he was dangerous."

An understanding passes between us, that Cheshire is taking his vow seriously.

"Okay." I nod before turning back to March. His ear spasms. "What do you need us to do?"

"Step away, step away, you must give me room to work, I need some space, so this won't hurt."

"It's going to hurt?" I don't move from my protective stance as he takes a step closer.

"Not her. No, it won't hurt her." March moves to the opposite side of the bed. Attie watches in fascination as mom's eyes begin to move behind her eyelids, as if she senses something changing.

"Hello, Diana," March mumbles as he pulls a vial from his jacket. There's yellow liquid inside, iridescent as it swirls around. "I'm going to bring you back."

There's no insanity in his words this time, as if he's a completely different person. I thread my fingers through mom's hands on the other side, and Attie takes my other one. We both watch as March touches a gentle palm against her forehead. He grunts in pain for a moment, but before any of us can react, the look is gone and replaced with concentration.

Cheshire stays at the foot of the bed, watching. He seems just as on edge as we are, his ears drooping as he watches.

March stays like that for long minutes, his fingers gracefully touching mom's forehead. Her eyelids start moving rapidly, her breathing coming a little faster. I clutch Attie's hand hard, afraid of what March is doing. I don't know if he's hurting her, or if he's filtering through her mind.

Before I can start to really panic, March removes his hand and tips the vial of yellow liquid into Mom's lips. Then we all stare, waiting. I have no idea what for, but I'm hopeful.

"Three times we circle the long hand," March mumbles.

"Three hours." Cheshire meets my eyes.

"Three hours for what?" I wrinkle my brow and look at March.

"Diana has three circles of the long hand."

"To what? To wake up?"

March shakes his head sadly and his ears droop. "To live."

My heart stops, and a sob catches in my throat.

"Will she wake up?" Attie asks, his voice hoarse but strong. "Before then?"

March points down, and we watch as mom blinks her eyes open. When she looks at us, they're clearer than they've been in years.

"Mom?"

"Oh, my sweet Calypso," she whispers. "My Atlas."

That's all it takes. Forgetting everything else in the room, Attie and I hug her close, being careful not to jostle her too much. Her arms wrap around us, weak but present. Distantly, I hear the door shut behind us, but I don't look. I'm too focused on the woman in front of me.

For a moment, I'm little again, and my momma is here, holding me, and telling me she loves me. For a moment, I forget everything. For a moment, three hours seems like forever.

"I've missed you so much," I whisper.

Attie climbs onto the bed and curls up on her other side, so gentle, so careful. I pull over a chair and take her other side, holding her hand close to my heart.

"I'm afraid I've missed so much, and I don't have very long." Even now her voice is raspy, as if it's painful to speak. "You've both grown so big."

"Do you remember where we are, Mom?" Attie asks, content to let her play with his hair. Normally, she would tell him he needs a haircut. Now, she just threads her fingers through the locks.

"I remember everything. I must say, it's so reassuring to know that there's a world with magic, and Hatters, and Cheshire cats." Her eyes flick over to mine. "One cat, in particular."

I can't help it. Years of not having my mom around has made me susceptible to it. I blush, my cheeks growing warm.

"He's an asshole."

She doesn't correct my language, or smack me on the hand like she used to. Instead, she smiles.

"Ahhh," as if my words hold all the answers. Maybe they do. "Do you remember the conversation we had when you were younger?"

I nod my head. "How could I forget?" Her words have been going through my mind since we came to Wonderland.

"Keep them in mind," she says, a tiny smile curling her lips, "next time you two share a look, and you think he's terrible. Sometimes the right one, makes your brain scream out no, even if your heart is saying yes. Don't trust it, not always. But you'll know when it's right."

"She has the hots for the Cheshire Cat," Attie teases.

"Shut up, little brother," I hiss, but I don't correct him, and both of them notice.

"Oh, my sweet girl," mom says, cupping my cheek with a frail hand. "It's far more than that."

I look down, away from her knowing eyes.

"It doesn't matter," I mumble.

"It always matters."

For a moment, we let those words hang in the air, but we don't have much time, and things are already diminishing. My mom's body grows a little bit weaker, and I watch as she seems to whither before our eyes.

"You will bring this world peace," she whispers. "Both of you. Accept the help Wonderland is giving to you, and bring them through this to the other side."

A tear slips from my eye, and I hastily wipe it away.

"What if I can't be who they need?"

"You already are, Calypso. You're everything and more. Both of you are important to this world."

None of us speak for a few minutes, content to sit in silence and let mom rest her voice, but the need to use this time, to keep her here for a little bit longer, pulls at me, so eventually, I speaks again.

"Attie has a crush on a girl at school," I begin, determined to make the most of it.

The hands tick away on the clock in the room, their soft sounds meeting my ears and matching the pace of my heart. Sometimes, we think we have time, to love, to live, to cherish. Forever can be this unattainable concept hanging over everyone's heads. I'll love you forever. Best friends forever. Together forever.

But what we fail to realize, when we say the words, is that forever isn't long at all.

Forever can begin and end in three turns of the long hand.

Or in just one second.

"She's in the band . . ."

Chapter 35

CLARA

I sit in my chair, watching as everyone funnels into the tea room. The mood tonight is somber, stifling. I can feel the pain echoing through the hall and it makes my heart skip a beat. This is the pain I want to take away, but I can't. That isn't my role.

I watch as Cal and Attie stroll in, Cal's arm around Attie's shoulders. Both of them have eyes rimmed in red and splotchy faces. The urge to reach out to them, to tell them I'm sorry, overwhelms me, but I refrain. Those words never help. I've seen enough of the dead now to realize that. But at least, we can give them one last moment, stop the clock for a single second, so that they can see their mom again.

Diana sits poised at the table, a bright smile on her face, so much healthier than she looked in that bed upstairs. Her eyes are bright as she waves Attie and Cal over and embraces them. They stay close as they take their seats.

When Absalom walks inside, we all tense. Hatter stands from his chair in a rush, fear on his face.

"What has happened?"

Cal and Cheshire tense, and I realize they knew, but with the events that happened, they were unable to tell us. Cheshire hadn't moved from the hallway while Cal and Attie told their mother goodbye, except to return March to his cabin.

"She saved us," Cal says, meeting Absalom's eyes. I don't ask about how the old man I knew is now a woman. I can bring that question up with Hatter later, but I suspect it has something to do with the purging.

"It was my time, Hatter," Absalom adds. "We all have our times."

"You've been the prophet since before I was born," White comments. "What does that mean for Wonderland?"

"Wonderland always has a plan."

"Of course, she does," Cheshire growls, shaking his head. "Like we're nothing more than chess pieces on a board."

Absalom merely smiles as Cheshire plucks some sweet bread from the safe plate and drops it in front of Cal. She doesn't even seem to notice, her agony written across her face at the loss of two important people. She keeps looking back and forth between her mother and Absalom.

Wonderland has a way of taking that which you thought was safe. I've learned that intimately while I've been here. I'm sad that Cal had to learn it, too.

Hatter takes his seat again, and I wrap his hand in mine, acting as his anchor. When emotions get too high, his madness has a tendency to creep back in. I've accepted it completely, but I know the madness bothers him, so I do all that I can to help keep it at bay.

My Sweet Hatter.

The tea table is full again, various creatures and people added to the Red Queen's victory, but I can feel the battle brewing. War is coming, and we'd better be ready for it. The real training will begin soon, and we'll need everyone on our side to win.

This is only the beginning of the end.

Chapter 36

The tea party is as painful as watching the light fade from my mom's eyes had been. Now she sits beside me, her eyes so bright and clear that it makes me happy. This is how I will remember her, talking to a creature that's half crocodile, half man, swapping stories of the swamps she visited in Louisiana once. Her hair is swept up in a messy bun, and she's wearing the dress she met dad in. I'd seen the pictures. I know exactly what that blue and white polka dot dress means. Mom is going home. I don't know if Wonderland's Here After is the same as Earth's Heaven, but I hope it is. I hope mom gets to be happy on the other side.

The tea party flies by way too fast, and I find myself clinging to my mom's arm when Hatter announces it's time to go. Clara watches with sad eyes as she stands, and begins to lead the other creatures away.

Absalom comes to our side and bows her head before mom.

"You've raised such mighty children," she says. "Wonderland will forever be in your debt."

"No," mom replies, smiling up at us as we flock to her side. "They were always mighty. Even without me."

Absalom smiles. "Of course, Diana. I would very much like to talk more with you in the Here After."

Mom nods even as we begin to move towards the archway in the back of the room, following the other creatures. We wait until only mom and Absalom are left, watching as Hatter leads each person through, and Clara hugs them all. Cheshire, Jupiter, and White stand beside her, watching. When we draw near, they all reach out to embrace Absalom. She puts her hand on Cheshire's face, speaks words I cannot hear, before she turns to me one last time.

"I won't be here when you fulfill your destiny, child of steel," she says, a smile curling her lips, "but give Alice hell." Her eyes flick to Cheshire one last time. "Don't give up, Calypso. Hearts are feral creatures. Sometimes, it takes a little time to convince them of their feelings."

I nod my head and smile as Hatter offers her his arm, and walks in through the spinning tunnel of light in front of us.

Finally, it's just mom, and my tears begin to flow down my face all over again. She pulls Attie into her arms first, both hugging so tight, I doubt they can breathe.

"You're such a bright young man, Atlas. Never let anyone steal your courage. I'm so proud of the man you're becoming, and I'll always be with you, whether you see me or not."

He nods his head where she holds him against her. When he pulls away, his face is red, his nose running.

Mom turns and embraces me just as hard, and I wrap my arms around her slight frame. She's so tiny—Attie and my height came from dad—that it feels like I'm holding her to me more than she can hold me.

"You are everything I've ever imagined, Calypso," she whispers. "And then so much more. I'm sorry you had to take care of Atlas when I couldn't."

"Don't apologize, mom," I croak. "You couldn't help it."

"Still," she leans away. "I'm sorry. You've done so much. You've always been so strong. I'm so proud of you, baby. Don't you ever forget that."

I hug her tighter, and pull Attie into the embrace until there's no end, and no beginning.

"I'm going to miss you," I whisper. "We both will."

"And I will always be here for you when you need me. Right in here." She presses her hand against our chests, over our hearts. "You will both do great things. And I'll always be by your side, cheering you on. Remember that. I love you both so much."

My shoulders shake with my sobs.

"I love you, too," Attie and I say at the same time.

I feel like I can't breathe, as if I'm watching her die all over again, but somehow, this part is comforting. Most people don't get the opportunity to know if their loved ones move on, if there's something out there other than death. We know there is, and as Attie and I both step away one final time, we watch as our mom turns towards the swirling lights.

She stops beside Cheshire and places her hand on his face. He lets her, no smirk on his face, no mask to hide behind.

"It's not your fault, Cheshire," she whispers, barely loud enough for me to hear. "Take care of my baby's heart."

And then she's moving forward. Hatter offers mom his arm just as a shape appears in the swirling lights. Attie and I both gasp at the same time as the shape forms into someone we haven't seen for so long, it hurts. He's insubstantial, so faint, we can see through him, but still, he's here.

"Oh, Jimmy," mom chides, a grin on her face. "I just knew you would be late."

Dad laughs and looks over her shoulder towards us. He smiles, lifting his arm to his heart and bowing his head.

"I love you two," he says, and I swear I can feel his hug even from the other side of the room. I know Attie feels it, too, when he hugs me tight against him. We both watch as Dad offers his arm to mom, and she takes it, so that she's connected to Hatter and him.

They step through the light, into the Here After, and I smile.

At least, they're both okay.

I hug Attie just a little bit tighter, and when Cheshire looks over at me, I hold out my arm for him, too. He hesitates, but he moves closer, until I can wrap my arm around him.

Everything.

It has to be everything.

Even if my heart can't survive it.

Chapter 37

Time moves both at a snail's pace and flies by in Wonderland. A week is gone before I know it, and yet, it seems like it's been forever. Our days become a mishmash of discussing strategies and training for battle. Hatter thinks we should learn how to use a blade and insists that I exercise with the Vorpal blade until my arms are numb from holding the sword aloft. White focuses on discussing any allies we can find, as many as still live. We need help, that much is clear. But my role isn't for any of that. I have one job: take down the Jabberwocky and Alice.

To say that I'm nervous is an understatement. I'm a mechanic. I can swing a mean wrench, but it's very clear from the first moment that the Hatter faces off with me that I'm far from ready to swing a sword.

"Elbows up," Hatter orders when my arms begin to drop from exhaustion again. "Back straight. Grip tight."

"I'm trying," I growl, sweat dripping from my brow.

"Try harder."

He doesn't give me any warning before he swings an intricate sword at me, it's purple glow mesmerizing. The first time I'd seen it, I'd been enamored with it. Now I can't stand the sight of the thing.

I just barely lift my arms up to block his swing. My arms shake with the force as the steel clashes, and I grit my teeth.

"Where's your muchness?" Hatter growls as he dances backwards before attacking again.

"I don't know what the fuck that means!" *Clash*. My arms give under the force of the Hatter's strength, but I focus on keeping my elbows up, my back straight, my feet planted before I dance away.

I can feel the eyes focusing on us as we go back and forth, me the offense, Hatter the defense. We've run through this drill what feels like a hundred times, and still he pushes. Behind me, Clara dances around with her blade like an expert, as if she's been practicing since the moment she arrived here. I suppose she probably has. If Hatter is this determined to teach me how to sword fight, he no doubt runs Clara through the same drills.

"Halt." I drop my arms in exhaustion, and the Vorpal blade drags the floor as I stumble away before laying down on the mat.

"Come on, sis," Attie teases where he practices swinging an axe. Someone gave my little brother an honest-to-god battle axe. I could wring their necks. "It's just a little sword fighting."

"Shut up, lumberjack," I grumble, panting for breath.

The days are filled with learning different weapons. Yesterday, we trained with bow and arrows before Hatter dismissed both of us from that. Apparently, neither of us have the skills needed there. Attie had been so disappointed. Secretly, I'd rejoiced. Bow and Arrows are a distance weapon. I prefer close contact.

Jupiter and White sit on the other side of the large weapons room. Jupiter has her eyes closed in concentration, that signature golden globe around them as she focuses on pushing it larger. Sweat coats her body same as mine, her face pinched with pain. Whatever it takes to use her powers, it takes a lot of. Maybe that's what the Hatter means with muchness. I can't even really guess.

Cheshire has been conveniently distant, even if he never seems to be far from where I am. It's as if he can't stay away, but he wants to, and I can't blame him. I've never gotten to thank him for bringing March to my mother's bedside, and each time I try to bring it up, he pulls a little further away, as if the reminder of the kindness he'd done for me rattles him. Still, I push, and I don't turn away. The Cat is stubborn as hell, but he can't deny the feelings between us, the pull. I don't like it, either, but I've come to terms that it's already too late. Jupiter thinks it's some biological compatibility between each of us that makes the draw so strong. Clara theorizes that it's nothing more than Wonderland knowing who works together. Me, I think it's all bullshit. But I do know that something pulls us together. We just get to decide if we accept it or not. Unfortunately for me, my heart accepted it before my brain did, but the last words I'd had with my mom had opened my eyes. It does no one any good to fight the inevitable, especially when it feels so right.

"Again," Hatter commands, bracing his feet apart and lifting his sword.

I glare at him from my spot on the floor, my arms like Jell-O, and my body drenched in sweat.

"I'm done." I wipe my forehead with the back of my arm and push my hair out of my face.

"The Red Queen won't give you a chance to walk away."

"At the moment, Alice can go fuck herself." I drag myself into a sitting position and sheath the Vorpal Blade. It sings as it slides inside, a sound I can't attribute to anything but a sword. There's an echo in my bones at the action, as if the blade is letting me know it understands that it's done for today. I don't know if it's sentient, but I pat it in appreciation just in case. Never hurts to be on someone's good side.

I barely spare the Hatter another glance as I leave the room and focus on where I want to go. Before long, I'm at that window again.

The roof of the Hatter's house has become my favorite place. The stars are mesmerizing in their firefly dance. And when the stars aren't out, like now, the sky is just an endless stream of black. Still, the sky pulses with an unseen energy during the day that soothes.

I climb through the window and carefully make my way to my favorite spot, before laying with my back against the warm shingles. How has my life become this new normal, of staring at a sky with no sun on top of the Mad Hatter's house?

I'm on the roof for barely a minute, when I feel that I'm not alone. I don't even turn my head.

"I'm not in the mood for you to stare at me some more, Pussy Cat."

Cheshire doesn't respond to my jab as he picks his way towards me and takes a seat, lounging backwards as if we're on a couch rather than a roof.

"You okay?" he asks instead.

This time I turn my head and meet his electric eyes, so bright even in the darkness of this world. "Is that a serious question?"

A tiny curl of his lips, as if he wants to smile, but he fights it. Of course, I'm not okay. I'm in a fantasy world, fighting to save it, and I lost my mother a week ago. He doesn't push for a different answer.

We sit in companionable silence for a few minutes, neither of us daring to break the calm. But eventually, everything breaks.

"When I was younger," Cheshire whispers, and I turn my head towards him, "I never expected to be a Son, or to become immortal. I was a wild child. Danica was the sweet one."

"You aren't born a Son?"

"No. Wonderland chooses her Sons, just as worlds choose all their children. She deems who will work for which job. And if you're picked, you know that any dreams you might have had, probably won't come true."

"What did you dream of?" I whisper. "Before you became the Hands of Justice."

His jaw ticks with my question.

"I dreamed of being free."

And suddenly, I understand exactly who Cheshire is. He was forced into a role he didn't want, obligated to fulfill that role, and now there are prophecies that dictate what exactly his life will become. It's no wonder he's fighting so hard against the destiny Wonderland is trying to give us.

"You know, I had dreams, too, once."

"What does a goddess dream of?" Cheshire finally turns his head and meets my eyes.

"Before my mom got sick, I wanted to go to college, start my own business, maybe meet a normal guy who wasn't an asshole, settle down, and have a family." I smile. "But dreams can also change. When my mom got sick, and my life got turned upside down, my new dream became to be successful enough to raise Attie so that he never wanted for anything in his life. It's been a struggle, but I'm confident he'll get to go to college, and chase his own dreams. It's okay," I whisper, "to change your dreams."

His face relaxes for a moment, revealing the Cheshire underneath, but then the mask slams back down before my eyes.

"I still want freedom, from everything Wonderland throws at me."

I try not to let the words hurt me. I realize it's not directed at me so much as the idea of me forced upon him. Still my chest aches at the thought, and I turn back to the pulsating sky, focusing on the sounds of the forest in the distance.

This world, the man next to me, will be the end of me. I can feel it in my bones. Even if I succeed, if we win the battle, I have to leave, to take my brother home. This isn't his dream, and I won't force it on him, no matter how much I long to stay. I'm falling, and this time, there won't be anyone to catch me.

But that's okay. I have to give everything, after all.

"You promised me when we first got here, that you would make sure Attie gets home, right?"

"I did." His voice is barely above a whisper.

I turn towards him again, meeting his eyes with the seriousness of what I'm about to say.

"Whatever happens," I pause, trying to find my words. "No matter what happens to me, you take Attie back home."

"You can take him yourself," Cheshire replies, wrinkling his brows.

"Just promise, Cheshire. Please?"

He studies me for a minute, searching for whatever I'm hiding. He won't have to look deep. I'm an open book when it comes to Cheshire, but I'm written in the wrong language. He doesn't see, doesn't realize, so he nods his head slowly, before looking back at the sky.

"I promise."

Chapter 38

It's been a month since mom died, and it feels like it was only yesterday. The house is filled to the brim with creatures and people that White has brought back, all allies rallying to fight the Red Queen. We've somehow amassed an army, although messy and odd.

Attie has taken to the new creatures with gusto, training with whoever is available. He's become adept at the battle axe, practicing with the thing every day. I watch as he swings the axe towards a frog-like creature that leaves little spots of slime wherever he moves. It makes it difficult to keep my face straight when a glob of slime splatters my arm. I wipe it on a towel, barely hiding the disgust at the feeling.

"There's still one more thing you haven't done that you should," Clara says from her spot beside me. She watches as the Hatter runs a group of creatures through a drill. It seems that, although most of the people seem too odd or soft for war, they swing weapons with skill, just as dangerous as any other being.

On the other side of the room, Jupiter stands working out inside her golden dome, doing burpees as if her life depends on it. It's her newest goal, that no matter what she's doing, the golden dome stays up. She's able to hold it much longer now, and without as much thought. Progress, White says. She's making progress.

"What's that?" I ask.

I'm already drenched in sweat from my training session. Hatter let up on me once I started to get the hang of the sword, but he's started training me in some smaller weapons. I won't be an expert knife thrower like Jupiter seems to be, but at least I can disarm someone with a knife and attack with one.

"You haven't tasted the Reali-Tea."

"Do I even want to know?" I swipe my hand through my hair. Does this world ever stop asking for things?

"It's a tea that March makes that allows you to see memories." Clara glances over at me. "It's brutal, and hard to stomach, but both Jupiter and I saw different things that helped us in our missions. Perhaps, you could see the same thing." I frown. "We can use all the help we can get," she reminds me.

"Whose memories do I see?"

"For me, I saw Alice and memories of the Hatter. For Jupiter—"

"Alice and White," I finish, closing my eyes. "So, I would see Alice and Cheshire."

"In theory, yes."

My eyes trail to the other side of the room where Cheshire leans against the wall, watching a pair spar back and forth with spears. He tracks their movement, even though he appears as relaxed as a sleeping cat. Anyone who knows him, would realize he's much more like a feral jungle cat, than any lazy housecat.

"And you think it's necessary?"

Of course, she does. Clara doesn't bring anything up without it being important. She has the most analytical mind I've ever seen, which makes her an odd pairing for the Hatter in my eyes. But even I've seen her eyes flash with darkness in moments, as if by chasing away the Hatter's madness, she absorbs a little bit into herself.

Clara nods her head. "Cheshire can take you there, see if anything new is revealed, and you can come right back." She bites her lip. "Don't you feel it?"

"Feel what?"

"It's almost time. The war is coming, and we have to be ready."

I don't ask what she means, or how she even knows such a thing. Clara has been here longer than me, and I don't even know how long that is. I'm beginning to understand that Wonderland changes a person the longer they're here, far more reason to leave when it's time. Even now, I can feel the pull of the Vorpal Blade stronger than ever, as if we are one and the same. It's unnerving but has made the drills far easier when the sword feels like an extension of myself rather than a weapon.

"I'll ask Cheshire to take me."

I leave Clara to watch the Hatter dance around with his sword and walk up to Cheshire. The moment I start heading towards him, his eyes flick to me before quickly dancing away. Then it becomes a fight for him not to look at me, dutifully fixating on the sparring couple in front of him.

He still doesn't look at me when I stop a few feet in front of him.

"Clara says I need to drink the Reali-Tea."

"So?"

"So, you have to take me."

His ear flicks. "I'm busy."

"Too bad. Come on. I want to leave and get back before night falls."

I'd taken to sitting on the roof every night, my time away from the insanity. Almost every night, Cheshire joins me. Those that he doesn't, I can feel him near, hiding just out of sight, as if he's afraid to get too close. I've given up fighting the pull, my heart being a little shit and deciding it likes the Cat. It's a little more than "like", but I haven't thought the words for fear of what they mean. But Cheshire still completely refuses to acknowledge anything. I expect nothing less.

When I don't leave and continue to stare at him, Cheshire sighs. "Fine. But we make it quick."

"That's what I said." I roll my eyes and Cheshire's focus finally snaps to me, his hand reaching out lightning fast and grabbing my hip before pulling me into him.

"Roll your eyes again," he growls quietly in my ear, "and I'll have to bend you over my knee."

White hot desire slams into my body at his words, my heart threatening to burst from my chest. When he pulls away the smallest amount and looks into my eyes, I see the challenge there. We're surrounded by people in the room, but still, I accept his challenge. I lean harder into his body and tap him on the nose. He blinks at me.

"Promises, promises," I whisper, before pulling away and heading for the door.

A soft growl behind me brings a smile to my face even as I feel him follow me. Cheshire doesn't like to lose, and I have no doubt he'll take the opportunity to challenge me again later. I'd be lying if I said I'm not looking forward to it, because I am. It's been so long since we had any action, our first collision bringing up all kinds of fears and making us stay away, but I ache for him more than I've ever ached for another man. And that tells me all I need to know.

Cheshire doesn't wait long for me to get on the porch before he grabs my hands and starts to Fade us without warning. Hatter had explained before that we can Fade from the porch to anywhere to make it easier, but no one can Fade in unless they were within a certain boundary of the house. Something about keeping the Red Queen at bay, but the wards come with a price. Apparently, to get more safety, you have to lose a little in between.

When we reappear outside of a decrepit cabin covered in vines and moss, I frown. I expected March's home to be nicer. Although, this certainly matches his appearance.

"Welcome!" March calls from inside, throwing open the door. He doesn't come outside, but we take it for the invitation it is.

We make our way quickly up the stairs and inside where the decay doesn't touch. I look around in confusion as Cheshire closes the door. When my eyes land on March, my eyebrows rise. "How the hell does that work?"

"The Cabin is charmed. March appears in one form inside, and another outside."

March giggles at the words. "Two forms, three to lose, nothing as hard as having to choose." More giggles.

I just shake my head and let it go. I'm not qualified to tackle that head case.

"We need the Reali-Tea, March," Cheshire says.

"Of course, you do. There's no other reason you come." There's a hint of resentment in his words, and I glance at Cheshire. He doesn't seem to notice, that or he doesn't care. I'm not sure which.

"Will you be able to leave the cabin once we defeat Alice, March?"

"Perhaps, perhaps . . ." He moves over to the kitchen area and starts crushing things in a chipped tea cup. I watch for a moment.

"What happens when we do?"

"I die." No emotions in those words. No anger, or sadness, or excitement.

"What?"

"One is dead. Two is begotten. Three is alone. And Four is forgotten."

"What does that mean?"

March pours something steaming from a teapot into the cup before coming to the table. He sets the teacup in front of me as I take a seat, and I look at the swirling red liquid that smells of chocolate, roses, and the metallic tang of blood.

"Drink up, Calypso," March says, his voice suddenly serious. I lift the cup to my mouth and take a drink, the chocolate flavor coating my tongue. "This one will be the worst."

"What?" I set the teacup back down, but it's already too late. I can feel the liquid as it travels through my body, feel whatever power is in my blood being drawn upon.

"Brace her, Cat."

Those are the last words I hear before the world snaps to black.

THE FIRST THING I REALIZE WHEN I OPEN MY EYES IS THAT I'M NO longer in March's cabin. Wherever I am is so white it hurts my eyes, so sterile and yet at the same time, filthy. The paint is peeling from the walls, the floor is cracked and missing pieces, dirt seems to cover every available surface.

A man walks into the room, dressed in a doctor's coat. He closes the door behind him and locks it, peeking through the window for a moment before he lowers the blinds. And then, as if by magic, a woman appears next to him, so weak, he's half carrying her. Her pale-blonde hair covers her face as she droops, and he sits her down on a ratty couch.

"You're going to have to feed, Alice. I can only push so much power into you without the feed."

The woman lifts her head and for the first time, I see her, so frail, her arms so thin it hurts.

"What . . . do . . . you . . . mean?" Even her words are weak, so quiet I can barely hear.

"My blood," the blond doctor says, pulling a knife from his coat. The poor woman doesn't even flinch as he lifts it. He slices it across his wrist and holds it out to her. Her lips curl up at the sides in disgust. When she doesn't lean forward, the man grabs her by her hair and forcibly places her mouth there. She fights for a moment, but she's so weak, she accomplishes nothing. What the fuck am I seeing?

"Drink, Alice. My powers will fuel you, strengthen you, and you will become something so much more." The man's voice is sensual, persuasive, so much that even I can feel a draw to him, but I'm not weak, and so I watch in anger as he releases Alice's hair, and she grabs his wrist on her own.

When she pulls away, I watch as her once blue eyes disappear within inky blackness and a smile touches her face.

I'm jerked violently backwards into another scene. This time, it's chaos as doctors, patients, and attendants run screaming. They don't make it far. Horrified, I move out of the way of an angry Alice, her hair flying around her in a phantom wind, her eyes black as night, blood dripping down a blue dress. People run from her as she slashes out with a large kitchen knife, ferociously stabbing anyone who gets too close, slitting necks that give out an arc of blood splatter across her face and the walls.

"You will all pay for what you've done to me. You will all die," she snarls.

She passes a patient, a girl that can't be older than fifteen. Instead of leaving her there, she squats down beside her and lifts her chin.

"Are you angry?" Alice whispers, her voice gentle.

"Y-yes."

Alice hands the bloody knife to the child, the same age as Attie, afraid in a hospital gown.

"Then do something about it." Alice stands and continues her massacre, swinging arms now tipped with claws. She bares her teeth at a doctor attempting to sedate her, the points sharp as she sinks them into his neck.

The little girl stands and charges into the fray in the opposite direction, but she only finds the dead and the doctor who made Alice drink, the one who I suspect is the Jabberwocky.

"Where are you going with such a big knife, little girl?" he asks, so calm in the face of this child armed with a bloody knife.

"I'm going to make them all pay." Her voice is so tiny, so weak, that I can barely hear it over the screaming, but she holds the knife up in front of her. She throws herself at him, the knife lifted, but she doesn't make it very far.

Faster than I can track, he has his hands around the little girl's throat as he squeezes. She claws at his hand as his eyes begin to glow, begging him to let her go. The knife clatters to the ground.

"There can only be one Alice, child." Tears prick my eyes as he drops her lifeless body to the ground, as if she's worth nothing more than trash. He continues his path down the hallway, whistling as he goes.

This time, when the scene changes, we're no longer in the building. I recognize the colors of Wonderland even if I've never seen the castle in front of me. It looks like melted candle sticks, like blood is dripping down its sides. We're in some sort of garden, blood splattered across the green grass. Alice stands in her blue dress, now more red than anything. A man stands in front of her, handsome, a thin crown on his head. Her Jabberwocky stands at her flank, a tiny smile on his face.

"Alexander," Alice mumbles. "You said you would wait for me."

"It's been years and years, Alice." The man's voice is strained, his eyes flicking to the side where the king and queen are restrained, their crowns on the ground beside them. "I waited, but you never came back."

"I'm here now," she chokes out, lifting a blood-coated arm towards the man. He doesn't take it. He instead backs away.

"You're not the Alice I remember," he says shaking his head. "It's too late. Stop this massacre," he pulls a sword from his hip, "and maybe I'll let you live."

Tears fall from her black eyes as she watches someone she obviously cares about hold a sword towards her. I watch the exchange as the Jabberwocky leans down and whispers in her ear. I don't think I'll be able to hear it, but when he speaks, the words are crystal clear.

"You could destroy them all."

I slam backwards out of the scene so hard my breath rushes from my body. The scene flies past me until I'm staring at the trees, the sky brighter than I've ever seen.

A little boy, somewhere around eight years old, comes running from the undergrowth, and I melt when I see the grey and blue cat ears on his head, and the tail trailing behind him. A little girl, a little bit younger, comes out behind him, laughing in glee, as she tries to catch him. Matching cat ears with bright green stripes sit on her head and a tail similar to Cheshire's follows her.

"You can't catch me, Dani," Cheshire teases before scaling the tree with tiny claws. I watch, a small smile on my face, as the little girl tries to follow, and fails.

Before she can get too upset, a hand reaches down and lifts her into the tree top. Childish giggles reach my ears.

When the colors swirl this time, I'm afraid of what will happen. I wouldn't have been shown such a happy memory if it didn't end in tragedy. I know that, and still I clutch my chest when the scene sets again.

"Dani, wake up."

Cheshire appears as he is now, fully grown. His sister lays in his arms, her chest not moving, a gaping hole through her sternum. Her eyes are still open, glazed over, as she stares at the black sky.

"Such a shame," Alice pouts, "that the Hope Bringer had to die, isn't it?"

I turn towards her, anger in my body at what she's done to Cheshire but when I reach out to strangle her, my hand passes right through. This is only a memory, only the past. I can't change history.

Cheshire gently sets Danica's body on the grass before he lunges at

Alice. He stops a foot from her, his arms outstretched, ready to shred her to pieces. It's as if there's a force field around her as she looks at him, a grin stretching her face.

"Beautiful, no? You want to punish me, but you can't. Sorry, Cheshire, but you won't stop me while I kill every last person in this world."

Alice turns, laughter leaking from her lips. Cheshire screams into the air before slashing out his claws at the nearest topiary in anger. He shreds the flamingo shaped bush, anguish on his face, tears leaking down his cheeks. I ache to reach towards him, as fruitless as that would be, as he collapses beside Danica's body, and cries for her.

"Dani, wake up."

The scene changes slowly this time, as if prolonging the torture. I hastily wipe away the tears that roll down my cheeks and take in the scene.

We must be inside the castle now, grotesque art and golden statues everywhere. We're in a bedroom, a great canopy bed taking up a large portion of the space. The blond man, the Jabberwocky, lounges on top of the mattress, naked, a sheet covering his groin. He's all rippling muscle, should probably be attractive, but I see him for the monster he is, the beast he becomes flashing in my mind.

Alice sits at a mirror, a silk red robe wrapped around her, dark circles under her eyes. She's clutching her chest in agony, tears leaking from her eyes.

"Alex," she whispers, her skin so pale, it's almost translucent. "They got my Knave."

"You didn't need him anyways," the Jabberwocky says. "You have me."

Alice doesn't answer him as she barely holds herself together, but when she catches her reflection, she straightens and wipes her face, sliding a mask into place.

"I am a Queen," she tells her reflection, tilting her chin up. "I am a Queen."

The Jabberwocky stands from the bed, the sheet forgotten as he comes up behind her and kisses the back of her neck.

"You're so much more than that, my love." He meets her eyes in the mirror. "You are a world breaker."

I'm thrown backwards out of the scene violently.

⁂

When I came to back in March's cabin, it was to find myself wrapped in Cheshire's arms and drenched in sweat. For a moment, I panicked, and tried to push myself from his arms in a hurry, but he'd only held me tighter, whispering that I was okay, that the visions were over.

Now, we walk through the forest, choosing to avoid the Bandersnatch rather than heading back right away. I can't get the visions out of my mind, the carnage that follows Alice. I see young Cheshire and Danica over and over again, laughing and carefree.

Freedom. Cheshire's dream has always been freedom.

But what if freedom comes with giving into your desires?

"I'm guessing you saw some shit after you drank the Reali-Tea?" Cheshire asks casually beside me.

"Truth," I mumble, not looking at him. I focus on putting one foot in front of the other.

"I'm sure you saw some things about me there."

"I did."

He grabs my arm and pulls me to a stop, the sounds of the Bandersnatch far enough away that my ears don't even twinge when they shriek. "Care to tell me which ones?"

I glance up into his eyes, attempting to hiding the haunting quality I know is there. "Not really," I whisper, the blood, the death all flashing through my mind.

"Ah, it's all the bad ones then." Cheshire sighs and pulls me towards him. I'm surprised when he wraps his arms around me and hugs me tight. "I'm sorry you had to see that."

"It's not your fault."

I mean those words. None of this is his fault. I'd been angry, so angry when we first landed in Wonderland, but now I realize that White was right to bring me here, even if it wasn't in my plans. Attie is having the time of his life, and even though we lost mom, we got to spend her last hours with her knowing who we were. That wouldn't have happened at home.

Cheshire has done everything in his power to make us comfortable, even if he won't admit to that. The cat hides behind his mask, always avoiding the emotions, while also drawn to them.

I lean up and kiss him gently on the lips, feather soft, as if afraid he'll push me away. I feel his tail curl around my hip, barely brushing under my shirt to tickle. When I lean back a little, I meet his curious eyes.

"What was that for?"

"For being you." I touch my fingers to the side of his neck, caressing, teasing.

His fingers clench in the material at the small of my back when I lean up and kiss his Adam's apple.

"This probably isn't a good idea," he starts, and I feel his claws gently resting against my spine when they peek out.

"I'm tired of good ideas. I need a bad one." I nip his throat, and a soft rumble comes from his chest.

"You're playing with fire," he warns as his fingers slip up my spine, trailing those claws so feather-light along my skin.

"I know." I push his leather jacket from his shoulders, and he removes his hands on me long enough to let it drop to the forest floor. "I still won't say your name." The challenge hangs between us, and for a moment, I think he's going to pull away.

And then he's growling and throwing me over his shoulder. I squeal and wrap my hands around his back as best as I can. He moves towards one of the large trees, one of the ones that doesn't hiss at us, and begins to climb, one-handed, up the side. I gasp as the ground grows further and further away.

"What are you doing?" There's panic in my words, but Cheshire doesn't comment on it as he slows and carefully sets me down on a branch wide enough to stand on. I slam my back against the trunk, clutching at the bark.

"I'm a cat," he growls, caging me in. It makes me feel safer, and I clutch onto him instead. After all, a cat always lands on its feet. "I like the trees."

"Okay . . ."

I'm completely confused. I thought we were about to get intimate, and now we're up way too high in a tree, and the Cheshire cat is looking at me as if he's right at home.

He leans down and kisses my throat, nipping the skin there as his hands begin to roam. I groan as I cling to his shoulders, afraid of falling but trusting him to catch me. A stupid decision really. He would probably let me fall for fun.

"Relax," he whispers against my skin.

"Easy for you to say," I growl. "I'm not made for trees."

"I won't let you fall, little goddess."

He pulls my shirt over my head, and the bark presses against my back as he drops the material towards the ground. I don't even watch where it goes as I pull his own shirt over his head and throw it away before popping his leather pants open. His own fingers loosen my jeans and shove them down my hips. My balance teeters as I work on kicking them off, but true to his word, Cheshire's arms keep me safe and prevent me from falling.

His mouth returns to my neck as one hands trails down my abs to tease my clit, stroking so soft, I growl.

I reach into his pants and free his cock, stroking the steel and drawing a groan from him.

"Fuck," he speaks against my skin as he slips a finger inside me. "You're gonna make me lose control."

"Then do it," I pant. "Give me all your feral."

"You don't want all of it." As if to prove his point, he curls his finger inside me, and I gasp. "You don't want me, little goddess."

"Don't fucking tell me what I want," I hiss, squeezing his length in my hand. His hips thrust forward, and his chest rumbles in answer.

Before I can blink, I'm falling, but not from the tree. Cheshire abruptly lifts me and sits down on the branch before pulling me over his lap, stomach on his legs. My head spins as I face open air, and I clutch hard at the branch, Cheshire, anything I can hold on to.

"What the fuck are you doing?" Panic fills my body even as I feel his hands caress my ass, gentle touches that do nothing to curb my fear.

"I told you earlier I was going to punish you." His words are so matter-of-fact, I lift up enough to give him my driest look. He chuckles as his tail flicks in the empty air and gently curls around my neck, like a feather boa.

"Dangling me fifty feet in the air is punishment?"

His hand swipes down, barely skimming, close enough to torture without touching me where I really want him to. That signature grin stretches across his face.

"That part isn't the punishment." And then his finger dips inside me again, and I gasp. My adrenaline from hanging so high, combined with the desire Cheshire strokes, makes my head spin. I grasp hard at the tree limb, my eyes sliding closed from the sensation. Slowly, so slowly, Cheshire strokes inside me. When he adds another finger, stretching me just a little wider, I relax a little more across his lap.

That's my mistake.

The moment I relax, his fingers leave my core. Before I can groan, his hand comes down across my bare ass, and I cry out. I lift up again and twist, snarling. "What the fuck?"

His fingers go back to stroking me, as if he hasn't just left a handprint on my skin. "Punishment," he purrs, "can be so much fun."

"I'm going to murder you," I snarl, but the infliction is lost a little when he curls his fingers inside me again, and I moan. This time I'm ready for it when his fingers leave me and smack across the opposite cheek. When he circles my clit, I bite my lip hard.

I can feel his length against my waist, twitching as he plays with me, as he teases. In my position, I'm at a complete disadvantage, his arm locked around me, keeping me in place and keeping me from falling at the same time. Those traitorous fingers dip inside and around, never focusing too long on one spot, never letting my orgasm build.

"I fucking hate you," I growl, a moan slipping out at the end. Cheshire leans down and bites me right on the ass, the sharp sting causing me to twist around. "Did you just bite my ass?" I ask, surprised.

"That's not all I plan to bite." Another smack.

"Enough," I growl, completely wound up, my orgasm frustratingly out of sight. "Fuck me already."

His fingers circle my back entrance, and I tense, hard, against him.

"Is it enough?" he purrs. "Do you crave more?"

"I crave you," I admit, and I'm rewarded by another stroke inside me.

"What do you crave?"

"Everything."

His fingers move in three sharp thrusts inside me, and I moan.

"You want everything, little goddess?" he hums, one long caress.

"Yes," I breathe. His fingers begin to thrust inside me, slow at first, gaining speed until it's both pleasure and pain, ecstasy and agony. My lower belly tenses, and I cry out, my legs shaking with the feelings.

"Tell me what you want," he growls, leaning down and biting my cheek again. "Tell me."

"You," I cry, clutching madly at the tree, my body growing both tense and liquid as my orgasm swells inside me.

"Say my name."

Nice try, I think, but I can't say that out loud. The pleasure is too much as his fingers continue to slam inside of me, bringing me higher and higher until I'm a mess of nerves. He chuckles at my non-answer but doesn't slow. Thank God, he doesn't slow.

"Come for me, little goddess." The words are a deep rumble, his pace never slowing as he brings me to the edge, and I crash down over it. I groan as my body shakes, my core gripping his fingers as he slows his punishing hand. He slips his fingers free and lifts me, setting me on his lap so that my legs straddle his, and then he's pushing inside me, slowly, achingly slow. I contract around him as he sets me on his cock, panting hard, my hands clenching onto his shoulders.

"Fuck," I moan, my feet dangling over the sides of the branch. I won't be able to get any purchase like this, and he knows it.

"So beautiful," he groans, leaning forward and pulling my nipple into his mouth. I grind against him, the best I can do, and we both tense. He lets my nipple go with a pop before nipping the underside of my breast. I throw my head back as his hands lift me the smallest amount before dropping me down again. "So perfect."

Cheshire licks a trail up my chest to the sensitive skin where my shoulder and neck meet, nipping at the spot where he'd marked me last time. The mark is gone now, faded away, and I clench around him at the reminder as he kisses the spot.

This time, when he lifts me up, he thrusts up into me. I gasp as he repeats the action, the sound of our skin slapping together turning me on even more.

"Won't you say my name, little goddess?" he whispers in my ear, his lips trailing kisses. I turn my head to the side to give him better access, threading my hand through his hair to touch his ears.

"Say mine, first," I manage, grinding down.

"Always a competition," he chides.

"Put us on the ground, and I can give you a real competition." My voice is so breathy, it sounds like one long moan even to my own ears.

"Then I lose my advantage." As if to show me that advantage, he lifts me and slams me down again. I lose what little breath I have. "I like you like this, helpless, at my mercy." His tail trails across my nipples, and I lean back a little further, keeping my hand locked in his hair.

"If you think I'm helpless, you don't know me that well," I groan, bracing my other hand against the branch behind me and using the leverage to lift my hips and roll.

Cheshire smirks and keeps a hold of my hips, continuing the roll for a moment before he lifts his left hand and grabs my hair. His grip is gentle but forceful as he brings me forward again and presses his lips against mine. I accept him completely, opening my mouth, so his tongue can sweep inside. He lifts my hips and grinds me down with one hand, the feelings intense as he kisses the life out of me. I'm certain I'm going to die in this moment, even if I'm going with a smile on my face.

I spread my free hand over his chest, right over his heart, before I break the kiss and lean down. It's my turn to nip his skin and lick my way to that sensitive spot he likes to mark on me. I don't give him any warning. I bite down, hard, and a savage snarl tears from his lips. Both of his hands grip my hips before he powers into me, over and over again. I scream even with my teeth clamped around his muscle, even as I tighten and tumble over the edge again, my eyes closed tightly against the waves of pleasure flowing through me.

Tingles jump along my body in that moment, spreading along my skin. When I open my eyes, we're no longer in the tree. Instead, we're on the forest floor, on a bed of leaves. He'd Faded us. Cheshire doesn't give me time. I'm still milking him when he flips us so that I'm on my back. His claws come out, and he buries one hand in the soft earth. The other wraps around my neck. I curl my legs over his shoulders before he thrusts into me again.

I scream out in ecstasy as he powers into me, bruising, feral, but I accept it all. I accept everything he has to give.

"Say it," he snarls, his face stretching with his intensity. "Say it!"

I can't speak if I want to. Hell, I can't even catch my breath.

I cry as he lifts my hips higher in answer, his cock hitting the spot inside me that tightens my whole body, another orgasm building fast after the last one.

His fingers squeeze around my neck, barely restricting the flow, before letting go to wrap around my thigh. The dried leaves dig into my back, but I hardly feel them as I slowly begin to crack beneath this man, my heart beating hard in my chest.

"Open your eyes," he commands, and I obey without hesitation. He looks wild above me, his eyes slit like a cat's, glowing so bright, I almost close my eyes against it. "You want the feral," he grunts, "I'll give it to you."

Fur sprouts along his shoulders first, spreading, revealing the stripes, hiding the mark I'd left on his skin. His claws sharpen as he pushes my legs up, never slowing his brutal pace. I watch that fur travel down, down, until he's above me, giving me everything.

I shatter around him, my core clamping down hard on his length as he pumps inside me with three sharp, bruising thrusts, and snarls his release. He spurts inside me, warmth spreading as he twitches, before collapsing on top.

His weight is heavy, comforting, my body like jelly beneath him. We stay connected as his fur slowly fades, his claws slip away, and his eyes return to their normal electric. He lifts up the barest amount, meeting my eyes fully, a tiny smile on his lips. I lean up to kiss his chin, my breath sawing in and out of my chest. Delight flashes in his eyes, his smile widening, as he says the one word that makes my heart stop.

"Calypso."

Chapter 39

Finding our clothes proves a little more difficult than expected. Cheshire ends up having to scale the tree to retrieve our shirts, both hanging in the branches and swaying with the phantom breeze. I watch his muscles ripple as he moves up the tree without hesitation, moving with such swiftness it takes my breath away.

I strap the belt to my hip that the Hatter had made me, the weight of it comforting now, the Vorpal Blade singing as I keep it close. When Cheshire drops down in front of me in a crouch, before standing up with our clothing in his hand, I reach out with a smile to take my shirt and pull it on.

"Next time," he purrs, "you should wear just the belt and the Vorpal Blade and pose for me."

"Naked with a sword, got it." I grin in answer.

His tail flicks back and forth behind him as he pushes against me, backing me against another tree. This one hisses, and my eyes widen, but Cheshire only thumps it on the side.

"Knock it off," he growls at it. Surprisingly, the tree shuts up. I raise my brow at him in amusement, and he winks.

"I can handle my wood."

I snort and kiss him quickly on the lips. Then, everything comes crashing back in, the battle, the threat, the role I have to play, and the pressure bears down on me. Suddenly, I feel like I don't have enough time. Before I can catch it, before my brain computes and warns me about the stupidity of my words, they slip out.

"I love you, Pussy Cat."

I clamp my lips shut, but it's too late. I know it's the wrong thing to say as soon as they leave my lips. Cheshire tenses against me and stumbles back and away. I feel so cold so fast, that I actually shiver. I fight the urge to reach out, knowing that he would back away more. It's always a bad idea to corner a feral creature. Cheshire is no different.

"Don't," he says, shaking his head. His face looks pained as he meets my eyes. "Don't do that to yourself."

I swallow past the thickness in my throat, trying to calm my frantic heartbeat. This moment, this is the moment that everything could change.

"I'm not telling you because I expect you to say it back," I whisper. "I didn't mean to tell you at all."

"So, you didn't mean it?" For a moment, both relief and pain cross his face, and I cringe. For a moment, I consider saying yes, that I didn't mean it, and make it all go away, but then that would be a lie. That would make me a coward, and I'm the savior. A savior can't be a coward. It's in the unwritten rules.

"I didn't say that. I just said I didn't mean to say it."

Suddenly, anger replaces the panic on his face, and he takes a step towards me again.

"You don't love me," he snarls. "You can't."

Something about Cheshire and me always dances in anger. In answer to his, my own fury flares up, and I bristle hard.

"Don't tell me how to feel, Cat."

"You don't love me."

"I've dated enough assholes to know the difference between wanting to fuck someone and wanting to do it forever," I growl. "You saying it isn't true doesn't make it any less true."

"That's the worst idea you've had." There's so much pain in his voice that I want to take a step forward. Instead, I push back harder against the tree, until the bark bites into my skin.

"Don't you think I know that?" I whisper. "Don't you think I've agonized about this very thing? Don't you know me enough by now to know that I fought against it every step of the way? But it didn't matter. I still fell for you, even with your asshole attitude and your annoying need to push me away. It didn't matter, because it still happened. I'm not asking for you to love me back," my voice trails off, because that's a lie, too. I want Cheshire to love me back. I need him to. Instead, I say, "You don't have to say it. This doesn't change anything."

His claws slide free as his hands clench, drawing blood from his own palms. It drips to the forest floor in bright splashes of red.

"It changes everything." He grimaces. "Everything."

I straighten, growing serious, blinking against the tears that threaten to fall out of anger and pain.

"You're right." I watch Cheshire, his breath heaving in his chest, pain written across his face, his blood drip, drip, dripping to the dead leaves. "You're right." I hold out my hand in front of me. It shakes, my own heart beating a rapid rhythm in my chest. I can feel it in my ears as he looks at my outstretched hand and then back to my eyes. "So, let's tackle this together. You and me. No expectations. No commitments. We can just see where it takes us."

The shaking in my hand grows worse when his eyes flick back to my hand, the shake travelling all the way through my body, until I feel as if I'm drenched in a cold sweat. I'm not forcing him to choose, I'm asking him to stay open, to just give it a chance, to not push me away. I don't say anything as he stares at my fingers, as the look of longing passes his face, but he doesn't reach out.

I don't dare speak, waiting for him to decide, waiting for his palm to slide against my own.

His eyes flick up to mine one last time, so much agony written there, and I know his answer before he speaks.

"I can't."

Slowly, he Fades away, leaving me there with my arm outstretched, in a dangerous forest I don't know. My hand drops back to my side, and the first tear falls.

He left me in the woods, far from home, with my heart flayed open.

Chapter 40

I don't know how long I stand there, uncertain about which way to go, but it turns out, I didn't even need to start walking. As if by magic, creatures surround me, dressed in armor numbered by suits of cards, their faces smooth. Then one of them opens their mouth, and I look away, too freaked out by the teeth there.

When Alice strides from between the trees, I tense, but I'm not surprised.

She's wearing a bright-red dress, crystals sewn into it so they catch what little light there is in the forest. It hugs her curves down to her knees before flaring out in a dramatic swoop. Her hair is messier than I expected, appearing brittle and dirty. Dark circles mar her normally ethereal face, her lips chapped and bleeding.

Alice tsks, looking me up and down. "Awww, did Cheshire leave you here all alone?" I don't answer. I don't ask how she knew Cheshire was the one with me. She glances behind her at the Cards and points at me. One of them storms forward and slides the Vorpal Blade from its sheath. He doesn't use his bare hands. He wraps it in a thick cloth before putting it away. I don't resist. I'm connected to the blade now. "Silly cat doesn't care for anything," she glances at me again, "or anyone."

I don't speak, focusing on Alice and Alice alone.

"Oh," she coos. "This should be fun."

With a snap of her fingers, the Cards point their weapons at me, jagged spears and clubs with nails sticking out of them. The weapons have never been cleaned, bits of gore still hanging from them, splatter across the handles.

"Come along, girl. I have plans for you."

I don't really have a choice. One of the Cards pokes me with his spear. I growl at him but move, following along dutifully. I can't take on this many people, no matter how certain I am that I can fight. Hatter's biggest lesson was knowing when to strike. This isn't that time.

They march me through the forest, the trees visibly shrinking away from our party. Not once do the roots rise to trip any of us. We move in the opposite direction I'd pictured the Hatter's house, and the further we move, the surer I am that I can feel the pull back there. Unfortunately, we're moving away from the feeling, and I start to wonder how anyone will even know I've been captured. Will they rally the forces? Or continue on as usual, wondering where I went?

Alice doesn't walk. A queen never does, I suppose. Before we get too far, a Bandersnatch bounds out of the trees and lowers itself to its haunches, allowing her to climb on and sit sideways on the beast. It doesn't shriek once, completely under Alice's control.

She leads us along a pathway through the forest, the ground a dark-red color that I fear is probably blood. When the grotesque creations start, I barely hold down my vomit. Bodies are strung everywhere, crucified, hanging, and the smell makes me gag. Alice only smirks when I barely hold it down. The bitch thinks all this death is funny.

When the heads start, I have to look away, focusing on the blood-covered ground rather than the scenes around me. The first ones were just skulls, but the closer we get to our destination, the fresher they get. I suddenly realize why the Red Queen says, "Off with their heads" in the story books back home.

The castle from my vision comes into view moments later. I'm not surprised by the sheer size of it, nor am I intimidated. I rightly assumed she would bring me here. I'm also assuming she won't kill me right away. Alice's strongest weakness is her pride. She'll want witnesses for my death, want everyone to see Wonderland's last hope slain.

Alice leads me straight to the dungeon, and the Cards throw me inside. I land on the dirty concrete hard, scraping the palms of my hands, before I pull myself up and put my back towards the wall.

When Alice steps inside the dungeon, she's not alone. Blond hair, blue eyes, and muscles for days, the new person stands before me in all his glory, all his grotesqueness. I meet the eyes of the Jabberwocky, who looks me up and down, a leer on his face.

"Look at you," Alice taunts. "What can you do? Powerless, human, so easily killed?" She steps forward and runs a claw down my face while the Jabberwocky watches. I don't flinch, meeting her bottomless black eyes head on. They don't chain me, underestimating me, thinking that I have no power. I lock eyes onto the cord wrapped around Alice's wrist, glowing a soft gold color. When I meet her eyes again, the corner of my lip quirks up.

"I may be powerless and human," I say, lifting my chin, "and you could easily rip my heart from my chest, but I'm still going to be your downfall. All of Wonderland demands it."

"Wonderland knows nothing," Alice snarls in my face.

I don't answer her again. I just smile a little bit more.

"I can't wait to thrust my hand through your rib cage in front of all your friends. I hear you have a little brother here. It would be a shame if something were to happen to him."

I don't rise to the bait, even though I severely want to punch her in the face. Clara warned me that she'd once shot Alice with an elephant gun, only for her to get up like nothing happened. A punch would make me feel better, but it would only get me killed faster. I need her to take her time.

When I don't respond, she growls and turns, storming from the dungeon and leaving me in my spot against the wall. The Jabberwocky strolls forward, too close for comfort, and I turn my face away when he breathes on me. A forked tongue flicks out to taste the air, tasting me. It tickles against my cheek. I shove him away, and he moves back a step, although I'm sure it's him humoring me rather than any actual strength I have.

"Touch me again, and I'll rip the tongue from your throat," I growl.

"Oh, I plan on touching you," he groans, adjusting himself in his pants. I scowl in disgust and clench my fist, ready to punch him in the dick if he comes near me. "Maybe Alice will let me play before I eat you."

There's a wicked light in his eyes as he says the words, and I realize he thinks he's being sexy. What a pig.

"Jab," Alice calls from down the hallway, and I raise my brow.

"Best run along to your master," I tell him, and a fire ignites in his eyes, their depths glowing a sickening yellow.

"I have no master."

"Jab!"

My smirk spreads to a full-on grin. "Are you sure about that?"

The Jabberwocky growls low in his throat and turns to follow Alice. The dungeon door slams shut on my laughter with an ominous click.

Chapter 41

WHITE

The house is full of buzzing energy as everyone rallies together. Our forces have grown exponentially in the last few weeks, creatures from all over Wonderland coming together for our final battle. This is it; if we lose this battle, all hope is lost.

Everyone has been assigned their weapons, armed to the teeth. Most brought their own armor but those that didn't have any, were supplied with suitable attire. The armory is practically empty save for some weapons that will be distributed as extras to the most skilled fighters.

Jupiter and Clara have their heads together, discussing what they can do to join forces, what each of their roles will be in the battle. I would prefer Jupiter stay back, stay in safety, but I know I can't ask that of her. This is everyone's fight. No one sits out.

Atlas sits in the corner, polishing the battle axe he's taken to like an extra arm. He wields it far more expertly than I ever have, a natural.

Cheshire strides into the armory alone a few moments later, and I wrinkle my brow in confusion. I hadn't seen them arrive.

"Where's Calypso?" I ask, thinking I must have missed her entrance. I've been watching for them, but I could have missed them with all the activity.

"I don't know." Cheshire dismisses my question so quickly that I bristle. "She should be here soon."

"What does that mean?" Jupiter asks, and the room grows quiet. Everyone turns to look at Cheshire where he grabs a sword and begins to go through drills.

He doesn't answer the question.

Clara takes a step forward, safely out of the way of the swinging blade, but close enough to draw his eye.

"You left her?" she asks, her eyes sharp. The Hatter steps up to her side. Jupiter and I do the same. Attie looks up from his place in the corner.

"What's the big deal?" he growls, swinging the blade until it sings. "She'll be fine. She's close enough to the house to make it."

Clara gasps at the same time that Jupiter covers her mouth. I feel myself harden towards my friend, my brother, and my fury builds.

"Why would you leave her in the woods alone? With everything happening?" Hatter demands, stepping within Cheshire's swinging arc. The blade narrowly misses his chest and Cheshire growls at him, swinging the next arc just a little bit closer. "She's the final key, Chesh!"

"I don't give a fuck!" Cheshire snarls, finally dropping the sword. It clangs as it hits the floor. "I'm sick of the back and forth. I'm not letting my life be decided for me."

I take a step forward, anger in my very soul, ready to strike him as hard as possible in the face. He deserves far worse. Jupiter's hand on my stomach is the only thing that stops me.

In the end, it's Clara who steps forward and meets Cheshire's eyes.

"Shame on you, Cheshire," she whispers. "If anything happens to Cal, anything at all, then this world dies, we all die, and you leave another brother without a sister." Chesh flinches at her words, but she doesn't stop. "That's on you. All of it. Because you can't be bothered to see what's right in front of you."

Cheshire swallows. "I alone make my destiny," he whispers, his voice thick.

Clara looks up at him sadly. "And you alone will destroy it."

Chapter 42

CHESHIRE

They leave me alone in the room. Every single one of them. It suddenly feels like I've lost everything. And it's no one's fault but my own.

The creatures funnel out of the room, leaving me standing there like an asshole to stare at the sword on the floor.

I'm lost in thought, when Atlas stands from his place in the corner. I didn't even realize he's still in here with me.

"You left my sister out in the woods alone," he speaks, throwing his battle axe over his shoulder, "knowing that she's the most important person to save your world?" A frown mars his face as he meets my eyes, and faces off with me far too courageously for a fifteen year old. "Knowing that she's already given her heart to you?"

I freeze beneath his words. "What makes you say that?"

Atlas scoffs. He actually scoffs at me.

"Please." He rolls his eyes. "I know my sister, and she's never looked at a guy the way she looks at you. Even when she's pissed with you, it's still there. Thing is, you're either too stupid to see or you pretend it's not there."

I don't know how to answer, so I slide my mask back into place and straighten.

"You don't know what you're talking about, kid."

"Don't I?" he asks, looking me up and down. "If anything happens to Cal, you won't have to worry about dying with Wonderland. I'll kill you myself."

"A Son of Wonderland can't die," I parrot, a reflex.

Atlas sniffs. "We'll see about that. If she's hurt, or," he gulps, "dead, I intend to rip you limb from limb, whether it kills you or not."

As he walks away, I don't say the words in my throat, that if she's dead, or hurt, over my childish fear . . .

. . . then I'll deserve every bit of pain coming my way.

Chapter 43

Jupiter

Flam had gone out to search for Cal, going right where Cheshire had said he left her. She should have made it back rather quickly, and the fact that she hadn't was the telltale sign that something had gone wrong. Sure enough, when Flam returned, he confirmed she was no longer there, and that there had been the scent of Bandersnatch and roses.

Cheshire's face, when he'd been told the news, had crumbled, but it's hard to feel sorry for him. I understand his resistance to the prophecy, but putting Cal in danger over it is terrible.

We're all sitting in the armory, the most open space. White laid out some pillows to make it more comfortable. Cheshire is pacing the length of the room.

"I can just go get her," he growls, never slowing his pace.

"We don't know where she's at yet," White says, cradling my head in his lap. "That's the whole point of this."

There's anger in his eyes when he talks to Cheshire, his brow creased. I reach up and smooth the crease away, and he looks down at me, adoration clear in his eyes.

"Everyone calm down. Cheshire, stop pacing." He immediately stops at my words and looks at me. "I need to be completely relaxed, and I can't be with you all arguing and pacing."

I close my eyes, relaxing my body as much as possible, willing myself towards Cal's energy. White gently massages my temples, and I drop under quickly, the powers stronger than they were when I first learned of them. When I open my eyes again, I'm in a familiar place, and Cal is standing in the corner.

"Cal."

She drops into a crouch with my words, prepared for a fight. Her training has done her good. She's alert and bright.

"Jupiter?" she whispers, squinting at me. I look down and realize I'm hazier than normal. I try and relax more, and I come into focus. "How are you here?"

"Dream Walker, remember?" I wink before taking stock. "Are you hurt?"

"No. They haven't been back since they dropped me here." Her eyes flick to the door where a guard stands. Fortunately for us, he seems uninterested in the rumblings of an insane prisoner.

"Good. We're gathering the forces and headed your way. Cheshire won't be able to Fade inside the castle walls. They're runed against such things. But we're coming as fast as possible."

"How is he?" she asks, biting her lip.

"About like you probably suspect," I admit. "Hating himself for hating himself."

Cal sighs and scrubs her hand down her face. "The cat is certainly stubborn."

"That he is," I agree. "I'm just glad you weren't hurt because of it. Atlas is worried. He threatened Cheshire with his battle axe."

"He didn't!" Cal smiles at the thought, a small chuckle slipping free. "For some reason, that makes me so happy."

I laugh, but a sound outside the dungeon catches our attention. It sounds like a door opening, luckily not Cal's. Someone screams in the distance.

Neither one of us are smiling anymore.

"Cal," I say, bringing her attention back to me. Her eyes meet mine, and I see a vast array of emotions there. Worry, fear, anger, but most of all, determination. Cal is as strong as her namesake. Alice won't know what hit her. "Remember, we're coming to get you." She nods. "Your only objective for now is to stay alive. Can you do that?"

A feral light enters her eyes, making me realize just how perfect she is for the Cheshire Cat. "Fuck, yeah, I can. It's time for battle."

I reach out my hand for hers and she takes it, the tingle barely there but still apparent nonetheless. As I begin to fade away, we both smile, and my last words seem to echo.

"Let's give them all hell."

Chapter 44

I sit in the dungeon, taking in every detail, searching for any weaknesses in my prison. I may be a captive, but I'm not helpless, no matter what Alice may think.

The only weakness I can determine is the Card outside my cell, but he doesn't even react to me when I berate him in an attempt to make him open the door. To be honest, I don't even know if the thing has ears to hear my jabs.

When I realize there aren't any weaknesses within the cell, I start to think about Alice and the Jabberwocky. The Jabberwocky needs Alice, from what I understand. The power exchange is a symbiotic relationship–Jupiter's words–as both benefit from it. Now that the avenue is cut off after Jupiter's enchantment, it has to be a sore spot. Alice also seems to care for the creature, even though he's very clearly using her. Alice's biggest weaknesses are her pride and her need for revenge. If she was smart, she would have killed me the moment she had me alone. Instead, she wants to make a spectacle of it, dangle me in front of those that wronged her like a broken chess piece. It's stupid, really.

Keys jangle outside my cell, and a Card throws the door open.

"What's up, Ugly?"

No response. Maybe they *are* deaf.

He grabs my arm roughly and drags me from the cell and through the halls. I very purposely avoid looking at the walls. The paintings are graphic and morbid. The walls seem to bleed, and I step in a puddle of it before I can sidestep it. I slip, but the Card keeps his hold on me. I'm actually thankful. I really don't want to land in the wall blood.

We enter a large room filled with various creatures. All of them are just as grotesque as the artwork, and they turn as a unit to focus on me.

"Ah, there she is." Alice grins from her place on an ornate golden throne, her dress a ballgown now. I must have been in the dungeon for a while because it looks like it's nighttime from what I can see through the window. I think I see the dancing firefly stars. "Right on time for the show."

"What show?" I ask suspiciously. When the crowd breaks, I see at least a dozen creatures tied up in the center of the room, all kneeling before Alice.

"The opening scene, if you will." I glare at Alice, but she doesn't care. Maybe she doesn't even see. She's too caught up in being the main event.

The Jabberwocky stands beside her chair, his hand on her shoulder, a constant reminder of his presence. My lip curls up at that. I must have hit a nerve earlier. He's in a classic power pose, as if he thinks he's in charge.

The Card shoves me down on the steps that lead up to the throne. When my knees crash down on the marble, chains appear out of nowhere to clamp around my wrists. I fight the panic at the new position. *Weaknesses. Look for weaknesses.*

"Bring the first creature forward."

The first creature is a deer-like humanoid creature. She's young, a child even, and I instantly tense. She cries as an older similar male fights his bonds behind her. His screams fill the halls as he attempts to go to the child, who I realize must be his daughter.

"No," I whisper, already knowing the direction this is going. "There's no reason to."

"There's every reason to," Alice tsks, and brings her hand down in a forward motion. A Card steps forward, a club raised over his head.

"No!" The sound of the club hitting flesh makes me gag. The abrupt end to the cries brings tears to my eyes. I yank at the chains in an attempt to protect, or to strangle Alice. I'm held fast as the Card moves over to the sobbing father. His eyes meet mine as the club raises. "I'm sorry."

"Save us all, Child of Steel," he says, the words reaching my ears as the club falls.

I sag in my seat, tears leaking from my eyes at the brutality.

"I'll succeed in destroying everyone," Alice speaks, as if giving me some profound advice. I turn, the chains just long enough to allow me to face her even if it's uncomfortable.

"Why? Why even do this? Why kill so many innocent people?" My voice is strong even if my body feels weak.

Alice laughs. "No one in Wonderland is innocent, girl. Each person is guilty. And the Sons more so than anyone else."

"What is it that they've done that merits death?"

"They brought a little girl here and then sent her back," she snarls, standing from her seat. "And they left her, forgot her. But she never forgot!" Her face twists with savage anger as she takes a step forward. "She . . . I remember everything. They left me to rot in a padded room!"

"And so they should all die? There isn't anyone you care about?"

Alice frowns, a grimace really. "Everyone I've ever cared about is dead, save Jab."

The Jabberwocky smiles fondly at Alice when she looks at him, but even I can see the look in his eyes, that he doesn't really care about Alice at all. Just like everyone else, he has an ulterior motive. Alice is nothing more than a means to an end.

"I don't think your precious Jabberwocky cares about you as much as you do him," I comment. There's a brief flash in his eyes at my words, when he focuses them on me like a predator. Alice only laughs, but I continue. "If he didn't need you, he'd be stabbing you in the back right now."

"How could you even know such a thing?" There's humor in Alice's words, as if she thinks I'm an idiot, but still her eyes flick to Jab.

"She's just a stupid girl," the Jabberwocky says, shaking his head. "You know I love you."

"I've spent a lot of time around men who take advantage, around people who use me. I run my own business, and one that men think they can run better. Do you know how many men I've fired for trying to railroad me, trying to take my business away, trying to steal my hard-earned money, trying to hurt me? I know what a person looks like when they have other plans, and your Jabberwocky has it all."

Alice looks hesitant for a moment, looking at Jab who does nothing more than smile, the cocky bastard. She shakes it off and snarls at me. "Your tricks won't work, girl. I'm the Red Queen, World Breaker, and the Sons' doom."

"No," I say, shaking my head. I look at the Jabberwocky, realizing who the real threat is. "You're still a scared little girl, too blinded by her own pride and revenge, to see that your funeral is right around the corner. If Wonderland dies, you'll be dying with it."

Alice stares at me for a second too long, looking deep into my eyes as if searching for my truth.

"I tire of this game. Jab, let's teach the girl a lesson about how she should speak to her Queen."

When the Jabberwocky smiles, I straighten my spine and lift my chin. My only objective is to survive. I can do that.

"My pleasure, my Queen."

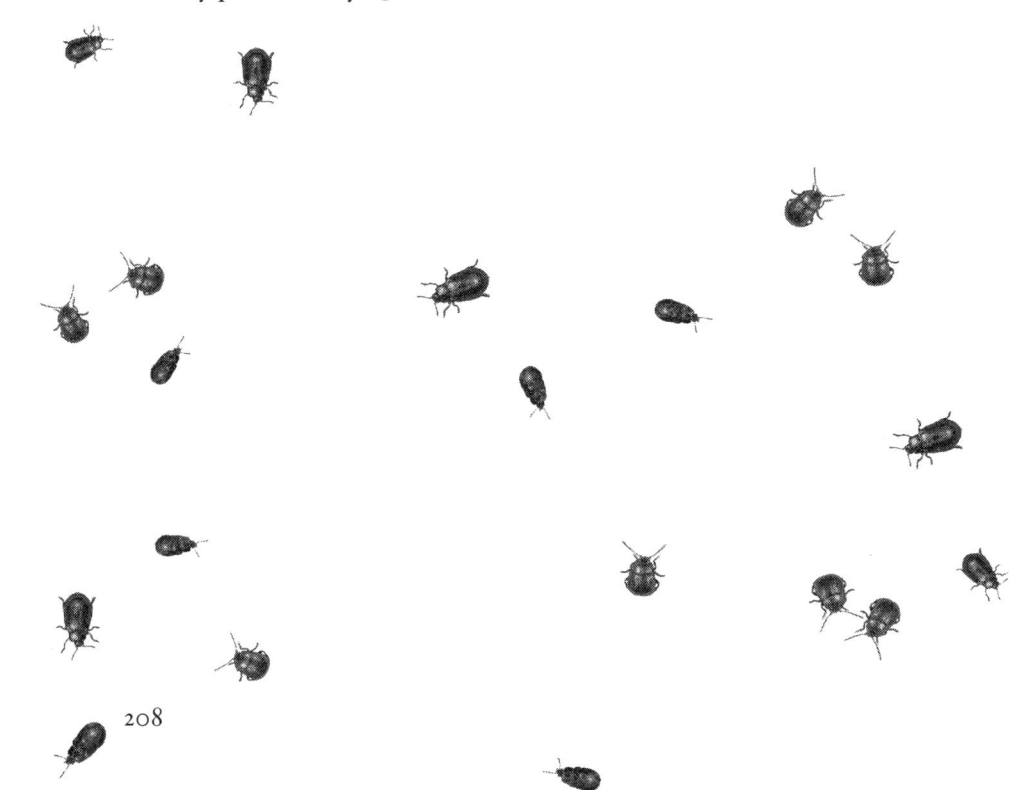

Chapter 45

CHESHIRE

I watch as everyone readies for battle, donning their armor and sharpening their weapons. After Jupiter's dream walk, and finding out that Cal is in Alice's clutches, I've been anxious to get moving. We're wasting time when I can just Fade there and rescue her, no matter if they don't think I can.

White has managed to bring together a massive army, various creatures traveling from safe houses and strongholds in a last-ditch effort to save Wonderland. It feels pointless, as if this war will be won with nothing more than a strong woman with steel in her spine.

Before Alice returned, I'd been more than just the Hands of Justice, leading the old King and Queen's Armies, leading the White Queen's army when needed. I'd been the general of all.

I touch the small Spade tattoo on my shoulder with the memory, the mark I'd been given as the general. But I'm not the general anymore, because I had failed. The old King and Queen are dead. The Prince is dead. Everyone is dead.

I'm leaning against a tree, watching White help Jupiter and Clara with their armor. Clara's armor is the same deep purple as the Hatter's, intricate, strong, and so light, it feels as if you're wearing normal clothing. I know the material well. Jupiter's set is in green, just like White. I'm dressed in my blue metal, the feeling of it both relaxing and uncomfortable. It's been a long time since I've worn the battle outfit.

There's a matching set for Cal, in blue, when we rescue her.

That thought makes me seize up in confusion. I both like the idea of her wearing my colors and hate it, as if it's already decided. I suppose it is. Cal's words come back to haunt me, and shame floods my system.

I'd left her there, with her arm outstretched, asking for nothing but for me to be open.

And I'd left her.

Hatter steps forward in his dark-purple metal, the scrollwork carved into it revealing that he's a Son, and a leader. Once upon a time, the Hatter had led his own legion of soldiers, before his madness had taken over. His battle helmet is cradled in his arm, purple and gleaming. When he holds out his hand with my battle helmet towards me, the blue flashes in the small amount of light, and I frown.

"That isn't mine. Not anymore." It has the spikes down the center that scream General, the etches of skulls that claim my role as Justice. Even the epaulets on my shoulders have the skulls.

Hatter shakes his head.

"You're still the General. And you have an army to lead." He sweeps his arm over the vast number of soldiers filling the clearing around his home, all eyes turning towards us as we talk. They watch with bated breath. Clara and Jupiter turn, and for the first time, I realize how warrior-like they look. Their hair is braided tightly to their skull, their weapons strapped onto their body in every available place. Clara has the King Breaker strapped at her hip, the gun heavy and imposing, but she doesn't act as if it's heavy at all. Jupiter has a sword strapped to her back, and knives along her thighs and hips. "This time, you're marching for more than Justice."

"What do you mean?" I look back at the Hatter, at his harsh gold eyes. There's still a madness in there, swirling, preparing for battle. If there's ever an opportunity to let it out, this is it.

Clara steps forward, a smile on her face. "You're marching for Love," she says.

Jupiter nods her head. "And the future."

"For Time." White grins, holding his helmet aloft.

"And for Revenge," Hatter adds, the hard glint in his eyes sparkling.

Flam and Doe move forward then. Neither of them wear armor, but they don't need it. They'll be shifting for the battle. Armor would only impede that.

"You march for all of Wonderland," Doe says.

"And for those that have perished while we fought," Flam adds. We share a look of understanding, of the loss we have suffered.

The Tweedles stand off to the side, dressed in their normal outfits, smiles on their faces. I glance at them, almost expecting them to add to the proclamation.

"We're only here because of the deals," they say, and I shake my head. Wasn't really expecting anything else there.

Then Atlas steps forward, his massive battle axe over his shoulder and a helmet on his head. His expression is hard, that of a grown soldier rather than a fifteen-year-old kid. I don't know when that happened, but Wonderland has nurtured him. That might not be for the best.

"You march for my sister," he says, his gaze fierce.

Atlas had been fitted for his own armor, the golden metal gleaming beneath the light. A dragon decorates his chest, the sign of the Berserker.

Hatter nods his head. "We march to save our world." His eyes shine as he meets mine. "You march to save your own."

I look into each of their faces, taking in the courage, the strength reflected back at me. There's no other soldiers I'd rather march into battle with.

Gingerly, I take the helmet from Hatter, staring at my reflection in the metal for a moment. Then I turn and thrust the helmet into the air.

"For Wonderland!"

Hundreds of helmets thrust into the air with me and as one, they yell their battle cry.

"For Wonderland!"

Chapter 46

I pull myself to my feet, my hand clamped around my stomach after a particularly brutal kick there. I'm not sure if I have a broken rib or not, but it hurts to breathe, so the chances are pretty good there's something damaged in there. Hopefully, it's only bruised.

"Have you had enough?" Alice asks, that smirk on her face as if it's glued there. "Do you know how to address your Queen?"

I straighten to my full height and lift my chin.

"Go fuck yourself," I spit.

Her smile widens as she snaps her fingers. The card to my right swings his club at me. I manage to jump backwards, but that only serves to bring me into contact with the one behind me. His club slams into my back and sends me sprawling across the marble. I bite back my groan of pain, my tongue suffering as blood wells in my mouth. I spit it out and glare at Alice on her throne.

Stay alive, I tell myself. *Let them get here. That's all.*

I can feel the Vorpal Blade calling to me, telling me to only will it to me, but I hold back. Not yet. Not until the cavalry arrives. Then I'll slaughter them all.

Behind me, her hostages lay beaten and slain. I'd had to watch every single one of them as they nodded their heads in acceptance, understanding that they would be casualties of the war, praying that I'd make them the last ones. Alice will pay dearly for that.

My arms shake as I push myself up. Slowly, achingly, I get to my feet. Alice watches, enraptured as a stream of blood drips from my lips, before I straighten. I make myself appear weaker, more fragile than I am. Alice thinks I'm made of paper; she doesn't realize I'm made of steel. That will be her downfall. I exaggerate the shaking as I meet her eyes, a grimace on my face for her benefit alone.

The sound of a horn in the distance makes me sigh in relief even as Alice stands and turns towards the sound. How we can hear the horn within the castle walls, I have no idea, but it's clear as day.

"What was that?" she asks Jab, frowning in the direction.

I chuckle, the action making my ribs hurt, but my laugh only gets louder. I can handle the pain.

"Speak, girl," she snarls at me. "Tell me."

"It's your doom," I say between chuckles, a grin on my face. "Your doom is coming."

"I should kill you now!" She takes a step towards me.

"But then, where would the fun in that be?" I ask, my grin stretching wider. "Why not do it in front of everyone who cares about me? Really set in the pain."

Alice rolls her eyes but nods.

"That's an old trick, but you're right. I do so want to see the look on Cheshire's face when I put my hand through his mate's chest. What a glorious sight that would be."

"Don't be stupid," the Jabberwocky interrupts. "Kill her now and get rid of the threat."

Alice smiles at him, but there's a hardness to her eyes that wasn't there before.

"Are you questioning my decision, Jab?"

That mask slides back into place, hiding the growing fury at her words. He doesn't like her orders, but he has no choice. He needs her just as much as she needs him.

"No, my Queen."

Alice nods and turns to the Cards surrounding me. "Bring her along."

When Alice turns away from me to make her way towards the

gates, I can't help but grin at the Jabberwocky and flip him the bird. His fury leaks out from behind his mask, but before he can move towards me, Alice calls his name. I make the hand sign for him to shoo and laugh out loud.

Weaknesses. So full of weaknesses.

The horn sounds outside the gates.

Chapter 47

I'm shoved through different gates than we entered the castle, onto a massive cleared field. The ground is painted like a chess board. Oddly enough, it's still grass, like someone takes the time to paint it often to keep the black and white color.

Alice and the Jabberwocky stand in front of me, as if they're trying to block me from view. I stand on my tiptoes even as I work my wrist from the manacle. Someone didn't check to make sure they were tight. When one frees and the chain jingles, I expect Alice to turn and see, but she doesn't, too focused on the army before us.

Cheshire stands at the front of a great battalion, glorious in gleaming blue armor. A battle helmet crowns his head, spikes down it like a mohawk. The armor is sexy and form-fitting. I liked him naked, but damn, he looks good as a warrior.

Cheshire's eyes roam over the growing crowd behind me as Alice's minions filter out of the gates to spread out. I don't turn to look. I know besides the Cards, there are Bandersnatch and other various creatures. I'm certain I saw a few Chimera in the castle, so they're no doubt there, too.

Cheshire's eyes meet mine, and he takes in the blood dripping from my mouth, the crazy hair, the bruises I, no doubt, sport. I'm just thankful I hadn't been hit with one of the clubs full of nails.

"Look here," Alice goads, always one for the theatrics. "Cheshire finally comes. And to think, all it took was stealing his human."

Beside Cheshire, Hatter and White stand, dressed in their respective armor. Jupiter and Clara stand with them, all in front, all battle ready. Each one wears the intricate armor. When my eyes find Attie in a golden suit, they widen, and panic takes hold. But then he meets my eyes and he winks, his battle axe thrown over his shoulder. My little brother knows what he's doing, no matter how much I want to wrap him in a bubble. Jupiter and Clara won't let anything happen to him.

"Let Cal go," Cheshire calls across the distance, "and I'll make your death quick."

Alice laughs. "You can't touch me." She grins. "You haven't been able to for years and years. What makes you think this time is any different?"

That signature grin spreads across my mate's face, and I know this is gonna be good. I work my opposite wrist from the manacle, slipping it free but holding my hands as if I'm still chained.

"See, I used to think prophecies were for the weak," he says, his eyes meeting mine, but then he looks back at Alice. "Until I met a certain goddess that changed my mind."

"A goddess?" Alice scoffs. "She's nothing more than a weak little human."

Laughing, Cheshire says, "You don't see it, do you?"

Alice turns at his words and looks at me. I smile at her while I tense my body, knowing exactly what's about to happen.

"My father named me after the goddess Calypso," I grin and drop the chains. Her eyes widen as I flip her the bird, ready as strong arms appear around me. "That means I outrank you, bitch."

Before Alice can scream or order her Cards to attack, we're already gone, Cheshire Fading in and out so fast that no one even knows what happened until I'm standing on the other side of the battlefield, listening to Alice's scream of rage.

"You still don't have the Vorpal Blade," Alice snarls.

Beside her, Jab seems to double in size, morphing before my eyes, bones snapping so loudly, I can hear it from here. I watch as he grows larger than a house, and a disgusting dragon-like beast stands beside Alice. He's black and iridescent, beautiful even, if it wasn't for the ugly mug. His face is part dragon, part goat, or some other odd mixture. It's hard to pinpoint what he is. Thick black wings flank his sides as he shakes out the effects of the change.

Flam whoops from behind me, and I turn in confusion. He starts stripping off his clothes as Doe watches, more and more skin revealed, all tattooed. I watch in fascination before Cheshire growls. I roll my eyes. Doe grins.

"You have no right to growl at me, Pussy Cat."

Cheshire actually looks ashamed for a moment. "I'm–"

I hold up my hand, shaking my head. "Nope. Now's not the time," I say, meeting his eyes. "Let's kick their ass first, then maybe we can talk."

Cheshire nods and faces forward. "That, I can do."

Chapter 48

The Jabberwocky braces himself behind Alice, massive and intimidating. To top it off, when he opens his mouth, I'm pretty sure his teeth drip some sort of venom. Fucking fantastic. More creatures leaking fluids.

"Why didn't anyone bring the White Queen to battle?" I ask, curious.

"We don't know if she could recognize which side to fight for," Hatter says from beside me. "Unfortunately, she's lost to us."

Clara hands me pieces of armor and helps me to start strapping them to my body. I expect it to be heavy, but it's so light, it feels almost like spandex. The best part is, it reflects a brilliant, electric blue. I grin as Cheshire watches me get clothed in his color.

"Keep looking at me like that, Cat," I warn. He only winks, and I can feel all his dirty thoughts about the armor. Who would have thought I'd feel sexiest completely covered?

I studiously try to keep my eyes from Flam as he strolls forward naked, but it's a bit of a losing battle. He's completely covered in tattoos from head to toe. I have maybe a second to try and decipher them before he starts morphing just like the Jabberwocky, expanding in size. I grimace at the bones start popping before staring, dumbfounded, at the massive beast when it shakes itself.

"What the fuck is that?" I ask, staring at him in awe.

Flam is similar in size to the Jabberwocky. He's the same shape as the dragon-beast, hints of black here and there, but besides that, they're nothing alike. Flam is covered completely in bright pink feathers, just like a flamingo. He's like a giant pink-feathered Jabberwocky, and I'm so shocked, I don't know what to think.

"Ah yes," Hatter comments thoughtfully. "The Flamingo is only half flamingo." He smiles at he looks up at Flam.

Doe stares at the odd creature, clear adoration on her face. "His father was a Jabberwocky," she comments. "Guess that's my cue."

Without another word, Doe changes before my eyes, until she takes the shape of a giant Dodo bird, shaking herself just like the others. She's lacking most of her feathers and heavily scarred. When her eyes meet mine, her beak curls up in a smile that makes me nervous. She's just as intimidating as her big, pink husband.

"Anyone else going to turn into a massive creature, so I'm not surprised?" I ask, meeting everyone's eyes.

White laughs and shakes his head. "My form isn't great for fighting."

"It's cute, though," Jupiter chuckles, winking at him.

"I am *not* cute."

Cheshire snickers beside me and adds, "Cute little bunny rabbit."

"No one calls me Bunny except for Jupiter," White snarls so fiercely, I actually take a step away from him. He seems to shake himself and looks at me apologetically. "Sorry, Calypso."

"It's cool." I remind myself never to call the man a bunny.

Cheshire doesn't even react to the snarl, and I watch as the skin of his hands and face cover with fur, completely morphing. His claws sharpen as he meets my eyes.

"Do you have a plan?" he asks.

I nod, a smile on my face. "I do."

Clara and Jupiter step up and link their arms with mine, grinning.

"Let's make this prophecy our bitch," Jupiter speaks, nodding her head.

Clara turns to the Tweedles standing off to the side. Both are staring around, clear hunger on their faces.

"In case it isn't clear," she tells them, "Everyone on the opposite side are enemies. Don't touch any of our side but destroy Alice's army."

The twins grin in answer.

"With pleasure." Their voices combine and do that weird, creepy thing. Fucking insane, those two.

Cheshire slides a blue helmet onto my head, similar to his. I smile at him.

"Whose idea was it to put cat ears on my helmet?"

He winks, and I know my answer. Laughing, I turn with Jupiter and Clara. Attie stands behind me, a golden helmet on his head, a smile on his face.

"You'd better be careful," I tell him. "Stay with someone at all times."

"I won't be the one dying today, sis," he says. "Besides, I'm only the backup."

I'm tempted to ask what he means, but there isn't time. Behind us, Alice's army shouts their battle cry as they begin running forward.

"Let's give them Hell!" I shout.

"For Wonderland!" Clara screams, and everyone joins in.

Together, we begin to run.

Together, we sprint into battle.

Chapter 49

"Get me to Alice!" I scream. Someone presses a sword into my hand, not the Vorpal Blade, but something to swing until I have it. Cheshire flanks me, his aqua-hued sword held steady in his hand. Jupiter and Clara separate from me, Hatter and White taking up their flanks as the two armies crash together in a wave of metallic clangs and blood.

The smell of pennies fills the air, screams starting almost instantly as soldiers from both sides fall.

We slam inside the battle and begin to fight our way through, pushing with one goal in mind. Alice stands in her large dress, as a Card slides armor over her head. She still wears the skirt, but now she wears intricate pieces covering her chest, her shoulders, her neck. Skulls decorate the shoulder armor in a grotesque display. She smiles as she sees me moving closer.

Above us, the Jabberwocky and Flam slam together in a ball of venom and feathers, screaming their rage as they attempt to tear the other to shreds.

I'm surrounded by so much aggression, so much death, that I'm amazed I'm not heaving in disgust. Instead, I'm focused on one thing, and one thing alone.

Alice steps forward, and a circle clears around her just as I break through, Cheshire at my side. The others fight at the edge, dropping Cards and beasts as they go. Cheshire snarls and leaps towards her. Alice watches in amusement as he slams into a glass wall, or some sort of force field that keeps him back. He can't reach forward and strangle her like he wants to, but that's okay. I'll be doing it for him.

"I've waited so long to see this world die," Alice says, drawing a sword from her back. I don't react except for a tilt of my head. "How pleasant it'll be while everyone is gathered together in one place. I'm going to take pleasure in killing you, Calypso."

I laugh, even as Alice flicks her wrist and sends Cheshire skidding backwards and away. His snarl is the only thing I hear, but he doesn't move to attack again, knowing it's pointless. So he waits, and watches, stalking the edge of the circle.

"Still so blind, Alice," I tell her.

"I'm the Red Queen," she snarls. "The Queen of Hearts. And you will bow before me as I cut the head from your body."

I can feel Cheshire's growl as if it's in my own chest, even though he's at least five feet away. A connection seems to slide into place at that realization, and I can feel his frustration.

And then a golden dome begins to spread around us, locking Alice and I inside. Cheshire leaps to get in, but it closes before he can, sealing up. I turn and see Jupiter, her eyes closed as Hatter, White, and Clara protect her sides.

Alice looks up at the dome in Horror as Cheshire presses his hand against it where I stand.

"Hope Bringer," she whispers, and I watch as shock crosses Chesh's face, stumbling back with those words. His eyes flick over to Jupiter where she sits, completely surprised, and I remember his story.

Danica had been the Hope Bringer. And now, Wonderland has finally chosen another.

When he looks back at me, I nod, hoping he understands that I have this. Just in case, I press my hand against the dome, and he does the same. If something happens to me, at least I got to meet the Cheshire Cat. At least, I got to give him my heart.

Alice seems to come to her senses, and she rushes me. I don't know how she moves so fast in the dress she wears, but she might as well be wearing pants. I dance out of the way just in time, her sword barely missing my hip.

Behind me, the sound of a gun going off has me glancing into the battle, to see Clara pointing a hefty thing at the Jabberwocky in the sky. He roars and dives for them, but Flam slams into him from the side, keeping him from the battle below.

I can't tell where anyone else is because of the battle pressing in around the dome; except for Doe. I see her bite a Bandersnatch into two pieces before screeching and slamming through a group of Cards.

Alice rushes me again, and I lift the sword to block her blow before we start to dance around the globe, avoiding each other's blade.

"You're going to die here," Alice taunts.

I don't rise to the bait and continue my defense, barely doing more than keeping her at bay.

"Why don't you fight?" she yells, thrusting the sword forward. I twist out of the way and move to the other side of the dome. "Stop running!"

"The reign of the Red Queen will end," I say, blocking another jab. Alice is decent with a sword, but she wasn't trained by the Hatter. She's slow to attack, and she leaves her side open when she does. Without her minions to fight for her, she's at a disadvantage, but her pride makes her sloppy, her need for revenge makes her weak. She's only focused on me, and me alone.

I move a hint too slow to dodge one of her strikes, and she nicks my hand, a thin line of blood springing forth. It's a flesh wound, nothing more, but the sight of the blood excites Alice and makes her think she has the advantage.

Alice raises her sword again, but this time I don't move out of the way. I lift my arm into the air and pull on the string connected to me just as the golden dome falls around us. The army starts to push inwards just as Cheshire springs inside, protecting my back.

A singing fills the air, as if someone plucked a guitar string and left it to ring. And then the Vorpal Blade slides between my fingers, the call of it vibrating in my hands, happy to finally be able to come forward. The silver gleams in the light, picking up on the sources around us, absorbing it and bringing a pale-blue glow with it. It's comfortable in my hand, no longer a weapon as much as an extension of my soul. It gives off a slight vibration, urging me to complete my duty, to fulfill my prophecy.

Alice's eyes widen, and she reels back, but she's too slow, and the Vorpal Blade wants blood. The dress finally slows her down as she trips over the hem and stumbles.

"Wait!" she cries, raising her own sword, but she always leave her side open. It's a simple thing to parry her sword to the side.

Without a second of hesitation, I thrust the Blade forward, every creature she brutally murdered dancing in my mind. That little deer girl's silenced scream echoes in my mind, even as the Vorpal blade sings. For every death in Wonderland, for every end that Alice has brought, I fight for that. Alice's armor gives under the steel, the Vorpal Blade piercing straight through her sternum. The sound it makes, a scraping wet squelch, unnerves me, but I don't have the luxury of letting it stop me. Too many have died at her hands; I refuse for there to be any more deaths. I twist the handle of the blade, embedding it deeper, in an attempt to make sure she can't heal from it. She can't be allowed to live. She can't be allowed to fulfill her destiny. This world will not be broken.

She gasps and looks down at the sword protruding from her chest, the silver-blue handle looking out of place. She's so confused, shocked, as she stares at the blade. Around us, the sounds of the battle pause, as everyone looks at the Red Queen. When she looks at me again, I watch as a single tear trickles from the corner of her eye, and my heart squeezes even though I know she's a monster.

Just when I'm uncertain of my next move, she begins to flicker, her image in front of me flashing between the Red Queen I know and the twelve-year-old Alice. She flickers like a glitch, as if she can't decide what form to land on.

"What's happening?" I ask Cheshire, stumbling back, leaving the sword in its place as I stare in horror at the image of a child appearing.

"Wonderland is trying to reclaim her." His voice is solemn as he watches. "The last time she was part of Wonderland completely—"

"Was when she was a child," I finish.

Alice flickers once more as the woman before she settles as a girl, her eyes so blue it makes my chest hurt. The Vorpal Blade sticks through her small chest, black blood rushing around the wound. Her eyes flick to Hatter's when everyone steps forward, and those blue eyes glaze over. Her sword clatters to the ground, a harsh gasp leaving her throat.

"You promised," she whispers, before she collapses to the ground in a heap of blue material and pale-blonde hair.

I cover my mouth in horror and turn away only to see the Queen's army collapsing to dust around us. They die with their Queen, her power the only thing keeping them on this plane.

I never expected the sheer dread I feel as Alice's body glows bright white before it's gone, too. The image will never leave my mind, and I'll never escape it. Clara meets my eyes and slips her hand into mine, an understanding passing between us.

It takes something from you when you destroy another person, even if they're evil, especially when they used to be innocent.

Above us, the Jabberwocky screams in outrage at the turn of events and flings Flam away from him. I look up just in time to see him dive right for us.

Chapter 50

"Watch out!" Cheshire snarls, seconds before he throws me backwards. I go airborne, a scream lodged in my throat, as the Jabberwocky misses me and grabs Cheshire instead.

Before my feet hardly touch the ground, I'm sprinting forward again, pumping my arms as hard as I can.

"No!"

I throw myself after the Jabberwocky, trying to grab the spikes on his tail as he speeds by. My fingers graze them, and miss. I land on the ground with an oomph, before pushing up.

I hear Cheshire's scream of outrage, knowing he's trying to Fade, but the magic of the Jabberwocky prevents it.

Flam swoops down, and I brace myself as he wraps his claws around me, gently, before we're lifting into the air, and leaving the ground far behind us. The battle scene disappears quickly as we enter the cloud layer and chase after the beast in front of us.

"We have to catch him!" I yell, hoping Flam can hear me over the wind. My hair whips around my face, pulling free from the haphazard tie I'd put it in.

Flam is fast, fast enough to keep up with the Jabberwocky and slowly gain on him. I squint my eyes, focusing on the black monstrosity in front of us.

"When I get close enough, I'll throw you onto his back," Flam says. I have no idea how I can hear him, or how he can talk in this form, but the voice is definitely raspier than usual. "Be careful," he warns. "If you fall, I'll catch you."

We draw close enough that I see Cheshire pull his knife and stab at the Jabberwocky's clenched hand. The beast roars in outrage and squeezes his fist tighter. Cheshire's grunt of pain reaches my ears as he pushes against the hold around him.

Closer, I think, tensing. *Closer. Closer.*

Without warning, Flam rears up and throws me forward. I don't get much time before I'm in the open air, barely below the cloud layer now, as I fling my arms wide and focus on the spines of the Jabberwocky's back. For a moment, I think I won't make it, that I'll drop into a freefall and have to hope that Flam can catch me, but then my hands wrap around one of the spines on the Jabberwocky's back, and I clutch to it hard. I slam into his rough scales, and it knocks the air from my body.

He roars the moment I touch him and immediately, goes into a barrel roll. I hang on for dear life as we flip through the air, focused only on staying on his back. Flam said he would catch me, but I'd rather not test that theory yet. My fingers slip the barest fraction just before he stops the roll and goes right into a nosedive. My stomach flips, the air rushing past us, slapping at my face so painfully that it makes tears leak from the corners of my eyes. I don't panic. Instead, I pull myself to the next spine, closer to his neck and to where Cheshire is clasped in his claws. My fingers close around another spine.

The Jabberwocky gets so close to the ground that I think his plan is to crash into it before he shoots into the air again, straight up. He intends for it to throw me off, but it only makes his spines act like a ladder. I scale five more of them before he realizes his mistake and evens out.

He turns his neck around and meets my eyes, the sickly glowing yellow swirling with hatred. He must realize he isn't going to shake me, so he attacks the only thing he can.

Cheshire.

I watch in horror as he curls a claw inward, piercing Cheshire's chest. His shout of pain rends the air and cuts off. There's a sickening gurgle from his lips, and I scream, trying to get closer, but I'm still too far away.

We might as well be miles apart. The Jabberwocky smiles at me, his forked tongue flicking out as if he's mocking me, and he realizes exactly how to hurt me. He won't throw me off. I'm too determined and have Flam hovering just out of the way to catch me if I fall. So, he attacks me another way. Cheshire is limp in his hand, his head lolled back and moving with the wind. The Jabberwocky leers at me, so confident so high in the sky.

He drops Cheshire.

I don't hesitate. I don't take a moment to think about the stupidity of it. I dive over the side of the Jabberwocky, my gaze focused completely on Cheshire, as he falls, unconscious, below me.

I press my arms into my body, making myself as aerodynamic as possible, as I speed down, down, down, the ground growing closer and closer. When I draw near Cheshire, I reach out my arms and wrap them around him, seconds before Flam dives underneath us. I grunt in pain as we land on his back, instantly reaching out for the spines in his feathers. I wrap myself tightly around the spine and Cheshire, determined to keep us onboard. Flam heads for the ground, fast enough that my stomach flips and roils, but I hold it down.

Cheshire isn't moving. His chest isn't rising and falling.

He can't die, I remind myself, but it does little to curb my panic.

The moment Flam touches down, I slide from his back in time for the Jabberwocky to slam down to the ground in front of us, crouched like some sort of gargoyle.

"Take Cheshire!" I yell at Flam. "Keep him safe until he can heal."

Flam dances away, with Cheshire in his claws, out of danger. I raise my hand into the air, calling for the Vorpal Blade again. Just any sword won't do. The Jabberwocky must be taken down with this one. It flies from where I left it, where Alice had fallen, and it slides into my palm just as I charge at the hulking beast slithering towards me. It's still coated in the Red Queen's blood.

I dive out of the way just as his hand swipes past in an attempt to catch me in his claws. The quick reflexes the Hatter has fostered since I arrived in Wonderland kick in, and I'm already diving out of the way of another attack. His tail tries to slam into me, but I duck under it, and jerk sideways in order to avoid his stomping feet. The Jabberwocky isn't as useful on the ground, his size a weakness. I'm able to dance just out of sight, to keep him from skewering me.

"You cannot win!" the Jabberwocky snarls. "I will have this world, and every world with it!"

"We've already won!" I snarl and thrust the sword into the soft underbelly above me.

He roars in pain and fury, stomping his feet, trying to squish me like a bug. No dice, dumbass. I'm already gone.

I twist from the other side, stabbing the sword in again. The sound it makes as it slices through skin and scales makes me cringe, but I yank it out with a squelch and dive again.

Flam roars behind us, distracting the Jabberwocky for the second I need. He looks in Flam's direction. I dive underneath and come up right under his neck, before slamming the sword home in his chest, right where his heart should be. He growls with pain, but he doesn't drop like I expect.

The Jabberwocky laughs when I back away, pulling the blade with me.

"My heart is on the other side, stupid girl."

Great. That would have been a nice bit of information to know before I came to battle.

His claw swipes out faster than I can track and throws me backwards across the flattened grass. I grunt in pain when I slam down, certain something must be broken. The Vorpal Blade flies from my grip to land precious feet away. Darkness dances at the edge of my vision, threatening to take me under, but I push myself to my feet, and face off against the monster before me.

"Why fight so hard?" he asks, tilting his head, a sinister grin showing his fangs. "This isn't your world. Just let it die."

"I refuse to let a bully win," I growl, opening my hand for the Vorpal Blade. It comes to me without hesitation, and I drop into a fighting stance.

He growls, and lowers himself in a crouch, ready to storm towards me. "I'll enjoy using your bones like toothpicks."

Before he can rush me, shouts and yells fill the air, and I look around in confusion. The remains of our army swarm from the trees and the field, their weapons raised as they circle the Jabberwocky.

He snarls and beats his wings, trying to lift into the air before any of them can climb onto his back. I watch in amazement as Hatter and White come out of nowhere, and lasso a massive chain around the Jabberwocky's neck, jerking him to a stop. Symbols etched into the metal glow a brilliant green as they work to yank him back down to the earth. He touches down with a fearsome roar, fighting against the restraints.

"What the fuck?" I mumble. Anger fills my body the likes I've never felt before. This beast, this monster is the sole reason for hundreds and hundreds of deaths—no, thousands! —and he's hurt my mate in the process. I snarl and sprint into the fray, between the soldiers moving forward until I'm in front. The Jabberwocky's eyes roll until they meet mine, fear reflected there for the first time. He realizes his mistake, thinking that this world is his for the taking. Wonderland belongs to the creatures, to the beasts, to the forest. This is no place for the likes of him, and now he will understand.

With a screaming battle cry, I bring the blade down on the Jabberwocky's neck, only to be met with resistance and a shallow cut. He roars in pain and fights hard against the chain. All the soldiers focus on keeping him landlocked, none raising their weapons. Only the Vorpal Blade can kill a Jabberwocky. Only the savior can deliver the final blow. I pull the sword free and hack again, and again, and again.

The Jabberwocky's screams turn to gurgles, and still I hack and scream in outrage, tears leaking from my eyes with the extreme emotions flooding my body. Rage, fear, determination, Love, it all takes over until I'm a mess. Blood splatters my face, and arms, until I'm covered in it, drenched in the gore of a monster. I don't flinch from it. I revel in it.

"Cal!" Someone yells, but I don't turn. I keep swinging. "Cal!"

"What?" I snarl, whirling to meet Clara's eyes where she stands behind me.

She's much the same as I am, covered in blood and bits of gore, her hair hanging in strands around her dirt-smeared face.

Anger still fills my body, the Vorpal Blade calling for more blood,

Wonderland urging me onwards, my viciousness taking over. I can taste the blood that covers me. It should disgust me, but right now, I don't care. It's just another sign of victory.

"You did it, Cal," she says, speaking slowly, like she's talking to a spooked animal. "He's dead."

I look down at the mutilated flesh beneath me, surprised to see the Jabberwocky's head completely detached, his yellow eye glazing over with death. The mouth is open in a silenced scream, the fear still written across his face.

"You're sure he can't come back as a zombie?" I ask hesitantly. I'm not sure what is possible, not after the stories of Alice standing back up after a massive gunshot.

Jupiter laughs at my words, and my eyes flick to hers. She's a little cleaner than Clara but not by much. Her hair is completely loose from the braid, flowing around her shoulders like a flame.

"He won't be a zombie," she promises. "I can feel it. His power is gone."

I breathe a sigh of relief and turn to look for Cheshire, but I don't get the chance. Screams fill the air before I can ask where my mate is.

"For fuck's sake, what now?"

I twist around and look into the crowd of soldiers, just in time to see Tweedledum and Tweedledee begin to rip through them.

Chapter 51

Clara looks down at her wrist in alarm, searching the smooth skin there.

"The deal! The deal is done!"

Jupiter frantically checks her own and meets Clara's eyes.

"Fucking really?" I growl, raising the Vorpal Blade again. It's completely coated in blood, but it sings for me, ready for more. Can't catch a break in this place.

The Tweedles focus their eyes on Jupiter, hunger on their faces, as they push through the soldiers attempting to bring them down. It's useless, their power far greater than the creatures of Wonderland. They move through together as a unit, intent on their target. The Hope Bringer squares her shoulders.

"Come here, little girl," they talk as one, growing closer and closer to us.

Jupiter growls. "My powers are depleted." She meets first my eyes and then Clara's. "This is gonna have to be a fight."

That Hatter and White take up our sides, Doe standing guard behind us. We have to make up an interesting party, battle-weary and covered in blood. Flam lands in front of us in a crouch that makes the ground shake beneath our feet. His feathers are ruffled from the battle, a few of them sticking out at odd angles. There's a deep red gash on his right flank, but he acts as if it's not even there.

"Move aside, Half Breed," Tweedledee hisses.

"Or we'll eat you, too." Tweedledum keeps his eyes focused on Jupiter, as if seeing her means capturing her.

"If you touch any of them," Flam growls, his tail swiping back and forth. "I will destroy you."

They hesitate. "You wouldn't touch us."

"Try me."

Tweedledee hisses, and they turn their attention to us. Tweedledum meets my eyes.

"Mark these words."

"This is not over." Dee curls her lips.

"We are the *Lost*, and we will have your power." Dum finishes by baring his teeth, before they turn, intent on heading into the woods, but they don't make it far.

Attie steps in front of them, and my heart stops. Before I have a chance to run in his direction, or even move to do so, the Tweedles pull up short.

Attie swings his battle axe, still shiny and sparkling, at the twins. I gasp as it takes off Tweedledum's head with a sickening slurp before the head falls to the ground with a thump. Tweedledee hisses in agony and lunges forward, but Attie swings again prepared, until two heads sit on the ground, and black blood splatters the ground. His golden armor sports the spray, giving the color a rusty appearance.

"What the ever-living fuck?" I growl, racing towards Attie and yanking him away. "What were you thinking?"

Attie looks at me funny, his eyebrow raised. "I told you, I'm the backup."

"What does that mean?"

Hatter steps forward then, a grin on his face. "Atlas carries the Berserker axe," he says proudly. "He had one mission today, and that was to keep his eyes on the Tweedles at all times."

I turn on the Hatter. "You ordered my little brother to kill the deadliest creatures?" I snarl.

I'm ready to wring his neck, punch him in the nose, anything, until a harsh grunt comes from behind me.

We turn as one, and my eyes land on Cheshire, where he leans heavily against a tree. There's still a gaping hole in his chest, blood flowing from the wound without resistance. His ears are drooping, his tail limp behind him, and he meets my eyes with faded blues. The electricity there is dull, no longer as bright as a livewire.

"Justice is done," he whispers, a harsh gasp.

I'm already sprinting forward before he drops.

Chapter 52

Sitting at the tea party table, the amount of people attending today makes me uncomfortable. All victory comes with a cost, and we were not immune to that. We lost countless soldiers to battle, and every Card that fell, also, sits at the table, finally released from Alice's curse. The table isn't big enough and so we had to find crates and stools, anything people can sit on, to cram into the available space. There are even some people sitting on the floor, because we ran out of seating.

The table is overflowing with food and teas, every variety imaginable. For once, we have an entire section of the table safe to eat, and I tear into the meat pies with relish. They're not as good as the ones my mom used to make, but they still hit the spot. I make sure to drink lemon-flavored tea today, remembering my mom's smile when she'd stepped through the portal. She would have loved the celebration.

Hatter and Clara sit in their usual spots, the head seats always occupied by the hosts of the tea party. Jupiter, White, Flam, and Doe sit opposite me, relaxed smiles on their faces for the first time I've ever seen. There's a collective relief that fills the room, as if suddenly, the sun has begun to shine again.

It hasn't, not outside at least. The sky still stays unbearably dark, even if the plant-life glows a little brighter.

The doors open, and the mumbling of the guests quiets, all of us turning to the doorway. Cheshire stands there, his hand clamped over his chest where a bandage still rests. A Son of Wonderland can't die, but he can feel pain. With a wound like Cheshire's, it'll take time to heal, time to rest. Now, the wound is mostly a shallow thing, probably will be healed by the next day, but for now, he keeps it wrapped with a bandage under Jupiter's orders. No one can resist the new Hope Bringer.

Cheshire isn't the reason that everyone grows quiet, however. It seems we have one last guest to this tea party that has everyone standing from their seats and placing their hands on the weapons they all wear. I don't move for mine, knowing that it's pointless.

The little girl is no longer a threat.

Alice walks hesitantly around Cheshire and looks up at him, a tiny smile on her face.

"Hello, Cheshire." Such innocence in those words that I feel my eyes mist. Wonderland had stolen all that Alice had become after she left, leaving behind only the little girl. She's still Alice, still capable of great destruction, but she no longer has any power to do so.

"Hello, Alice." I'm surprised at the softness in Cheshire's voice as he gestures for her to go before him. Her little shoes make soft clicking noises as she makes her way down the table, closer and closer to our position. There are only two empty chairs in the whole room, and both of them are beside me.

"Should we be worried?" Clara whispers, but I shake my head.

There's nothing to worry about anymore, not from Alice.

Her little blue dress is clean and wrinkle-free as she slides into the seat two spaces from me, Cheshire sliding into the one closest. Alice leans forward and meets my eyes.

"Calypso." Her little voice brings the first tear over my lashes, but I don't move to brush it away.

"Alice." There's a thickness in my throat that I didn't expect, but I saw her in the visions. I know she didn't mean to turn into such a monster even if she was twisted before the Jabberwocky. Having twisted thoughts and actually acting on them are two different things. Sometimes, fate is a real bitch, and little Alice was the victim of the wrong side.

Still, I don't expect the words that come out of her mouth.

"Thank you," she whispers, and there's an awkward shuffling of the other tea party guests at the words. I can feel their confusion, matching my own, and their anger at the crimes this little girl committed as a woman. I understand it all, but they also haven't seen what I have. Only Jupiter and Clara could know.

"For what?" I ask quietly.

She smiles, and I can see the first bit of mischievousness in those eyes.

"For making me a part of Wonderland again."

And then she pours herself a cup of lemon tea as if she's done it a million times and sips it quietly, not meeting the stares of any other creatures.

I suck in air and fight the emotion threatening to spill out. Cheshire, with his awareness, reaches over and curls his tail around my ankle and places his hand on my knee. I can breathe easier, and I look up at him gratefully.

"Pretend it's just another day," he whispers. "Or the emotions will consume you."

Focus on one good thing. His words come right back to me, and I follow the advice.

I nod my head and look over at Attie on my other side. He's been mostly quiet since the battle, far too mature-looking for his age. He'd returned the armor to the room, and the axe, even though Hatter told him it was his.

"I have no need of it for now," Attie had replied to him. "So, keep it, until it's necessary."

There'd been so much strength in those words, when any normal teenager would have gleefully taken home a battle axe to show off to his friends. But Wonderland has changed us. It's uncertain whether it is for the worse or for the better.

"I think there's something important to address," Flam comments, popping a piece of bread into his mouth.

"What's that?" I ask, tilting my head.

"Who will rule. The Old King and Queen are dead. Their legacy gone with Prince Alex. And the White Queen is in no position to rule anything."

"Can she be helped at all?" Jupiter bites her lip with her question, thinking through the possibilities.

"I don't think so, but if anyone can find a solution, it would be you, Hope Bringer."

Jupiter blushes with his words but nods her head in understanding.

"I think it should be Clara," Atlas speaks up, meeting everyone's eyes. "It makes sense. She's been the one in charge since I arrived here."

Clara shakes her head. "I'm not in charge, and I'm certainly not a ruler. Besides, I don't like the word 'Queen'."

I snort, a grin spreading across my face. For a moment, I forget that little Alice is sitting beside Cheshire.

"Well then, All hail Empress Clara Bee." I wink at her. "Or whatever title you want.

Alice sighs, and I tense, looking over. "An empress sounds lovely," she says, that childish lilt echoing in the room. "Empress of Wonderland."

I relax, a smile on my face.

"All in favor of Empress Clara Bee?" I raise my hand and everyone in the room follows suit. Clara watches in astonishment as every creature raises their hand, or hoof, or paw into the air. "Seems like it's unanimous."

"Well," she mumbles, glancing over at the Hatter. "Seems I'm in need of an Emperor."

A grin stretches across Hatter's face, so silly that I can't help but laugh. He stands and jumps up onto the table, his combat boots making the dishes rattle as he kicks plates aside.

He turns in a circle, addressing us all.

"As is the custom for proposals, I will now perform the *Flutterwacken*."

I watch, shocked, as he starts dancing on top of the table in something that reminds me of the chicken dance rather than some romantic proposal. I cover my mouth to hold in my snort, but I'm too late, and I fall into a fit of laughter.

Clara isn't much better. She's laughing along with everyone else, delight in her eyes as he kicks china off the table. When he actually flaps his arms like a chicken and makes a sound in his throat so close to a rooster that it's insane, Clara actually falls out of her seat, tears leaking from her eyes.

Hatter stops, so much happiness on his face that I can't contain all the emotion. I bite my tongue in an attempt to stall it and only succeed in making it bleed.

"It's alright, sis," Attie says in my ear. "We won. And this is how it should be."

I nod my head at him and watch as Hatter leaps from the table and picks up Clara from the floor. He doesn't kneel. Instead, they stand face to face, as lovers, as rulers, as equals.

"Clara Bee, you were meant for me. Will you be my wife? Will you be my . . . Empress?" Clara laughs as he slides a large purple rock onto her finger, the stone seeming to glow from within.

"My dear Hatter, it's about time. I want you completely, with or without the rhyme."

She wraps her arms around him, and they kiss, the moment so beautiful, it hurts. There's so much love there, so much trust, that I find myself looking for an escape.

As the room erupts in furious cheers, and a line of congratulations is formed, I whisper to Attie that I'm okay, before I slip from the room.

Chapter 53

CHESHIRE

I feel the moment she leaves the room, slipping away as if she can't stand to be in here. I watch Clara and Hatter for a few minutes longer, nodding my head at them as they turn and receive the applause and congratulations. They deserve it, and I'm certain there won't be better rulers than those two. Clara has a knack for emotions. Even now, her eyes flick towards the door where Cal disappeared.

To be honest, I'm just relieved it's not me in their positions. My life is already restricted enough.

For a second, I stare at Jupiter as she laughs at something White said. My first instinct was to be bitter when I learned she's the new Hope Bringer, but I realized that Danica would love her and wish her the best. Her quirkiness would have made them fast friends. I'm sad that Wonderland replaced her, but I choose not to look at it as replacing, as much as birthing a new power to protect the land.

Jupiter is the logical choice, and the emotional one.

I slip from the room in search of Cal, trusting the connection we have to find her, until I come to the usual window. When I climb from it and gingerly step onto the roof, I'm not surprised to see her with her chin on her knees as she watches the stars. The wound on my chest aches, still visible but mostly healed. The Hatter had slipped me some of his special brew to keep Cal from worrying. She'd sat by me after the battle, when I was too weak to open my eyes, even after what I'd done to her.

I take a seat beside her, and we sit in silence, listening to the sounds of the forest. It's more docile now, the shrieks of Bandersnatch nonexistent, the Beezles buzzing as usual. And the stars seem just a little bit brighter tonight, as if even they celebrate.

"I have to go back home," Cal whispers suddenly, and I turn to look at her. I'd thought we might have more time before we had this conversation. My chest aches when she meets my eyes. "Attie needs to grow up in a normal world. Finish school. Achieve his dreams."

I frown and look down at my hands, where they clench against my pants.

"I know."

Cal bites her lips and looks back at the stars. When she speaks again, I recognize the heavy timber of a prophecy, the words sinking into my soul.

"Child of metal, fire in your soul,
You'll take out Alice and save us all.
Open your heart and love complete,
The journey won't be easy, and you'll know defeat.
Wonderland asks for everything you have,
She'll demand your heart, and that you take the Cat's mask.
You must surrender it all to succeed in this war,
The third, the mate, the chosen liberator.
Your love will be deep, which will help you succeed,
Love Justice and Wonderland, but then you must leave."

I LET THE WORDS RING IN THE AIR, SETTLING INTO MY BONES WITH their demands. Another prophecy to act on my life, another damned prophecy.

"Where did that come from?" I ask, already knowing the answer.

"When you left Absalom's house, she told me."

"Makes sense," I growl quietly. "The Caterpillar was never one to give up."

Cal looks down again, her dark eyes meeting my own. There's such sadness there, even on a day where we should be celebrating, but I know battle is not something that goes away. I see every creature I've ever punished. I've no doubt that Cal sees her own punishments.

"What's funny," Cal whispers, "is that I didn't need the prophecy to tell me that I loved you. I'd already been done for by then." I feel my body seize up at her words, fear coursing through my body. My tail starts to beat double time behind me, and Cal's eyes zero right to it. "I still don't expect you to say it back. There's no expectations between us."

I don't answer, keeping my lips shut. The words linger just on the other side of my lips, demanding to be let out, but I refuse. I won't do that to her. I won't make her stay when she wants to leave. I should have expected that my mate wouldn't be the same as Clara or Jupiter, should have known that there would be something that prevents us from being together. Even the prophecy demands Cal leave, as if she's not a part of my world after her job is done.

Cal slips her hand into mine, her fingers warm. I look down at where our skin meets, squeezing just a tiny bit, wishing I could keep her here with the simple action. *Stay, stay, stay,* my heart begs, but I don't give the bastard any air time. This isn't about me. This is about Cal.

I tug her closer to me, wrapping an arm around her body and lifting, until she straddles my waist. She doesn't fight it, completely at ease with me picking her up on the slanted roof. Her trust almost does me in, but I slide my mask into place, hiding behind it.

"If you have to leave," I purr, "then one last fuck is in order, no?"

I expect a smile, maybe a small one. I'm not prepared for the frown that mars her features or the tear that slips over her cheek. My chest aches as I watch the course of the drop, until it drips from her jaw. My hands cradle Cal's hips in my lap, loose, gentle. I don't know how to react when another tear falls.

"Cal—"

"Don't." Her whispered words are like a slap in the face, but I don't try again. When she leans down and presses her lips against mine, I don't respond, afraid I'll break her. So, the cheeky little goddess bites my lip, hard enough to draw blood.

I growl low in my throat when she pulls away, her glistening eyes meeting mine.

"No expectations," she reminds me.

The next time she kisses me, I open beneath her and immediately take control. She lets me, and I have the urge to bring her fire back, but perhaps, this isn't one of those times. Perhaps, I can stroke her fire higher without adding fuel.

I slip one hand around the back of her neck and into her hair, gently guiding her while I taste her. But I'm not made for gentle.

The thought of her leaving Wonderland forever, that I might never see her again, brings my beast out, and I start gripping her harder, and grinding her down onto my hard cock. The wildness creeps in, and my claws peek out when I break the kiss and trail down her neck. She gasps and leans back, giving me better access, exposing her throat. I lick her in reward, trailing my tongue along her pulse, kissing her sun-kissed skin. Need crashes through me, all-consuming. I slip my hand inside her shirt and circle one nipple with my claw.

Cal spreads her hands against my chest, her fingers touching the bandage there. She jerks, as if remembering why it's there in the first place, but I hold her hand against the beating of my heart when she would have pulled away. And then I'm rolling us, until her back lays flat against the roof, and I cover her with my body, her legs open around my hips. I don't give her time before I'm shoving her shirt up and pulling the tip of one tiny nipple into my mouth. Her back arches while I pop open her jeans and slide my hand inside to find her arousal. Her wetness coats my fingers, and I pull them free.

Her eyes watch, riveted, as I lick my fingers clean, a hum in my throat.

"You taste like divinity," I groan, a small smile on my face. She blushes at my words, fire igniting in her expression.

Sitting up, I help her pull her jeans down her legs and toss them away, until she lays before me on the roof of the Hatter's house, bare save for the shirt and bra bunched up. I pull my shirt over my head and toss it aside, not caring where it lands, before I'm shoving down my pants, freeing my erection. The urgency I suddenly feel takes over, as if Cal will slip right through my fingers.

We don't waste time once I'm free of clothing. I position myself at her entrance before gently sliding inside, slowly, torturously. We both groan as I sit fully inside, and I place my forehead against hers, holding her thighs tightly in my hands.

"Do you know what you taste like?" she whispers, her hands threading around my neck, one into my hair to caress my ears. I barely shake my head before pumping the smallest amount inside of her, drawing a little gasp from her lips. "You taste like wild honeysuckle," she groans.

I slam my mask back into place and slam into her hard, punishing, trying to dispel her words from my mind, but she only meets my eyes, the clever goddess. She knows what's she doing and doesn't back down.

"Sometimes, you smell like woodsmoke, like a blazing bonfire in the summer." My mask slips a little, and I slam inside her hard, bringing a cry to her lips, but she presses on. "Sometimes, your eyes glow in the way that makes me think of fireflies." Her voice is huskier, breathier, as I pump inside her, a snarl on my lips as she pushes forward. "Sometimes, I imagine you on the back of my motorcycle," her eyes twinkle at that, even as I set a punishing pace and her words get a little lost. "I think you would look good riding bitch."

I press my lips against hers in an attempt to stop her words, to push aside the emotions threatening to spill out of me, but it only serves to heighten them as she kisses me back without abandon, as she lifts her hips to meet every thrust.

So, I slam inside her harder, until we both groan with the pain and pleasure, until her small hand wraps around my throat and squeezes, her back arched up in offering. I take it, and slip down to wrap my lips around her breast, nipping, dragging a single claw around the shaking flesh.

"You can't hide from it," she breathes. "You'll always smell like wild honeysuckle and woodsmoke. You'll always taste like home."

I can't handle it. I can't let her see the mask slip away, so I react the only way I know how. I jerk out and roll her, trusting my instincts to keep us on the shingles when I yank her hips up to mine and slam back inside her, her chest pressed hard against the roof. I piston inside of her, the sound of our skin slapping mingling with the sounds of the forest. She's so beautiful, laid out beneath me, that I can't help but grab a fistful of her hair and gently tug her until she's on her knees, her back plastered to my chest.

"If I can't hide from it," I growl, feral words, "then I'll make sure you never lose the memories."

It's unfair, and wrong on so many levels, but I want Cal to remember me, even if we part and never see each other again. I want her to feel me, to long for me, to love me harder.

"Yes," she breathes, pushing against me even with the brutal pace I've set.

I slip my hand around and wrap her neck with my fingers, an anchor, as I jerk her head to the side, and kiss where her neck and shoulder meet. Her breath stutters, and I can feel her body winding tight, preparing to crash.

I have the urge to mark her, to make sure she always wears my badge of claim, even if I can't actually claim her. It's an asshole move, one I didn't think I was capable of, but as I feel her body shatter around mine, her cries ringing out, I clamp my teeth hard on her sensitive muscle. She jerks in my arms, her pussy milking me until I find my own release, roaring against her skin where my teeth break through, where blood wells in my mouth.

We're both breathing hard when I gently lay her against the shingles. I don't think about it when I lay down beside her and pull her against my chest. I don't think about her words as we watch the stars dance across the sky. I don't think about the mark on her shoulder, red and angry, my own rage manifested.

Instead, I close my eyes, and slide my mask into place, but it's already too late.

The mask is gone, broken into a million pieces.

I love you, Calypso, I think, but I don't dare say it out loud. *But I have to let you go.*

Chapter 54

It's a little odd that there's no tea party, but it's also a relief. Attie and I plan to leave the next day, after we've had time to say our goodbyes. We don't know how long it's been since we left our world. White explained it could have been days, or months, or even years since we left. I'm hoping it's only been days after imagining the fear that Rob must be feeling at our disappearance. He's been good to us; it wouldn't be right for him to think something had happened to us when we're alive and well.

Hatter and Clara are having a celebration, almost like an engagement party. For once, the tea room is filled with the living, creatures and people sitting at the table and clinking tea cups. It's all a big festive affair, one that makes me smile to be a part of.

Attie is having the time of his life dancing with a group of antelope-looking women. They'd pulled him up from his chair ten minutes ago, and still the kid hasn't made an excuse to leave their circle. I smile at the sight, glad to see him making memories, because that could be all we have when we go home.

Cheshire is leaning against the wall, pretending as if he isn't watching me. Every so often, his eyes flick over, and I catch them, before they dance away. He's been odd since our moment on the roof the night before, as if he's afraid of what I'd said. I don't regret them, but it would have been nice to have him close for the little time we have left. I would have liked that.

"Hi. Calypso, right?"

I turn my head and frown at the woman taking the seat next to me. She has cat ears on her head just like Cheshire's, her stripes bright green rather than blue. She's wearing a shimmering dress, and when she moves, I can see through her. It's as if she's a ghost. I nod my head at her, confused. I recognize her from my vision, both as a child, and dead in Cheshire's arms.

"I'm Danica." A small smile spreads on her lips, and I see the resemblance immediately. She is certainly Cheshire's sister.

"How are you here?"

She points to the Hatter where he sits with Clara draped across his lap. He's currently feeding Clara bits of muffin, sensually sliding the pieces between her lips.

"The Hatter used his powers so that those of us who wanted to come celebrate, could. I didn't want to pass up an opportunity to see my brother or the woman who captured his heart."

"Unfortunately, I don't think I'm that woman." I glance over at Cheshire again, his eyes fixed on us. He doesn't glance away this time. "I have to leave Wonderland."

Danica studies me for a moment, taking in every detail. She lifts her hand as if she might grab my own, but her fingers pass right through. She sighs but smiles, before glancing over at Cheshire, too.

"Love is an odd thing," she comments. "So full of hope. So full of wonder. There are many ways to love, and Wonderland is nothing if not a supporter of such things."

"What do you mean?"

Her brilliant-green eyes glow when she meets mine, a wide smile on her face.

"You know what I mean, Calypso, goddess of Wonderland." She glances up at the ceiling, where another painting depicts the creatures of this world. Again, no one seems to notice it, no one besides the Sons and me. "Have you ever wondered why you can see the paintings?"

"Yes." I stare up at the depiction of Cheshire, Danica right beside him. They look happy, as if it was done before Alice returned.

Danica hums, a glint in her eyes. "It's because they were painted by a Cheshire Cat, when he thought he was free." She smiles. "Silly cat thinks he lost that freedom."

Danica winks at me. Then she stands from her seat and walks over to Cheshire.

I watch, fascinated, as she opens her arms, and they hug, some magic making it possible when she couldn't touch me. Cheshire holds her so tight, I fear he could break her, but she holds him back the same, as they trade words.

It's a sight everyone in the room pauses to watch, a collective sigh at the genuine love and anguish in the simple touch.

Forever can be three turns of the long hand, I think, *or it can be just one second.*

We have to make sure we use what time we have wisely.

I FIND CHESHIRE ON THE PORCH THAT NIGHT, SITTING ON THE banister. The forest is alive with the sounds of its creatures, but thankfully, none of them make my ears bleed. He doesn't turn to look at me, hardly acknowledging my presence at all. The only sign he knows I'm there is a twitch of his ear in my direction.

I don't wait for him to run, or Fade, or hide behind his mask. I move off the porch and step in front of him, looking up into his eyes.

"Come with us." I force the words out, knowing what I'm asking but asking anyways. It's selfish and goes completely against what I would normally do, but it's worth the risk. I can't help the hope that threads through my voice. "Come with us to our world."

"And what? Stay there?" Cheshire asks, already shaking his head. "I have a job here. Wonderland won't let me leave."

"Danica told me that Wonderland supports love and hope. I bet she'd let you go if you only had the courage to ask."

"It's not possible." His voice hardens. "I'm a part of Wonderland."

"But I want you to be a part of me," I whisper, holding his gaze, holding in the tears threatening to fall. *Stay strong, Cal. Don't let it out now.*

His face softens a fraction at my words. "There's no happiness for me, little goddess." His words are so soft, I can hardly hear them. "I'm not someone to live happily ever after with. I'm not that person."

I clench my jaw, those damn tears welling before I've even had a chance to push them back. They start to spill over my lashes, and Cheshire's face collapses completely, but he doesn't move towards me. The stubborn bastard stays on the banister, as if I'm not falling apart in front of him.

When I try to speak, I have to clear my throat to get the words out. I want to beg, to implore him to come, to choose me, to realize that coming with me is the freedom he's searching for, but that's not my place. Cheshire must choose on his own. I can't make the decision for him.

"If you change your mind," I whisper, my voice thick. "I'll be waiting for you tomorrow."

I turn and leave him alone on the porch. I don't give into my pain until I'm safely behind my bedroom door.

I remind myself that if I have to leave my heart behind in Wonderland, it's okay.

After all, doesn't the savior always leave a piece of themselves behind in the story books?

♠

I STARE INTO THE FOREST AFTER CAL LEAVES, FEELING HER PAIN even though she's safely inside. We have a connection at a level I can't comprehend, and I'm certain it'll tear me to shreds when she leaves, when the emptiness takes its place. All this time, I've fought against the prophecy. I didn't realize it would be my death.

Memories drop over me like rain, the emotions of seeing Danica tonight, and Cal asking me to come with her acting as a hammer to the walls in my mind.

"LOVING SOMEONE IS LIKE GIVING THEM ALL OF YOUR TRUST, AND *handing them your heart, hoping they don't break it," Danica says, her legs hanging over the branch she sits on, completely comfortable even at the top of the* tree canopy. "It feels like hope and warmth. I have to assume if you lose it, it'll feel like nothing is ever worth a thing again."

"Who has you speaking these kinds of things?" I ask, leaping from another branch to take a seat beside her.

A tiny smile curls her lips and she winks at me.

"That's for me to know, big brother." I scoff and roll my eyes. Her face gets serious for a moment, and she meets my eyes. "If you find it, hold onto it, Chesh. You don't want to lose it."

"No one could ever love an asshole like me," I tease, and she laughs again, that smile springing back to her face.

"Well, you're right there." When she looks off into the trees, our powers already calling us forth to some terrible crime, she closes her eyes to feel it. "Maybe," she whispers. "Just maybe, if you open your heart a little bit, the perfect woman will come in when you least expect it." A teasing grin. "Unless your mate is a prophecy waiting to happen."

THAT HAD BEEN THREE WEEKS BEFORE ALICE RETURNED, AND I forgot ever having the conversation. But now, it haunts me like a record, as I stare at the stars, and wish that I could take Cal among them.

Chapter 55

Attie and I stand at the edge of a shining portal, the colors green and white just like the rabbit hole had been. After Alice's death, the key to Wonderland was returned to White, whatever that means. So, now he can open a portal wherever he wants and lead us home. I much prefer this way rather than having to go back through the skin table room.

There's this overwhelming sense of anxiousness; I'm afraid of what's on the other side of the portal, afraid of what I'm leaving behind. I didn't expect it to feel like this, as if I don't know how to handle anything. I'm supposed to be strong. Instead, I've never felt so weak, so tired. When we get home, I'm taking a day-long bubble bath, maybe splurging on a spa day for both Attie and me. But there will be something missing, something important.

I frown and look around the crowd, Cheshire conveniently absent. Sadness the likes I've never known explodes in my chest. He isn't even going to come say goodbye. We won't even get to share a final moment.

Attie squeezes my hand in reassurance, and I focus on the touch. It's gonna be okay. I have to keep reminding myself that. We'll survive.

Jupiter comes up to hug me first, enveloping me in an awkward hug. "We'll come visit as often as possible," she promises, a smile on her face. "Besides, I really need some tacos. I miss tacos."

I laugh as she moves to hug Attie, and Clara takes her place.

"You'll always be a part of Wonderland even if you don't stay here," Clara says, hugging me tight. "Come back when you're ready."

I glance over at Attie, a smile on my face. "Maybe. When Attie has had a chance to live, maybe we could."

Doe and Flam hug us next, the Flamingo ruffling my brother's hair affectionately. "See you around, Berserker," he teases.

The Hatter nods at me solemnly, his arm wrapped tight around Clara while she blinks back tears. I look away fast, so that I don't do the same.

White smiles sadly when we turn to him and stare into the swirling portal. "All you have to do is step inside, and you'll come back inside your mechanic shop."

"Thank you," I tell him. "For everything."

"I'm sorry about bringing you in the beginning."

"No," I shake my head. "It's okay."

"Are you ready?"

I turn and look over the crowd one last time, searching for electric blue, or for that familiar grin. Nothing. He's not here, and there's no more time. I clench my jaw hard and turn back around, facing White.

"Ready."

Attie squeezes my hand hard, just as anxious as I am, and I take a deep breath, preparing myself for the journey ahead. Things will always be different, our lives forever changed, all because of a Hatter, a White Rabbit, and a Cheshire Cat. How will we ever manage normal again? We won't, but we'll have to.

We take a step forward, the portal starting to drag at us, preparing to pull us inside. I close my eyes, readying myself. Attie stands beside me, our fingers threaded, my rock. Everything is going to be okay. It has to be.

I go to take another step forward, to move inside the portal, when movement comes from my right, and a hand slips into my free one. I smile, turning towards a Cheshire grin, my heart flipping inside my chest. My eyes mist as I take in his leather jacket, those amazing ears, those electric eyes.

"You came," I whisper, my voice almost a croak.

"Didn't think I'd let you get off that easy now, did you?"

I laugh, and Attie whoops beside me.

"Come on, you're late," White says, gesturing for us to continue through the portal.

"Late for what?" I don't even glance at White as I speak.

"Who knows?" he grumbles. "Just hurry up."

I laugh, and as one, we step forward.

When the swirling white and green lights pulls us in, I can't help but think that fate is a funny thing. Sometimes, we fight so hard against it, thinking we know better. Yet, every now and then, right in the middle of the worst times, Fate hands you a Cheshire Cat and encourages you to love him madly.

I'm mad. You're mad.

We're all mad here.

And Wonderland will never be the same. . . .

Epilogue

CLARA

"What does an Empress of Wonderland do?" I ask, looking around at the table. We're sitting in the empty tea room, planning for the future. The only problem is, I don't know how to plan at all. If only Absalom hadn't perished in the war.

Flam and Doe sit on one side of us, Jupiter and White on the other. Hatter watches me as I speak.

"Rule," Flam answers, shrugging his shoulder. "Decide disputes. Protect the land and her creatures."

"That all sounds very easy when you say it, but I doubt it is." I sigh, rubbing my temple. I never thought I would be in this position, but at least I have people to help me.

"I expect every one of you to be on my council. I can't do this alone," I chide.

They all smile in response and nod their head.

Jupiter fidgets in her seat. "Do I get a fancy title? Cause that would be awesome!"

"You can have whatever title you want."

She thinks about it for a second, a bright smile on her face. "Chief Geek to the Empress."

We all laugh at that, and for a moment, I allow myself to relax. We did it. We won the war. Almost as if sensing I'm relaxing, a letter appears in midair in front of our faces and drops on the table. That's a first. I jerk as it gives off a little poof and watch as Hatter grabs it and rolls it open. His eyes scan the delicate writing, reading each line.

He stands suddenly, panic on his face. "There's trouble."

"Where?" I ask. "Is it someone else in Wonderland?"

"No. It's not Wonderland." His eyes scan the letter again, reading the words there.

"Then where is it?" Jupiter asks, leaning in.

"Someone fetch March." Flam jumps up at Hatter's words and nods his head, before rushing from the room.

"Where are we going now?" I sigh in exasperation. Seriously, we barely finished the last war.

"We need the fourth Son." Hatter's words ring in the room for a moment, and I frown even as he mutters "bloody pirates" under his breath.

"Forth?"

Hatter turns to look at me. When he speaks, his words echo in the room.

"One is dead. Two is begotten. Three is alone, and Four is forgotten."

That fucking rhyme. "But what does that mean?" I feel like I'm just asking question after question. I need a clear answer. I'm so sick of guessing what the mad ramblings of the March Hare mean.

"When Wonderland is called forth to defend,
and someone needs to protect her,
she will choose another Son.
She'll choose another Berserker."

His words ring with the notes of prophecy, of a long ago decision made by Wonderland. I tense.

"No," I growl. "No. Cal will never allow it."

"It's too late." Hatter rips his top hat from his head. "It's too late. The Fourth Son has already been chosen."

And suddenly, March is somehow in front of us. I shriek when he appears out of thin air, completely whole, not a single sign of rot on him. And he's out of his cabin. What the actual hell is going on?

"You rang?" he giggles, dusting off his coat.

I'm so tense, I don't know what to do except to stand and lift my chin. No. No, no, no. Not again. Cal and Cheshire deserve their happiness. They don't deserve this shit.

"Prepare," Hatter orders, his eyes meeting each of our own. I hold my breath for his next words, knowing they will change everything. Our battle is over, but another will begin. I can feel it.

"Who calls for our help? Who calls for the Berserker?" March asks, a grin on his face.

The Hatter pulls his sword and meets my eyes, his madness dancing just underneath. When he speaks, my heart shrivels in my chest.

"Neverland," he whispers. "The Daughters of Neverland are in turmoil."

The End
...or is it?

Every fairy tale has a twist.
You can think of it as you may.
Beasts and darkness await you.
Please enjoy your stay.

You're doomed upon the water,
you're doomed when you're on land,
take care if you're in the skies.
Be careful where you stand.

A new chapter has begun.
Open a new door and be a Darling.
Pick the second star to the right,
And fly straight on until morning.

ACKNOWLEDGMENTS

Without the support of my awesome husband, none of this would be possible. He keeps me excited every day and never hesitates to listen to me go on an on about my crazy ideas. My son is the reason I get up every day and write. One day, I hope to write something that I can read to him.

Thank you to my awesome ladies from the three-way. Katie Knight and Poppy Woods, how did I ever live without you? Seriously. I can't even remember what it was like before I met y'all and I hope I don't have to ever know again. I can't wait for what this year and many more have in store for us.

Thank you to the amazing readers and authors who make me smile every day. In particular, I would like to thank Jocelyn Sanchez, Claudia Coenen, Kit Tee, Adam Tennant, and all the members of my Street Team. I would also like to thank Nicole JeRee for not only being a great friend, but for, also, making my books always look so great.

Thank you to my ARC readers, Beta Readers, and anyone else who has a hand in this book.

Thank you to Michelle Hoffman for always doing amazing edits. Thank you to Ruxandra Tudorica of Methyss Design for always taking my vision and making an amazing cover. Not only do I consider you a friend, but by some level of sorcery, you make these amazing covers that capture exactly what I hope.

Thank you to Mallory Kent for being an amazing unicorn of a PA. You're exactly what I need and I'm even luckier to call you friend.

Thank you for being the first to be sacrificed by the three-way.

Finally, thank you to everyone who has taken a chance and read the Sons of Wonderland series. Without y'all taking that chance, this final book would have never been possible. Thank you for jumping down a rabbit hole with me and embracing the Sons and the Triad. I can't think of a better bunch of people than my readers. Y'all are my tribe. After all, we're all mad here. I'm excited to start the next adventure with you. See you in Neverland!

Stay Mad, Wonderlanders.

ABOUT THE AUTHOR

Kendra Moreno was born and raised in Texas where, if the locusts don't drive you mad, the fire ants and sticker burrs will. Iced tea, or aptly called straight sugar, fuels her for battling the forces of evil and washing the never-ending dishes her son dirties. She has one husband who listens to her spin tall tales constantly without fail. Although he doesn't always know what she's talking about, he supports her better than grandma's girdle. Kendra has one son who will one day read her stories. For now she's teaching him that books are meant to be cherished and not destroyed. Her three Hellhounds keep her company while she writes. If she isn't writing, you can usually find Kendra elbows deep in anything from paint to cookie dough.

If you'd like to have a place to discuss the book with other fans, head over to Kendra's facebook group where you can get updates on her work before anyone else.

You can also reach her on her website:
kendramorenoauthor.com

facebook.com/kendra.morenoauthor.7
instagram.com/writingbeast90

ALSO BY KENDRA MORENO

Sons of Wonderland:
Mad as a Hatter
Late as a Rabbit
Feral as a Cat

Anthologies:
Cupid's Playthings:
Supernova
At World's End: An Apocalypse Anthology:
Wings of Rage
Falling For Them Anthology Vol. 4:
Four Parts Super

Steampunk Reverse Harem:
Clockwork Butterfly

Continue on for a preview of Clockwork Butterfly...

CLOCKWORK BUTTERFLY
AVAILABLE NOW ON KINDLE UNLIMITED

Chapter One

"That's it, little machine. There you are."

Vic stared at the tiny mechanical creature on the workbench in front of her, concentrating hard as she tinkered with the small gears. She had been working on the project for days, a distraction from her father's anxiousness and her own excitement. Word still had not come of the news they have been waiting years to hear. Vic did not have the patience for such things.

Her cat, Gear, lay on the workbench beside her, watching with fascination as the butterfly wings flapped with the movement of the cogs. The soft grind of his own gears, those that made up his hind quarters, filled the small workroom. Vic had found him as a kitten, brutally beaten by some miscreants who had run the moment she had stormed into the alley. Steam had risen behind her, lending to the demon image they no doubt pegged her with. It added to the terrifying sight she had surely made, a woman dressed in trousers and a tunic, a pair of spectacle goggles on her head, grease smeared across her face. The puffs of steam that regularly came from her leg certainly helped. Vic was an odd woman for her time, raised around machines and preferring them to the boring social nuances of other human beings. Gear had become her companion after she had nursed him back to health. His hind legs had been mangled beyond repair, so she had built him new ones. The fact that they both had prosthetic limbs drew them closer, similarities and all that.

Gear purred when Vic reached over and scratched him under the chin, happy to steal some of her affection from the machine sitting under the magnifying glass. The newest tinker was a machine smaller than Vic had yet accomplished, a mechanical butterfly. As she wound the gears tight and leaned back, she held her breath expectantly. The tiny, stained glass wings began to flap, gently at first before speeding up as the apparatus began to run.

"We did it, Gear!" Vic exclaimed, lifting her goggles onto her forehead.

She pushed the magnifying glass out of the way and watched in excitement as the butterfly's wings flapped faster before rising into the air, the wings mimicking those of the real insects. The wings had taken some ingenuity. At first, she tried a fine layer of silk but found they were too porous. Eventually, she had found her answer in a micro-thin layer of stained glass. The result was a dazzling display of multicolored beauty, closer to a butterfly than she could have ever hoped.

Gear sat up and watched, enraptured with the moving parts. The butterfly took off into the air, and Vic clapped happily. The tiny machine fluttered around the room, sending glittering colors around the walls when they caught the light. It moved closer to Gear, clicking, teasing. Gear's tail whipped from side to side as he glared at the offending thing, agitated instantly at its incessant fluttering. Before Vic had enough time to truly celebrate the tinkering feat she had pulled off, Gear reached out his paw and batted the machine from the air. It immediately stopped fluttering and fell straight to the floor with a tiny clank.

"Oh no! Gear, what have you done?" Vic chided, squatting down and scooping up the butterfly. One wing tried to move again, but some of the pieces in the mechanisms were bent at wrong angles. She sighed, placing it back on the workbench. "Naughty Kitty." Gear just meowed in pride before laying back down, keeping a close eye on the machine in case it took off again. "This is going to take ages to repair."

Vic was just beginning to straighten out one of the cogs, the smell of grease and lubricant strong in her nose, when the door to her workshop burst open, startling her and making her drop the tool she had been holding. Her father rushed into the shop, tension across his shoulders. At first, she thought he might be upset or angry with something she had done or forgotten to do, so she immediately attempted to smooth things over.

"Father, I haven't been in here that long, I swear."

He waved her words away, a bright smile crossing his face.

"Both you and I know that you have been in this workshop since the moment you rose this morning, but that is not why I am here."

"It's not?" Vic asked dubiously. Her father was constantly trying to convince her to mingle with other people. He thought it was good for her social skills, and though he was not adamant that she act like a lady, he wanted her to have every opportunity if she so chose. In reality, social events made her feel like a bumbling fool when the other ladies looked down their noses at her, commenting on the state of her hair or her lack of petticoat. Dresses were not a favorite of hers, and so each moment wearing one made her feel terribly uncomfortable. The men were worse, coming up and asking her to dance every five minutes. She wanted to have a conversation, not waltz and listen to the men drone on and on about their accomplishments or assets. She particularly did not like having her feet stepped on. A lot of men were terrible dancers. One day, Vic hoped she could tell a man about her accomplishments, and he would actually listen with interest. Alas, she seemed doomed to end up a spinster. She did not mind so much. She would always have her machines. But her father would think it his fault if she did not join society as their station dictated, being the child of Lady Jenica. He had felt guilty a lot since her mother died, as if he was failing to give her the opportunities their station afforded them.

"No, my dear! I have received a letter!"

"A letter from who?" she asked, her own excitement growing with the obvious emotion leaking from her father.

"The High Council of Sciences and Exploration!"

Vic jumped from her seat,

"Well? What does it say?" She held her breath.

Her father stood there for a moment, letting the anticipation grow before he finally spoke.

"We have been fully funded!"

"No!" Vic laughed. "You are jesting."

"I swear it! Read for yourself." Her father passed the letter into her hands, and she scanned the document.

"That is the Queen's seal," she whispered.

"That it is."

"What does this all mean then? You are leaving?"

Vic was sad she would not get to see her father, but this had been his dream since she could remember. He had been fighting his entire life to get funding for an expedition to the Amazon rainforests where there were legends of a temple, the Temple of the Rising Sun. Those legends spoke of a great fire opal protected inside, potent enough to act as a power source capable of fueling dozens of cities at once. This was her father's moment, his dream come true. She would not hold him back.

"This means we are both leaving."

"Have you gone mad?" Vic asked, staring at him in confusion. "Would I not be in the way?"

"On the contrary, I have been tasked with picking the crew for the journey. I am in need of a Master Tinker, if you are interested."

"If I am interested?" Vic wrinkled her brow. "Of course, I am interested! When do we leave? What do I need? How long is the trip?"

"Patience, my dear. All in due time. For now, let us celebrate!" Vic could not stop the excitement that coursed through her body. She jumped up and down as her father offered his elbow. Her leg hissed and clinked at the pressure, the shocks absorbing the impact. She scratched Gear under his chin one more time, dropped some food in his half empty bowl, and looped her arm through her father's.

"Let us make haste," her father told her. "I have a lot of work to do."

Chapter Two

The next few weeks went by in a flurry of activity. Vic worked with her father to arrange for the letters to go out, requesting the service of certain renowned tradesmen. Vic was amazed that letters went to the Americas and, one in particular, to Germany. She had heard great things about Bram Schmitt, the up and coming German inventor. Letters had already begun to arrive with answers, and she was pleased when he was among those who had accepted.

Vic had her own preparations to make for the expedition. Three years ago, at sixteen, she'd garnered the attention of a local Master Tinker. He'd taken her under his wing, and at first, it had been something she was proud of. Until she began to work with him, that is. Master Frederick was a drunk, and a sordid one at that. He could be found most days passed out in his shop, a bottle of whiskey tucked under his arm with his snoring rattling the window panes.

An opportunity that started off as an honor turned into Vic running the entire machine shop. Master Frederick's patrons came because they knew she could fix their machines. She did her job, and she did it well. While Master Frederick had never taught her the things she had expected, she had learned so much more. Running a tinker's shop was the greatest experience, even if it took her a while before she was running it well. It helped that the Tinker Shop was a short ten-minute walk from her home.

Vic opened the door to Fred's Tinkering and immediately wrinkled her nose. The smell of whiskey and stale musk were heavy on the air. The scent of urine also permeated the shop, a rather terrible habit of the Master Tinker. She had heard he had once been the greatest Tinker London had ever seen. She was not quite sure where that man went, but the lump of flesh currently dry heaving over a bucket certainly was not him.

"Master Frederick," Vic spoke. "Are you well?"

"You're late," he groaned, waving his hand at the work table against the wall. There were various machines piled up: a typewriter, a steam-powered horn, and some other machine she had not seen before.

"That is what I am here to discuss with you," Vic started, keeping far away from Master Frederick as he heaved again. She had been the target of his vomit one too many times. She had no desire to repeat the event.

"Just get to work, girl. The patrons do not pay you to talk."

Vic frowned down at him, her anger getting the better of her. No, the patrons did not pay her to talk. In fact, they did not pay her at all. Master Frederick paid her a measly salary when he felt like it, and only if he did not piss it away on whiskey and the brothel. She straightened her spine and lifted her chin.

"No."

Master Frederick stopped heaving long enough to look at Vic. His cheeks were ruddy, and sweat was coating his skin and soaking into his clothing. His hair hung in strings across his forehead, dirty and unkempt. She was not sure when the last time he had bathed himself was, but the smell told her it had been far too long.

"What do you mean 'no'?" he growled. "I don't pay you to stand around and look pathetic."

"I am afraid I have to take my leave from my position, Master Frederick. My father's expedition had been funded, and I have been signed on as the Master Tinker." Vic shifted in annoyance, her leg giving off a small puff of steam at the movement. His eyes fell to the leg with a sneer.

"You're a cripple and a woman. What in the devil would make them think you would make a good Tinker?"

Vic raised her chin impossibly high. Master Frederick was often rude when he had been drinking, and it seemed this time was no different. It was a wonder he was ever sober enough to sign her on as his apprentice. The old fool would have gone under long before if he had not done her that service.

"I believe I have proved my worth during my time here, Master Frederick. I am taking the opportunity presented to me. I thought it prudent to inform you I would no longer be coming into the shop to do your work."

"Your job won't be waiting when you come back," he sneered before heaving into the bucket again. Once he caught his breath, he talked into the bucket, his voice a muffled echo. "I can find any other incompetent fool to take your place."

Vic nodded her head.

"It is a shame you feel that way, Master Frederick. I will take my leave now." She turned towards the door, but her eyes fell on the steam-powered horn. "The bell is cracked," she pointed out, a courtesy. The crack was miniscule, hardly apparent in the right light. With his eyes seeing double, it was doubtful he would find it. If it went unfixed, the horn would have a fuzzy sound when played.

"Good riddance." He dropped the bucket and slouched down on the floor. He pulled the bottle of whiskey towards him and took a long swig. Vic sighed. Some things never changed. It was likely he would not remember the conversation tomorrow. She grabbed a paper and pen from the workbench and scratched out a note for when he was sober again. She included the fix of the horn. Then she pushed through the door and breathed in air that was blessedly free from the smell of human disappointment.

London was not the cleanest city, the smell of horse droppings and steam coating your tongue long before you ever got a breath of clean air, but it was home. And Vic would be leaving it for the better part of eight months. She was excited for the adventure, and at the same time, she would miss the Queen's land dearly.

Since Vic would be leaving the city for so long, she thought it necessary to stock up on essentials she would need for the journey, including ordering a shipment of her favorite gear oil from the local shipyard. There were many vendors that sold the oil, but there was a rash of them adding water to the oil in an attempt to add to their coin. It never worked. Water and oil did not mix, and if one looked into the barrel, they would know instantly. Unfortunately, a lot of Tinkers did not think to look until the shipment arrived at their doorstep, and they found themselves in the possession of oil they could not use. Vic had stayed clear of anyone that was rumored to sell the tainted oil and instead went to the only man she trusted.

"Paolo," she exclaimed, walking into the shop close to the shipyard. Airships came and went around her, the hums of their propellers and boilers not quite masked in the small shop. Paolo had come to London, as a child, from Italy. His father was an abusive drunkard that his mother risked running from. She had left everything she had known to give her son a better life, and it had worked. His mother lived with him, a wife, and three children, and Paolo was one of the most successful vendors in London.

Paolo looked up from where he was marking in his log books—a task Vic had no urge to ever take on—and grinned at her.

"Victoria," he exclaimed, opening his arms. She immediately stepped into his embrace, accepting the warm hugs he was famous for. He smelled like oil and the metallic sting of metal, the best combination.

"You know I prefer Vic," she admonished, pulling from his embrace.

"I know. I just like to tease, is all. To what do I owe the pleasure?"

"I have a rather large order for you, I am afraid."

"That Master Frederick working you to the bone again?"

Vic grinned.

"Actually, this order is for me." She pulled a bag of coin from her belt. "I am the Master Tinker for my father's expedition."

Paolo clapped his hands.

"It is about time, no? Congratulations, Vic! You deserve it every bit." He looked down at the pile of coins, and his eyes bugged. "How much are you purchasing?"

"Eight months' worth of gear oil."

Tears sprang to his eyes, and he pulled her back into his arms.

"That is enough to pay the rent twelve times over. You have taken care of my family by bringing this order to me."

"I would never trust anyone else, Paolo. You are the best at what you do."

She meant it. Paolo mixed the oil himself, making sure the balance was always right for proper lubrication. There was no one else who did what he did.

Paolo kissed her cheeks, excitement in his eyes, before grabbing his notebook and writing down her order. After he took the details of the delivery address and date, he grinned at her.

"Stay there. I have something for you," he said, but before he could make his way to the back, the bell above the door chimed.

A man walked in, not many years her senior, dressed in a grey double-breasted sack suit. Vic immediately noted him as higher class than the men she usually dealt with. He did not once look her way as he pulled his gloves from his hands and walked up to the counter.

"Are you Paolo Ricci?" he asked, his voice rich and cultured. He was most definitely high class. Vic unconsciously smoothed down her trousers, noting the small smudges of grease on her sleeves she never seemed to be without.

"Yes, sir. What can I help you with?"

"I am in a need of an order of box gears, and see that it is delivered by tomorrow."

"I'm afraid that won't be possible, sir. It will take me at least a week to procure your order."

"Are you the best-known vendor, Paolo, or not?"

"Yes, sir, but–"

"Then I expect the order on my doorstep by tomorrow evening. See that it is done, or I will make sure everyone knows you are nothing but a fraud."

Paolo's face went white.

"Excuse me?" Vic interrupted, furious at the man's treatment of her friend. Class did not give a man permission to act a fool. "That is no way to speak to him."

The man turned towards her voice. His amber-colored eyes took her in, from the boots on her feet, to the trousers, the corset, and the goggles strapped in her hair. His expression immediately changed, his whole demeanor evolving into a smooth, dignified viper.

"What is a beauty like you doing in a dingy shop such as this?" he asked, his voice a purr.

"Paolo is the best vendor in the city. No one else could get you gears that fast, and that is exactly why you came to him. Perhaps you could use a little more class when addressing him rather than act like a boar," Vic said, holding her head high.

The man waved away her words and stalked towards her, stopping when they were merely inches apart. It was completely inappropriate for a man to be so close to a woman other than his wife, but Vic did not have delicate sensibilities. She was as stubborn as they came, and she refused to back down from this man, no matter his status.

"What does it matter how I choose to talk to my inferiors, Little Tinker?" His voice was soft and seductive.

"The true merit of man is not measured by his class." Vic met the eyes of Paolo who was watching carefully, waiting to see if she needed any help. "It is measured by how he treats his inferiors." She flicked her eyes back towards the well-dressed man in front of her. "Paolo will get your shipment as fast as possible, like he always does, and you will respect him."

"And if I do not?" he asked, tilting his head to the side. His eyes dropped to her lips and she fought against the sudden skip in her heartbeat. She was not attracted to this fool. She refused to be.

"Then I will make sure there is not a crate of box gears in this entire city."

The man's lips curled the smallest amount, and he inclined his head.

"Mr. Paolo, as soon as possible would be splendid." He dropped a large bag of coin on the counter, much more than his order cost. "I will await the delivery anxiously."

He turned back towards Vic and smiled.

"Good evening, Madam Tinker," he said, bowing and tipping his bowler.

Vic raised her eyebrows at the man.

"Good evening, Sir Boar."

The man laughed and headed for the door, pulling on his gloves. At the last moment, he turned back and touched his cheek.

"You have a bit of a smudge just there."

Vic wiped her hand across her cheek. Indeed, her hand held the telltale streak of grease, and she sighed. The man shot her one last appreciative glance before stepping out into the cacophony of airships and steam-autos, disappearing quickly in the crowd.

CLOCKWORK BUTTERFLY
AVAILABLE NOW

Printed in Germany
by Amazon Distribution
GmbH, Leipzig